Surfing Tsunamis

Anne Geraghty

The Tenth Bull

CONTENTS

'He approached me and in his glance I saw a hundred gardens.

'Where are you from?' I asked him.

He swayed from side to side like a ship without an anchor and replied,

'Half from the edge of the sea and half from the depths of the ocean.'

We took off our robes and lay with each other.

Our nakedness together changed me completely.'

Jalal al-Din Rumi (1207 - 1273)

Prologue.

You might think the worst storms happen in winter, when you tighten every muscle against a bitter north wind sweeping down from the arctic and your breath freezes on your lips before it's left your mouth, but no. The hurricanes, typhoons, tornadoes and tropical cyclones that uproot forests, smash down buildings, destroy farmland and send creatures scrabbling in panic for shelter from screaming winds, these storms happen in summer, often after an unusually warm night.

Nights like these, when the clouds keep in the heat of the day and you throw off sheets, stretch out and sleep naked, can fool you. You dream of a picnic under a blue sky, a cooling swim in a warm lake or a lazy afternoon reading a novel; not for a moment do you imagine in the morning you'll be running for your life. Like the halcyon days of a honeymoon can seduce you into thinking love is a walk in a perfumed garden full of roses with no thorns, a sail through calm seas under a strawberry moon, all soft caresses and sweet murmurings. If you've not read the signs behind the warmth of the night and the sudden silence of dogs, your lover's tight smile and slight turning away, you're unprepared when the storm unleashes its violence and smashes into you.

The worst storms of all, however, happen at sea. When you're out in the ocean, all landmarks gone, the only certainty the far horizon, that's when there's nowhere to hide from a hurricane. The ocean is completely white with foam, the air filled with driving spray, winds whip through you at two hundred and fifty miles per hour able to break apart ships built of the thickest steel – that's if you've not already capsized under the towering walls of water that slam into you again and again, nor fallen into the raging seas when your ship heels thirty degrees over on one side and then thirty degrees over on the other side with a whiplash that wrenches your eyes from their sockets and pulls out your eyeteeth, have not already drowned when your ship cracks into pieces under pounding hammer blows to the hull and all the while winds howl around you like demons intent on revenge against humanity for its neglect of the old gods.

You might imagine the way to go is straight to the nearest port. But here's the thing, when those dark clouds gather, the waves begin to grow and you see the violent weather heading towards you with the determination of a killer, being in the wrong port can be as perilous as being out at sea. In fact there are some ports so dangerous to ride out the violent weather of a hurricane at sea is safer than to stay. So if what you hoped was a safe haven happens to be one of those ports, and you've not read the signs and left well before the storm strikes, you face devastation. Though the warning signs you need to note are not only those of darkening clouds, warm nights and the geography of ports. As well as what's above, you have to read what's below.

Some storms have their origins in undercurrents way below the surface yet are so powerful they can shipwreck an oil tanker. Experienced sailors know these invisible undercurrents can't be seen when you're floating on the waves but they can wreck your ship all the same, drag you down full fathom five and leave scattered splinters of your precious cargo strewn across the seven seas. Though you can't rely on maps; we know more about the contours of the moon than the ocean depths. Which is why seasoned sailors have charts of the ocean etched into their bones from all the times they've nearly drowned.

How do I know this? Because I've spent a lot of time lost at sea, swimming adrift from all landmarks in oceans so tumultuous the crests of the waves are in the clouds. And I've had many near death experiences from drowning. I've been shipwrecked enough times to navigate even the Mariana Trench, the deepest part of which, the Challenger Deep, is deeper than Mount Everest is high by over a mile. Which is why when I met Dan and he smiled into my eyes with an invitation to fly with him through blue skies so vast you can lose everything in the emptiness, I smiled back and invited him to swim with me down into the *midnight zone of the deep ocean, where no light penetrates the eternal night; and the creatures who live there must swim forever blind or create their own light. Neither of us understood these were not promises - they were warnings.*

Chapter 1   Come Drown With Me

DAN

She's standing against the wall with long legs, shining hair, creamy skin and green eyes the colour of the first growth of spring. She turns. Her hair scatters moonbeams. She sees me and smiles. A poem flies across the room and lands fluttering close to my heart. I manoeuvre through the party towards her in moves I hope reveal my drummer's muscles and cool sense of rhythm. After all, dazzling beauty like this may be dangerous but to turn away from it is lethal.

'Hi. I'm Dan. Wanna dance?' I'm coming on too fast; she's only just walked in. She'll need a drink. 'Or a beer?' She's not a Sheila from a sheep farm. 'Maybe a glass of wine?'

She smiles. A sun I haven't seen since Australia shines on me.

'I've a bottle here.' She holds out a classier bottle than I've seen in the kitchen so far. I take it. The bottle is cold, still frosted from the fridge. 'I'll open it,' I say and turn in search of a corkscrew. I return and find a tall guy with dark hair is talking with her and leaning in close. I stand awkwardly holding two glasses and the opened bottle. Still talking, she turns, takes the glasses and holds them while I pour. Our eyes meet. I'm not sure if I'm a knight to the rescue or a moth to the flame. But all good things sit on the edge of a precipice, and when that smile shines out again, I could be a shorn lamb waltzing into a pack of starving dingoes for all I care.

'Cheers!' I say. I clink my glass with hers.

'Cheers!' she replies and looks over the glass at me as she drinks. 'Are you a friend of Carole's? I haven't met you before.' The other guy reads the signs and fades away.

I tell her I'm staying with Carole's ex-boyfriend, having just got back from Australia and launch into a witty and fascinating episode of my tales from the Aussie Outback. She laughs and tells me of her acting and drama teaching. That's the dialogue above ground. Underground we exchange age-old promises in a subtle dance only a wildlife cameraman might notice. I smile like I'm both innocent and experienced, and lean into her with just enough, not too much, closeness to let her know I'm sensitive as well as cool, that I'm a real man who knows how to make love to a woman so she *feels* the love. She smiles too. Though there's danger in those green eyes. They can perhaps see in the dark because they promise an adventure beyond the event horizon of any journey I've made so far, into wider freedoms than even travelling an open highway through bluegrass country, over mountains, headed further west than the sunset. Those eyes and that smile invite me to travel with her into the witching hour of a night with no moon, where in the darkness anything can happen.

No man in his right mind would refuse an invitation from such a creature, even one who likes to display his flamboyant peacock feathers in broad daylight. I lean in closer. Her hair smells of summer. I rub my cheek against hers. Slowly. Gently. Like when you lean over a drum and stroke it lightly with a brush for a buzz roll so soft it might be the ringing in your own ears. Maybe lovers do not meet as strangers after all but have taken full measure of each other in that first instant, because in the wordless honeyed language of those who are already lovers my body moves with hers and tells her, 'I'll follow you even into the eternal night of the ocean floor and stay with you there because…' I whisper silently, 'all our hearts are of darkness, if they come to light, we die.'

LIZZIE

It was a cold grey November day and I'd spent it on the sofa with lank unwashed hair - and this was the early eighties, big hair was a religion. Discarded cigarette packets, chocolate wrappers, half eaten sandwiches and stained coffee cups lay scattered about the floor. But this wasn't a gritty northern drama of life down the pit or on the dole, I'd just told my latest lover I needed more space. 'I love you but I'm not *in* love with you. I'm too immature and selfish. You deserve better.' The usual half-truths. He'd begged me to stay. 'We can get through this. Just give me another chance. I'll do anything to make it work.' The usual half-lies. But I'd shaken my head and turned away. 'You've broken my heart and I'll never love again,' he'd said. 'Yes you will and so will I,' I'd said.

I wished I'd been as confident as I'd sounded, especially as it had been a sweet love affair and I had no specific reason for ending it. Except that my desire to be desired had led me to shape-shift into what I thought *he* desired until I was trapped in a web of my own making and lost in my own intrigues, again. I can't even blame him, though obviously I'd tried.

He wasn't the first. I've left a string of discarded lovers in my wake for no reason I can fathom. There must be something wrong with me. Though when I turn to successful people for advice, life gurus, celebrities, CEOs of big companies and such like, people who have made it and therefore proved there's nothing wrong with them, they tell me life is about following your dreams, climbing mountains, forging streams. But what if your life has been a nightmare of falling off mountains and drowning in streams? No one gives motivational speeches about just giving up and surrendering to gravity. Especially as gravity doesn't take you the scenic route, you go the steepest way down. I have the scars to prove it.

It's dangerous to be left alone with a mind like mine for long, even when you're listening to Joni Mitchell, the mistress of break-up songs. Fortunately I'm saved from further meanders through my dubious inner world by the doorbell. I open the door to Carole. She walks in, sweeps yesterday's newspaper from a chair and sits down. She gives the discarded remnants of my vigil with sorrow a scornful glance.

'It's my birthday party tonight and I want you there' she says. 'Staying at home alone on a Saturday night is so…' she pauses for thought, 'so pathetic!'

I inform her that at least the knowledge of how low one can sink gives one an existential edge over those who, despite the evidence, naively imagine life is wonderful. She ignores my philosophical depth.

'I'm not going until you promise to be there this evening,' she says, interrupting my sorrow to demand a fag. 'It's for your own good, Lizzie.' She lights the cigarette, waves out the match and inhales. 'There's someone I want you to meet.' She stares at the ceiling then back at me. I recognise a meaningful look when I see one.

'Thank you for caring but I'm finished with all that.' My turn to inhale and gaze at the ceiling wishing there was a river I could float away on. 'I plan to dedicate my life to doing good, travel to war zones with medicine, rescue wounded orphans, mediate peace in the Middle East, save endangered species…' I see myself, a Mother Teresa in Levis standing backstage at the next Save the World rock concert next to Keith Richards who'll probably invite me back to his place. Carole has noticed my eyes are seeing into some other landscape.

'If you prefer to indulge in vacuous narcissistic fantasies on your sofa, rather than the real world of sex and shopping, that's fine by me. Just don't expect sympathy when you come weeping to me tomorrow.' She stands up. 'I've a party to organise.' She tosses her big hair and sweeps out. I toss my lanky hair and go into the bathroom.

I peel off my jeans, turn on the shower and let the water cascade over me. It's wise to wear waterproof mascara, even if only crying inside, so fortunately I emerge without black streaks down my face. You want your tears to be a sign of delicate sensitivity not unglamorous rampant grief. Angst ridden unkempt dishevelment is all very well as long as you look like you're only pretending to be a wreck, even when, like me, you're only pretending to be pretending.

The party is throbbing when I arrive with the base beats of Blondie's 'Call Me' pounding through the speakers. And so it is through a haze of smoke, music and alcohol, I first see Dan. He is dancing. Beware a lover who comes dancing.

DAN

I'd just returned from six months on a sheep farm in Australia. It's a long story. I was trying to escape my family and their pressure to join the family business, Brewin's Boxes – slogan: 'Our packaging contains it all.' I'd done my best. I walked the factory floor in a suit and tie, faked an interest in the crushability quotients of various corrugations, sat in meetings discussing marketing strategies and ad campaigns, made notes on a clipboard listing the cartons, packets and cardboard boxes piled high in all directions, but my mind wasn't on the job. By day I ticked off consignments of packaging, a foot soldier in the Capitalist project to fool us into thinking consumer choice is freedom so we chain ourselves to desks to market what we later buy with the money we make marketing it; by night I played the drums, a wild beast unleashing anarchic fury with a total lack of restraint in a band whose music was a savage indictment of modern capitalism and would bring society rocking to its knees. In my defence, it was the '70s, a lot of us spoke like that back then.

It became increasingly difficult to steer a course through life with two such widely diverging horses on my chariot and when I heard Topper Headon's drum rhythms in The Clash's London Calling with those opening military beats underpinning an anthem that called us to take up arms against the establishment, I was more than ready to enlist. It became suddenly clear, I must leave my day job immediately and find creative fulfillment on a self-sufficient farm, live in a geodesic dome off the grid or join a Marxist commune with no personal property – apart from a drum kit. Plus the gear a band needs to crack out the tunes. Not forgetting windmills and solar panels to power up the amplifiers. It doesn't matter how far from western civilisation you travel, you'll still need a bass beat to rock through your chakras and keep you dancing.

The band was on the verge of splitting anyway, due to creative differences, personality conflicts or too many drunken fights - take your pick. I packed my bags and flew to the other side of the world. I heard the music scene in Sidney was taking off and there'd be a fair few bands looking for a drummer. Partly because back then drummers were the ones who sat at the back and were ignored. Nowadays you have drum magazines, drum libraries, drum videos, drum downloads, a whole global community of awesome drummers, but back then strutting your stuff as a front man, singer, lead guitar, even bass guitar was way cooler than being stuck behind them banging cymbals and drums. Look at Ringo. But I loved the drums and didn't care. The Sidney music scene wasn't taking off, or rather my part in it wasn't. So I turned to Plan B: a sheep farm.

Sheep shearing is an art form, an athletic sport, a dance. In fact The Guardian newspaper once compared Bowen's sheep shearing to Nureyev's arabesques and Barbirolli's cello playing. Certainly it's theatre. The sheep shearers arrive at the shed at 7am. An amplifier and speakers are connected for a sound track of hard rock or brutal heavy metal with its stoner doom metal riffs at full volume. By 7.30am you're full on into four two-hour sessions with breaks in between. You hook up your high-tech sheep shears, grab a sheep by its front legs and shear the wool so the entire fleece comes off as one. Though until you're a fully fledged shearer you're a rousey and assigned other roles such as picking up the wool, classing it, pressing it, sweeping up the excess, moving sheep into the shed – and right down the pecking order, picking out the shit in the wool. There's loads of it in every fleece. I should know. I spent a lot of time getting up close and personal with the full bio-diversity of Australian sheep shit.

I never got to be a gun shearer, one of the guys who can shear more than two hundred sheep a day, that's about two minutes to catch the sheep, get it into position, shear it so the shorn wool is even and the sheep unharmed, then get it back into the pen, but I became good enough to hold my own. The world record is 456 full wool sheep in nine hours, held by Godfrey Bowen who invented the Bowen technique, now used the world over. Though these days the Australians have a biochemical way of doing it. You inject the sheep and the wool just falls off. No way is that progress.

By far the most fun though was the sheep shearing shindig. When your nearest neighbour is several hundred miles away, you do not pass up the chance of a rave when the shearers are in town. And no bash is complete without the beat of the drum. From Wagga Wagga to Woolgorong Dan's Drums called farmers and their wives to dance, and especially their daughters, those tanned, strong, muscular Sheilas who embraced you with arms of steel so your ribs cracked. Not that I minded. A few bruises were well worth it for a roll in the hay with one of them. Those farm girls might never grace the pages of a fashion magazine but they were long-limbed and fit, with healthy appetites for all sorts of fun and games.

Life is hard on Australian sheep farms, but I enjoyed it. The main difficulty was the scarcity of women. Within a hundred mile radius there were just three, the farmer's mother, the farmer's wife and the farmer's daughter. So when the boss found his sweet sixteen-year-old Joanne having more fun with me in the barn than people usually do baling straw, it was time to go walkabout. That's how I came to be back in England with a tan and blonde sun streaks in my hair. If that didn't pull the women, my tales of life in the Aussie outback and how to shear a sheep in two minutes would surely fascinate them. And if that failed, I had the drums. What kind of woman can resist a blonde sheep shearer who rides the crash and snares them with two bass drums? Yet when I saw Lizzie, I was the one who fell. Harder than a Kodo drummer hits the great o-daiko.

LIZZIE

We walked from the party together, through fine autumn rain. The last leaves were falling. Dan caught one and gave it to me. 'Make a wish,' he said, 'but don't tell me.' I liked that. Most men want to know what you're thinking, to colonise your inner world and grab your secrets so you belong to them. To be honest, so do most women. Not it seemed, this man. Though he could be a smooth player with some very slick moves. It made no difference; I'd fallen at the first hurdle. Even if he were a shark in sheep shearing clothing, that blonde sun streaked hair and those tanned drummer muscles had worked their magic, and I was up for this ride wherever it's took us.

We sit on the sofa. Dan rolls a joint. He lights it, takes a long drag and passes it over to me. He leans back, puts his feet up and smiles. I breathe in and hold the smoke in my lungs. Marijuana can sometimes affect me weirdly. While all around bliss out in cosmic well-being, I can get screwed up in cosmic turmoil. I hope this isn't one of those times.

A tension begins in my shoulders. It spreads down my arms. Perhaps if I sit very still it will go away. It doesn't. Of course not. When you really want to relax is when you tense up most because you're trying so hard to relax. I try hard not to try so hard, but the more I try to relax the more I feel the tension of this particular situation. And it is a very particular situation. Everything in my life seems to have led up to the conjunction of Dan, me, these green cushions, this blue sofa, my flat on this November evening, with these exact rain drops falling on the window-pane. All this has come together to make it a momentous moment, a life changing moment after which nothing will be the same again. I'm afraid I'll blow it and not live up to the momentous-ness of this moment.

I'm travelling way out there. This grass is strong.

But just as I'm about to worry about going so far out there I won't make it back, I'm hit by another insight: every moment is a momentous moment. Every moment everything changes. You can't step into the same river once let alone twice because it's never the same. Nothing is. My inadequacy to respond appropriately to the momentousness of each moment is possibly the only continuity because everything that ever happens changes us forever from what we were the moment before it happened into what we will be when the moment of it's happening has passed. Except we never get there. We're always in the moment of becoming, never one that arrives.

Dan stretches his arm along the back of the sofa behind me and gazes into my eyes with another smile. He has no idea that each moment we die and are never re-born, that we are nothing but shifting-sands, moving goal posts, transitory migrants in existential exile in a life that is a never-ending series of losses. Shall I tell him? 'I feel afraid,' I tell him instead. 'What of?' He smiles again, oblivious of the death he's just experienced. 'I'm not sure.' I look down confused about why I'm telling him this. 'I don't know. Loss. Death maybe.' He pulls me towards him. Perhaps he can sense my mind is overheating because he strokes my hair like a mother might caress a frightened child, persuading me I am safe from all harm.

The only sound in the sudden quiet is the rise and fall of our breath. The pulse begins to beat in our veins. Our heartbeats quicken. The field widens and deepens and spreads like a tide flowing into the mudflats of an estuary, silently filling the creeks, seeping over the banks until every landmark is gone. We float in a sea of feeling until, soaked in every pore, we slip below the surface and drown.

It's morning. I slip out of bed and into the kitchen. I make coffee and bring two mugs back into the bedroom. I look down at the man with sky smiles in his sleepy eyes. I know this will end in tears. It always does. Every love has its heartbreak because whatever we love will one day leave, change or die - or we will. The loss is written in from the beginning. Maybe Buddha was right, the way to find relief from suffering is to detach from our desires. But what if some things are worth suffering for? What if some desires are themselves to die for? What if love and loss do not cancel each other out but together create something unbearably precious? There's only one way to find out.

DAN

We left the party together and walked together in silence. What is there to talk about when your meeting feels like a karmic encounter written in the stars? Though if, as they say, we meet our destiny on the road we take to avoid it, then Lizzie and I must have been running towards each other long before we actually met. Whether running from fate, from ourselves, from pasts into futures we hoped would be brighter than where we were running from, or whether we ran simply for the hell of it, for the wind in our hair and the freedom of the road, I've no idea. Maybe a curve in space-time had given us a glimpse of each other, and we were running from that. I don't know. Though I do know, because I have the bruises to prove it, we were running from opposite directions so blindly and completely, we didn't meet, we collided. And when two bodies collide, they become entangled forever. That's quantum physics.

We sat on a sofa with more cushions than I'd seen in one place before and smoked some grass. One thing led to another and then another, until we fell back into the paradise our animal bodies have never left. Though that night I dreamed a forest burst into flame and creatures ran for cover from a fire that consumed all that could not run, crawl, swim or fly to safety from the raging heat.

One time I saw such a fire in a Eucalyptus forest. Not much escapes infernos like these. The fires start in the grasses low on the ground and spread quickly upwards towards the canopy as the flames travel up the Eucalyptus bark that hangs in long fibrous stringers. These burning bark strips, 'candlebark', are carried by winds to other parts of the forest. The fire is spread too by the eucalyptus oil that hangs in the air as a highly volatile blue haze and burns at twice the heat of the wood. Soon there's nothing left but devastation and smoke drifting over a dead forest.

Though a forest can never truly die. Eucalyptuses are old trees from the ancient Gondwana forest and have evolved many ways to live with fire. They have died and regenerated millions of times. In fact they are so dependent on fire to regenerate and spread, the aboriginal name for a Eucalyptus is 'fire loving tree'. Just a few weeks after a fire, the Eucalyptuses look healthy again and have sprouted masses of green new shoots. This is because while the fire is raging above ground, the heart of the tree lies waiting silently, deep underground. Far beneath the surface is the lignotuber, a root structure of ancient origin. This hidden heart is an old protection against fire, flood and being eaten. It holds vast reserves of food and can form masses of shoots but lies dormant while the tree is growing. When the tree is burned, the hormones that held the lignotuber in check are no longer present. The soil is warm. The ash bed is full of minerals. With the overhead canopy gone, sunlight reaches the ground. There are no plants left to compete for the nutrients and no insects, birds or creatures to eat the shoots. Without its leaves and bark, the trees themselves have no other focus, other than regeneration and growth. At last, the lignotuber bursts out of its confinement in the soil and erupts into daylight.

The night Lizzie later told me she'd drowned, I burned. And my heart, buried deep underground, burst open.

In the morning Lizzie brings me a cup of coffee. She smiles, her eyes the colour of fresh forest growth. Sometimes after forest fires, the first plants you see are orchids. They spring up and burst into colour more quickly than any other plant. Rare orchids blanket the hillsides with a dazzling display of colour against the smoky ruins of a forest now blackened tree stumps surrounded by grey ash. So much beauty amidst so much devastation - it breaks your heart.

LIZZIE

I climb back into bed. Dan takes his coffee and we drink in silence. The sun shines through the autumn leaves of the tree outside my window. Shadows dance on the duvet. Dan turns to me, smiles and leans over me. His eyes look into mine as he kisses my cheek. Without breaking eye contact and without smiling, I lean over and bite his shoulder. The marks of my teeth are pink on his skin. I turn away and gaze into the black coffee in my mug. A rule at my convent school was you must always look at the bottom of your glass when drinking. I never discovered why looking around the room while drinking was sinful, unless those priests saw an invitation to sin in every young girl's eyes, but for sure it wasn't to hide the terrifying vulnerability of having woken to discover in the night you've fallen in love with a stranger.

I can't be in love with Dan. I hardly know him. Yet I've woken to find a strange wonder is covering the world. It's like when you pull back curtains in the morning to see everything wrapped in a blanket of white snow and you want to laugh and jump from a height into the soft virgin snowdrifts. This is what love feels like, a fall into softness, a fall from speech into song, from certainty into confusion, from grace into grace. Though a free-fall is never free. Whether from paradise, onto snow, over a precipice or into love, a fall involves a loss of control. Tried and tested ways are abandoned. Stability, a firm footing, the status quo, whatever was standing before the fall, they're all gone and what was once solid tumbles into new uncertainties. Falling in love is not a cruise through the pearly Adriatic with cushions, refreshments, and an emergency handle to stop the ride when you want to get off; it's a sheer plummeting drop down mountains in the dark with nothing to hold onto except the ride itself.

But maybe Dan is someone who'll surf the waves with me and still be an anchor. Maybe he'll teach me how to fly so I never crash-land again. Maybe I can dream of a perfumed garden full of roses without thorns and wake to find I'm still there.

When you fall in love there's always a fantasy.

Chapter 2   Born a Long Way from Home

DAN

There's something about Lizzie, the way she moves, her smile, her smell, her skin, her touch. When we're together I feel I've come home to where I belong. The only other time I feel like this is when I play the drums and suddenly there's no drummer, no drum, yet it's all there anyway. You're not playing the drums, the drums are playing you. The river flows through the pulse of those rhythms wherever the river wants to go and there's nothing else you want to be doing and there's nowhere else you want to be - you're in the zone. Being with Lizzie is like being in the zone, except with the drums I have to play for some time before I get there, with Lizzie it's immediate. When we're together, watching a film, walking in the park, or just hanging out, we fall into a dream-field where anything can happen, yet what unfolds is so exactly perfect, it's all happening anyway. The zone. It's ecstatic. I love it. And I love Lizzie all the more for it.

LIZZIE

Dan and I are usually at my place; I have a comfortable home and Dan's sleeping in a mate's spare room. Though when Dan holds me in his arms and murmurs honey into my ears, the cushions and carpets fade into the background and he becomes my home. Perhaps love is not blind. Perhaps lovers see everything that matters in the first moments of meeting and fall in love because they already know each other. Certainly we wonder at the strange familiarity we feel, as if we've belonged to each other for aeons.

We pass more of ourselves over to the other for safekeeping. I tell him I play a confusion of parts and while most people live with what's around them in constant flux and the ground they stand on is solid, I live in a sea of change where the only fixed thing is the far horizon. He says, but surely you know who you are. I say, no, without the grounding of terra firma I lack the stable sense of self most take for granted, instead I'm a fluidity, a continually changing movement that rises and falls like the ocean. It means I can go with the flow with such ease I appear so cool people want to *be* me, but they're not around the next morning when my feet should be back on the ground to deal with laundry, timetables and electricity bills, and I remain lost at sea, carried by ocean currents too powerful to do other than float like flotsam from a shipwreck long ago. The answer is of course another party. Except it isn't. He shrugs and tells me maybe everyone's a bit like that. I say, but I don't think they're as afraid of being themselves as I am. He says, 'but we're all afraid aren't we?' and he tells me he often feels anxious for no reason he can fathom but hides his fear behind his drumming. He confesses he's even afraid he'll fall so deeply in love with me he'll lose himself then there'll be two of us missing at sea. I tell him to get lost anyway and he thinks I'm asking him to leave. I say, I mean, let's fall in love whatever the risks. But by the time I finish telling him there's nothing to fear but fear itself I contradict myself and tell him, yes we must be careful, love is the most dangerous poison and medicine of them all. He says, you're contradicting yourself. I tell him what do you expect? I'm a woman of many parts, several of them locked in perpetual conflict, and though he might be confused by me, he'll never be bored. He says he isn't sure if he prefers the security of the known to the excitement and confusion of the unknown because he likes to know where he is and sometimes he doesn't know where he is with me. I gaze into his eyes and tell him, get used to it, the one certainty is uncertainty, certainly since Heisenberg told us the very act of seeing changed what we were looking at from what it was before we saw it. Dan tells me in no uncertain terms what I can do with my intellectual abstractions before pulling me towards him for another round of getting to know each other in ways other than talking.

And when we make love, the trees dance and rocks turn to diamonds, rivers run uphill and music comes down from mountains, the moon sings and stones become gods. Not even quantum physics can explain that.

DAN

This feeling with Lizzie that I've come home is all the stranger because I've never felt at home anywhere before. My family home was a place of alienation and constriction, not a safe place to relax. At fifteen I read 'On the Road' by Jack Kerouac. It spoke to my generational soul like nothing I'd heard before and overnight my feeling of alienation was revealed as a gateway to freedom. Since then, my vision of home has been a hay strewn railroad truck on a long ride through endless plains to where I know no one and no one knows me. I'm with Marvin Gaye on this one, 'I'm the type of boy who's always on the roam, wherever I lay my hat that's my home.' I wanted to be that kind of guy, one who lives in the moment, goes with the flow of karma through the dharma, and even when holed up somewhere for a while, is always on the road without commitments or attachments. Because when you're born a long way from home, you learn to make your home wherever you happen to be. Freedom I called it. I hadn't realised that freedom to follow your desires is not the same as freedom *from* your desires. Nor that freedom because 'you ain't got nothin' to lose' is not the same as a total liberation from the karmic wheel of delusion, or however you like to describe an escape from the tough realities of life on Earth.

My wanderlust might have been a reaction to being boxed in by a family business where the packaging is more important than the product, or maybe it was due to a nomadic tendency in my genes, or perhaps something that evolved in the human spirit after WW2 and erupted in a generational sign of the times, but whatever the reason, the virtues of living sensibly, accumulating money, and getting it together with a 'proper' job hadn't figured in my plans so far. The search for freedom, love, authenticity, music, comradeship and fun mattered far more. With Lizzie I felt I'd found a partner in that quest. Together we'd run up mountains, dive into the ocean and dance over the horizon with the freedom to roam wherever the winds of circumstances took us, and still we'd have a home – in each other.

LIZZIE

I lie in the languid horizon between sleep and waking. The sun shines in through the bedroom windows. Trees rustle in the wind. I can hear children playing and the soft chirrups of winter birds. Dan and I have nothing planned other than a lazy breakfast and conversations over the Sunday papers. Maybe later we'll go for a walk, invite friends over, or watch a movie.

Dan is asleep. I turn on my side and trace 'I love you' along his arm. But Dan is not asleep. He opens his eyes and smiles. I stiffen. I've just violated the first law of cool, love only those who love you first. A fear streaks through my heart. It's uncool to be vulnerable. He might pull away from such neediness. He might think me presumptuous to speak of love so soon. Or worse, Dan's smile could be one of pleasure in the power he now has over me. He pulls me to him and kisses my forehead. 'I love you too, Lizzie,' he whispers.

I look into his blue eyes the colour of a sky so wide you risk losing your soul in the emptiness, and fall helplessly back into his arms. He's just said he loves me. Me. Lizzie. He loves me. Yet as I sink back into him there's still a fear. Love needs us as much as we need love, and I'm not sure I've got what it takes. Is there a choice? Falling in love can't be a choice like which sweater to wear or what film to watch, especially as to refuse an invitation to love is to consign vital parts of us, possibly the best parts, to oblivion. If abandoning the best of us is the price we pay for keeping safe, what kind of choice is that? Besides, the most dangerous path of all is to seek safety at all costs.

Dan and I have fallen too far to clamber back to safety anyway, even with crampons and ropes, so whether we like it or not, it's time to gear up for the heart-stopping ski off-piste down a black-diamond run at midnight that is human sexual love. And there's only one way to travel here - as your downhill speed picks up, you throw caution to the headwind, let the fall take over, and enjoy the ride. After all, it's not the destination that's the Promised Land - it's the journey. Isn't it?

DAN

Ask any drummer or bassist and they'll agree, the play between the drums and the bass is the backbone of any band. Even Robert Plant and Jimmy Page wouldn't have made it without the bass and drums of John Paul Jones and John Bonham. Their interplay is like a mantra, the more you hear it, the more profound it gets and the deeper it beats into your soul. Matt played bass guitar when I played drums back in Noise days. A lot of trust builds up between you that way. Matt and I are brothers.

While I was sheep shearing in the outback, Matt was getting it together in Manchester. Or rather with help from his parents, he bought a house and rented out rooms. I landed back in the UK at the same time one of his tenants was off to see his girlfriend in Greece and I took his room until he returned. It's a small room with a single bed and not much room for a drum kit, but that's OK. A drummer frequently has to travel without his gear. You can hitch a ride on a dusty highway with a guitar across your back, no problem - a drum kit? No way. Though you never travel without your beaters. You might be waiting for that lift, riding in the back of a truck or sitting on a night train to Georgia when a new rock ride hits you and you have to play that groove before you lose it. Some drummers can write stuff like that down but I'm not one of those. I have to rely on the cellular memory of my muscles. Fortunately I can play a rhythm a few times and some kinaesthetic body-memory lays it down in my system to be recalled when later I plug into a band.

I was soon well settled at Matt's, OK temporarily, but the moment's all we've got anyway so it's cool. I had my drumsticks, my portable high-hat clutch, the one of a shared kit at a gig will almost certainly be knackered, and spare drum keys, they're always going missing, all I needed was the kit itself. I paid a deposit at Jack's Instruments and became the owner of a Tama drum set, not the best but good enough.

Matt told me he'd left the band he'd been with. Due to creative differences, he said. Because he'd got it on with the lead singer's girlfriend, a mate said. He was getting another band together, had found a lead guitar and keyboard player, and was looking for a singer, a drummer, and maybe a rhythm guitar. That's when I landed on his doorstep.

I called up Chris, a mate from Crude Crewe days, as good a front man you're likely to find who also plays rhythm guitar. He was hanging loose having recently got back from learning to play the gimbri, a three stringed lute, in Morocco. So here we were, a new band, Matt on bass, Chris, front man and rhythm guitar, Steve, lead guitar, Oumar, keyboards and back up vocals, and a drummer, me. Several jamming sessions later we emerged as Obsidian. Apparently obsidian is a kind of glass formed in volcanoes and has the sharpest cutting edges of all knives. It's also used to manufacture the most expensive turntables in the world. And is jet black. For Oumar, whose grandparents live in Mali where his parents came from, though he's as Brixton as they come, that was the clincher.

A mate has a mate who runs a pub in Deansgate and was looking for a band to gig on Wednesdays. We checked it out, played a set we'd practised at the local community centre and were booked. You could describe what we do as new wave alt rock, with a punk-reggae Bob Marley meets The Clash undertone, or you could say we're suffering from identity confusion. Either way, the punters liked us enough to keep coming so we kept playing and sharing out the £50. What with the band and now Lizzie, life is sweet.

LIZZIE

We're walking back to my place after a meal. A full moon shines through the bare trees.

'Look at the moon!' I say. 'We'll be home soon and it will shine down onto us through our bedroom window.' Beside me, Dan stiffens and slightly pulls away. We're walking together but not as we were a moment ago. His silence slices into me like an obsidian scalpel. I get it. It's my home not his, my bedroom window not ours. I've presumed too much.

Dan takes his arm away from mine and blows on his hands to warm them. 'Lizzie,' he says, 'something's come up.' He pauses and puts his hands in his pockets. I stop breathing. A fear lodges in my throat. Losing him would involve more than a few days on the sofa with Joni Mitchell before pumping up my hair for another party. I wrap my arms around me and look at the ground. I don't want him to see the fear in my eyes. I steel myself for his withdrawal, from this walk, from me, from my life.

'Jim's coming back from Greece next week, I have to move.' He pauses. 'I was, uh, wondering if, uh, I could stay at your place for a while.' He scratches his cheek. 'Just until I get my own place.'

I smile. 'No problem. Until you get your own place, you're welcome.' I speak as if I'm easy and cool with it all, not as if I'd been expecting a hit in the solar plexus that would have sent me flying.

We walk home feeling out the contours of this new, and more dangerous territory. Whatever the psycho-geography however, it's clear we've already moved in with one another, and arrived in that place of almost unbearable togetherness where I can wound him as deeply as he can wound me.

DAN

When I asked Lizzie if I could move in for a while, there was a pang that I'd be leaving my lonely road to nowhere and sliding into a tame domesticity. Yet to move in seemed natural. I was spending most nights there anyway. Lizzie owned a flat with books, furniture, cushions and all the paraphernalia that goes with life in a city; I had none of that. When you're on the road hitching rides to wherever the road leads, you travel light. What do you really need anyhow? A strong pair of shoes, dry clothes, sleeping bag, backpack, torch, knife, your drumsticks, maybe a notebook and pen, and you're kitted out. These all moved with me into Lizzie's flat. Not the drums. She insisted I kept them elsewhere; she didn't want a load of musicians hanging around while she was trying to work. So they remained at Matt's in the basement. That was fine. The community centre had evicted us after complaints about the noise from the yoga class so we'd done up Matt's basement and practised there. A bit cramped but with egg boxes on the walls and carpet on the ceiling no one could hear us. And I certainly didn't want to be told, 'keep the noise down!' while deep in a shamanic frenzy calling up the spirits of the drum. As it turned out, my slide into domesticity was easy. Lizzie's soft pillows helped - laying your head on feathers is always going to score over a lump of rock on a mountainside whatever the rhythms you beat out to the howl of wolves under a star-lit sky in the wilderness. Besides, central heating relaxes parts of you even a long train ride to nowhere can't reach. But what I never expected, because I never imagined it possible, was with Lizzie, I didn't feel stifled by duty or boxed in by commitments, I was still travelling.

We'd go together to places I've known only on the road and alone, but without having to wander through city streets looking for a place to call home for a few hours or standing by a road in the rain waiting for a ride with a stranger. I'd never dared to hope for a travelling companion, someone who'd travel alongside me and value freedom as much as I do. I'd found her in Lizzie. I could lay my head next to a beautiful woman and call it home whether that home was the ride or the arrival.

I'd forgotten, a lover can wound you in many more ways than a stranger.

Chapter 3   An Ice Palace

LIZZIE

The sun is shining. Daffodils dance beneath trees with the first green of spring on their branches. I walk back from the supermarket through the park and sit on a bench overlooking the lake. Willow trees shiver in the wind. Ducks swim in the ruffled water. I lean back into the sun's pale warmth and smile. The evening before I'd come home to find Dan had written 'I love you' in daffodils all over my bed. Now our bed. Nothing explicit has been said, but we both know Dan is not about to find his own place anytime soon. I curve across the park through the gates and into my street, a quiet road with little traffic that could be a country lane in a village rather than a small corner of a metropolis.

I manoeuvre around uneven slabs, past familiar dustbins and the low walls of small front gardens. The first bees of spring are buzzing in the yellow forsythia and the bright red of the flowering currant. By the time I open my newly painted black metal gate, which still squeaks when I open it, the weight of living in a city has fallen from my shoulders. I walk up the small path to a Victorian house divided into flats. Mine is the ground floor. I bought it because of the garden out the back where, despite living in a city, on warm nights I can sit out and enjoy the dark solitude of the park in front of me.

I unlock the door and bring the shopping into the hall. I change out of my work clothes into my sparkly jeans and a new T-shirt. Time to make dinner. I place a large pot of water onto the stove and open a bottle of Rioja. I like to cook. It relaxes me as I wind down after whatever has been my day, especially with the promise of a lovely evening with Dan. While the lasagne boils, I chop the onions and garlic and fry them with the mince. I assemble what would be needed for the salad and unpack the parmesan and cream for the sauce. I am a plain cook but make everything from the best fresh ingredients I can find, as a result I've acquired an undeserved reputation as a good cook. The truth is, I cook well but within a limited range. My planned desert for example is an old favourite, plum crumble and custard.

Everything is done, the lasagne in the oven, the salad made and the crumble waiting to go in the oven later. I lay the table and light candles. The flickering lights give out a warm glow and when I glance in the mirror, a beautiful woman smiles back at me. Dan will be home soon, around 7 he'd said. I wriggle into the sofa's soft cushions. Dan and I are young, free and in love, possibly more in love than any two people have ever been before, and so free we can dance with wolves, set the house on fire or fall down mountains if we want to - yet all I wish for this evening is dinner for the two of us in the relaxing comfort of our home. The secret of happiness - to want what you've already got.

I pour another glass of wine. It's 7.30 pm. Where's Dan? He was checking out a venue to run a drumming workshop in an Arts Centre. Perhaps traffic has held him up. I take the lasagne out of the oven. I don't want it to burn. I pick up the Guardian and read how the world is trying to work out what it means to have a Hollywood cowboy for an American president. I put the paper down. I'm trying to work out what it means that Dan's not here even though it's now 8.15.

I pour another glass of Rioja and put some lasagne onto my plate. I pick at it. Maybe Dan's had an accident. Would the police know to call me? Perhaps he's forgotten we'd planned a meal and evening together. I push away the uneaten lasagne. Maybe he's met a sexy artist at the centre and has gone to the pub with her. I fiddle with the flowers on the mantelpiece. I blow out the candles. I sit back on the sofa and try to engage again in the strange politics unfolding on the other side of the Atlantic. It's too far away; trouble is brewing much closer to home.

At 8.45pm a car arrives. I peep through the curtains and see an old Ford Cortina. In it two people are laughing. One is Dan, the other I can't see because she has big hair that hides her face. I am peeking through curtains like an old maid while Dan is laughing in a car with an unknown woman. He leans over and kisses her on the cheek. He gets out and waves goodbye. She drives off.

DAN

I'm late for dinner. I'm not worried. Lizzie knows I'm not one for disciplined timetables. Never have been. My school reports said things like, 'Daniel has still not learned that work and play do not mix' and, 'If only Daniel applied himself with the same dedication he does to playing football his exam results would greatly improve.' That's why I never bothered with drum lessons and didn't 'work' at the drums, I 'played' with them. I learned the drums by listening to the masters, John Bonham, Charlie Watts, Ginger Baker and especially Keith Moon. Though I have more in common with Keith than just love of the drums. Keith's art teacher had described him as 'Retarded artistically. Idiotic in other respects.' I also failed nearly every subject and hated school. In my weaker moments I thought maybe I was just stupid, mostly I was angry because I knew I was not. Despite he had no idea I existed, Keith and I were brothers. We both burned with that strange passion labelled 'hyperactive'. These days we'd be diagnosed with ADHD and given Ritalin to make us sit still and 'behave'. Thank the God of the Drums we'd been born too early to be saved from ourselves pharmaceutically – at least not in that way.

Like Keith I abandoned the hi-hat cymbals and got a second bass, I used the grooves of R&B and Californian surf rock and played them louder and faster, and again like Keith, I played fills and accents over a wall of white noise from riding the crash. The difference was Keith Moon was a drum genius while I was, well… not. Though with my hyperactive energy and ability to roll out a noise loud enough to frighten horses, I could fool enough people to get into a band, the aptly named 'Noise'.

Despite my lack of genius, in fact the music critic of the local paper suggested I couldn't hold a backbeat if I tried, I loved our gigs at the Rose and Crown. Not that our audience would have noticed the arrhythm of any backbeat; they were generally pissed on the local brew or Newcastle Brown and for all they cared I could have been a hyperactive monkey in a random frenzy rather than a disciple of the high priests, Baker and Moon. But through the years I reckon I've learned enough of the art of drumming to earn a few pounds by teaching it. I go to look over the Arts Centre as a possible venue for drumming workshops. Bethany, who runs the place, shows me around. Bethany is beautiful with wild sexy red hair. I'm drawn to her, especially when she tells me she loves Obsidian and has seen us play a few times. There's nothing like a gorgeous fan to make you feel good about yourself. Plus she tells me she's interested in learning the drums herself and would welcome a drumming workshop at the centre.

It's hard to find venues for teaching the drums; most don't want the noise. Though I reckon it's not the decibel level that turns them off, it's the primitive passions those throbbing drumbeats evoke. So when I meet someone who's open to the jungle vibe, I love the play of it. Bethany's hair more than hints she's up for the hit of some primal energy-play, in fact she and I were having so much fun we went for a drink together. Like I said, discipline is not my thing.

I sense the alluring possibilities with Bethany, and naturally I'm tempted, but copping to how late it is, I pull back from the enticing brink and say I have to go. Though I don't say 'home to my girlfriend' because I'm still enjoying that brink. Bethany is driving in the same direction and offers me a lift. We pull up and I thank Bethany with a hug and a kiss on the cheek. There's more on offer and I let her know I appreciate it with a smile that says maybe one day, and jump out the car. I bound up to the house. I'm late, but hey, things happen - no harm done. I'm looking forward to gossiping with Lizzie over dinner before sliding between the sheets for more riding down that moonlight mile. It's all good.

LIZZIE

Dan walks in. 'Sorry I'm late,' he calls as he hangs up his coat. He seems not to notice the heavy silence stalking him from the sofa. He comes and sits next to me. 'Mmm, that dinner smells good. What's cooking?' He's referring to the dinner, not me. He reaches out to hug me. I'm stiff and unresponsive. 'Hey, are you OK? Is something up?' I can sense an aura of complacent self-congratulatory satisfaction around him that is somehow connected to the woman in the car. Yes, something's up. He rubs his hands and blows on them. 'It's cold outside.' Does he imagine a weather report will calm me down? My stealth bomber silence lets him know how wrong he is. 'Lizzie, I, um, it's just…' His voice trails away. He can't tell me what's kept him because he will then have to tell me about the artist with the sexy hair. He reaches for my hand. 'Look, Lizzie, I'm sorry I'm late when you've clearly gone to all this trouble.'

The trouble, my friend, is not in the cooking.

'Why didn't you call? Where have you been? What have you been doing? Who have you been with?' The beautiful woman I saw in the mirror earlier is gone. She's disappeared in an unseemly rush of angry questions.

'I, er, I, well… there were some interesting people there. I forgot the time.'

'You mean you didn't want to remember.' I stand over him. 'I saw you in the car with that woman so don't pretend to me you just forgot. You fancied her and stayed with her instead of coming home even though you knew I was making a meal for us. And then you wank on about the weather when really you've been aching to get it on with that artist and her big hair. And if you think a pathetic apology is going to sort this, you couldn't be more wrong!'

'Hey – there's no need to get hysterical.'

'Don't tell me I'm hysterical when you've fucked up this evening because you live in a delusional belief you are amazing and women are just dying to fall at your feet. Well I've got news for you, you are not a sex god, you're a narcissistic arsehole who can fuck off.'

Dan leaps to his feet. 'Who the hell do you think you are to speak to me like that?' He shouts with clenched fists. The threat of violence turns my rage into something so cold the mercury freezes.

'Leave my house immediately,' I say. My breath forms frost on all surfaces.

'Ah,' he says. 'So that's how it is.' He brings his face close to mine. 'I can see I am not welcome. Well OK, I'm out of here.'

An abyss cracks into existence between us. We glare at each other across the great divide, in his eyes a forest fire, in mine, a frozen wasteland. I speak slowly, one word at a time. 'Yes. This. Is. How. It. Is.' I'm an Ice-Witch spitting icicles into his heart.

Dan turns and pulls on his coat. He comes back one more time. His finger stabs the air in front of my face. 'Don't you ever tell me what to do. You don't own me. I owe you nothing. You're a demanding bitch who thinks she's always right, well let me tell you, you're making a big mistake!' He slams the door as he walks out.

The land splinters and crackles as it freezes down through the earth's crust into the mantle. In the sub-zero temperatures of the arctic, things do not bend, they freeze, become brittle and break.

DAN

Before I've taken off my coat, Lizzie goes crazy on me. I'm like, 'Hey, what's going on here? I'm just having an interesting conversation with a woman who happens to be a useful contact, and yes I like her, and yes I could see where we could have gone, but my focus is on working with her to create drumming workshops, not fucking her in the car park round the back of the Arts Centre. Why on earth would I when it's all happening with you?' But Lizzie keeps coming at me. 'Look,' I say, 'I'm just a bit late for Christ's sake, it's nothing more than that.' It makes no difference; Lizzie's gunning for me. 'Lay off,' I tell her, 'what's a cold dinner anyway? It's hardly the end of the world. I've done nothing wrong, back off.' But she's not listening and I get louder until words come out of me and I don't know what I'm saying. 'You don't know me, you don't own me, I don't have to justify myself to you or anyone, fuck the fuck off!'

Furies swirl around inside me. My body explodes with rushes of energy. There's so much pressure in my head, I can't stand it a minute longer. I'm out of here. I slam the door as I leave.

LIZZIE

Dan's walked out. I throw uneaten lasagne in the bin, stick unwashed plates in the sink, screw up the tablecloth and throw it onto the sofa. I'm off to bed. I'll clean up tomorrow. I click down the lock on the door and bolt it. If he comes back now he won't be able to get in.

I lie in bed awake. Adrenaline runs through me and into the sheets. If only sleep would carry me into sweet dreams, not this nightmare where Dan is a self-centred narcissistic arrogant arsehole. This is not the Dan I fell in love with. He's gone. Disappeared. And in his place is someone I never want to see again.

DAN

I walk through dark streets with furious conversations going on in my brain. What I should have said. What I shouldn't have said. What I meant to say but didn't. I kick at a tree stump on the edge of the pavement. If only she'd not gone off on one like a wailing banshee it'd have been alright. But she did. So it's not alright. And I'm angry it's not alright and want to smash furniture and kick bricks. It's raining. I'm wet. She started this whole thing but she's in the warmth while I'm pounding the streets in a biting wind. The cold, the rain and the injustice make me even angrier with Lizzie than I'm already angry with her for making me angry in the first place.

Only the spiritually dishevelled and morally unkempt wander city streets in the early hours of the morning, decent folk are in their beds, so if you're out and about in this pitiless rain then either you're working for one of the emergency services or you're up to no good. I'm up to no good. In fact I'm no good at anything. Not anything that matters. Bashing a drum with sticks is hardly what really matters. But then nothing and no one gives a shit about whether I'm good, bad or indifferent at anything. No one cares. Yet this is Lizzie's fault not mine. She started it. She went off on one, not me. I was just living my life. I'll go round to Matt's and beat a few drums. They won't let me down.

LIZZIE

I lie awake. The self-doubt kicks in. Maybe I read it wrong. Maybe the flush of self-satisfaction I saw in his smile wasn't about the hit he'd got from that woman with the hair, maybe I jumped to conclusions. Perhaps I should have been more persuasive and shown him with smiles that however big her hair she can't take him on the journeys I can. But I'm not wrong. He was definitely getting off on the attention she was beaming at him. I don't know why I hadn't seen it before but he's like so many other musicians I know, hooked on the heroin of being adored.

I yank at the duvet and turn over trying to escape the turmoil of obsessing about a man who seduces you with honeyed words and promises safety from all harm, then turns and sinks his teeth into you with the bite of a starving Rottweiler. I hate him. I plump up my pillow with the vehemence of a killer. Maybe I'm mad, as in crazily insane, to feel such rage when you could say all he did was come home late for dinner.

It's 3am. I go for a pee. It's icy cold outside. On my way back to bed I think of Dan trying his key, the door remaining locked and so he's wandering the streets all night. I unbolt the door. I stumble back to bed not knowing if this is kindness or weakness. After all, the law of the jungle is, 'kill or be killed.' And I should have learned that by now, the more vulnerable and easily wounded the animal, the more vicious and deadly are the ways it protects itself.

DAN

Down in the basement at Matt's I mash up enough grooves and shuffles to fill the Apollo several times over. That gets rid of the critical voices in my head, for a while anyhow. I'll never get rid of them completely. Though I'd like to. Especially the voices telling me I'm a failure and a fool who'd be better off being someone else entirely. Thank god for the drums. They don't beat down on me with a remorseless list of my failures and inadequacies.

I'm sweating from the action and grab a towel to wipe my face. Maybe my true love is the drum, not Lizzie. After all, our love affair began a long time ago. I lean back and remember the night I'd gone with some mates to a club where Cream were playing. Five of us, pimply schoolboys masquerading as street-wise ninja's, roughed up our hair and borrowed George's sister's psychedelic clothes. We practised hip talk by reading Oz, but try saying 'Groovy baby, it's cool, where are the chicks, man?' without giggling when you're a 15 year old wanker with spots. Fortunately George's sister was going out with one of the bouncers so despite the acne and uncool grins he nodded us in. The music was fantastic, but what did it for me however was when Eric Clapton and Jack Bruce left the stage and Ginger Baker took up the baton for a drum solo.

Most people imagine the drum solo is a break when the important guys go backstage for a pint or two, and whatever else might be going round, while the drummer bashes out a few rhythms to keep the punters happy. But that night in Salisbury, the Drum Solo was revealed as shamanic magic for the soul. Ginger Baker stroked, caressed, hit, smacked and beat those drums until a savage jungle pulse thumped through our veins. His arms became spinning blurs that forced us into a frenzy and compelled us to surrender to the primal rhythm that lies under all sound. There's only one way to listen to awesome polyrhythms like these - you feel them in your bones and dance.

Films of the late sixties show beautiful people wafting elegant arms in the air and swaying in tie-dyed kaftans to Pink Floyd or the Byrds with wide eyes seeing into an alternative acid coloured cosmos. But this was Salisbury - a guy going bananas on a dance floor wasn't something you saw often. A few adventurous folk in the provinces may have begun occasionally to trip the light fantastic and shake to the beat, but Ginger's drums forced me into spasms and jerks only seen in Wiltshire previously in ECT and epileptic seizures. A space cleared around me. Not that I noticed. Those drums made me forget myself and I remembered I was someone else - someone for whom the beat hammering into my soul was the one true religion. Though if I wanted to become an urban shaman like Ginger Baker, I'd have to first get hold of a drum kit.

Months of helping out in the factory, taking dogs for walks, cleaning cars and windows later I was at Macy's Music paying for a second hand drum kit. I struggled across Salisbury Town Centre in the rain carrying drum boxes and long metal poles pretending to be a roadie for the Rolling Stones and lovingly assembled them in my bedroom. I sat on the bed. I could do no more than stare at them. The Bass and Snare drums, the Tom Toms, Hi Hats, Ride and Crash Cymbals. They were magnificent. They were real. And they were mine. Matt popped round with his guitar and the rest of the evening was an ecstasy of jerking bodies and loud noise.

Since then, the drums have saved me from myself hundreds of times. They save me again. I beat the savagery out of me and play right through to the other side of my fury. Though I'm not sure if my detached calm is the serenity of wisdom or because I don't fucking care anymore. It could be I'm just knackered. I curl up on the sofa among the empty Rizla packs, cigarette burns and a variety of unsavoury stains left by previous inhabitants, and close my eyes.

Chapter 4   A River Runs Through Us

LIZZIE

I wake a second time with a bleak emptiness beside me and shiver in a bed empty of all warmth. I have lost my love. Perhaps I never had it. Perhaps I've only ever seen love through the distorted lens of my own longing and never known what real love is. It certainly doesn't seem to be where I've looked for it, in the sighs and ecstatic movements of sexual love. Maybe true love is a selfless transcendental love, the kind Buddhists go in for, where you serenely smile with compassion for all sentient beings and never get entangled in the vagaries of human sexual love. That way no broken dreams could stab into my heart ever again and accuse me of the most dismal failure of all, the failure to love. I stare at the ceiling in my own private Zazen. How could I have got it all so wrong?

I tried meditation at a Buddhist centre once. We sat in a circle and watched our breath. Though I watched the clock, impatient for the 'sitting silently doing nothing while the grass grows' to finish so I could move in on the meditation teacher. The muscles in his tanned arm had rippled when he banged the gong and sent decidedly un-meditative tingles up my spine. And when he explained how meditation can lead to a blissful state of nirvana, his slow Californian drawl and long flowing locks spoke more of the beach parties and stoned cool of a surfer than the saffron robes and shaved head of a monk. He seemed to take kindly to my advances however, though it might have been compassion for a sentient being in need, and took me for rides on his motorbike. To teach you how you can meditate even on the road, he'd said, hoping to expand my consciousness beyond desire and the illusion of worldly pleasure. I took him home with me. To teach you how you can meditate even in bed, I'd said, wanting him to feel the unworldly pleasure *in* desire. After all, I told him, you can't get away from the material reality of the body, which is literally what matters and no illusion. And I leaned in as if to kiss him and bit his lip so he'd know for sure. Anyway, I told him authoritatively, you can't be alive with a dead body, and that body is sexual - sex is the fact of life on this planet. I think I got through to him because the last I heard, he'd left the Buddhists and gone off to a Tantric Ashram in Pune.

Maybe sex and love are not so different after all. In which case I may not be quite as fucked up as I think I am. Though, if you think about it, to think you're fucked up is pretty fucked up. Perhaps it's best not to think too much. Not with a mind like mine anyway. Though neither thinking nor meditating changes the fact that I'm lying in a cold and empty bed and Dan has gone.

Dawn streaks across the sky. I get up, shower and dress for school. Today I'm to teach a class of twelve year olds for two hours. I've planned an improvisation game of what would happen if we were on a desert island together. I'm already on a desert island.

DAN

I thought I'd lie awake for hours but the next thing I know, it's morning. My shaving gear and toothbrush are at Lizzie's. I have to go back there sometime so I guess now is as good a time as any. Maybe she's calmed down after a good night's sleep.

LIZZIE

I'm eating tasteless toast when a key turns in the lock and in walks Dan. He takes off his coat and stands by the table looking down at me. 'If you want coffee, there's some made.' My voice is as flat as a dream that's died. 'Thanks,' he says, and goes into the kitchen. I twist in my chair and stare after him. 'I have to leave for work soon,' I say. He returns with his coffee. I look for a sign he's ready to apologise. I don't see one.

He pulls out a chair and sits down. 'Shall we start over?' He scratches his chin. He's nervous but that doesn't mean he's not ready to slice an obsidian scalpel into me.

'I don't know,' I say.

He puts his elbows on the table and clasps his hands. 'Let's see if we can sort this out. I don't know how but I'm here.' Whatever his words, his eyes look at me with suspicion. I take a sip of coffee, put my mug down and wait. There is the ticking of the clock, the whoosh of cars in the street, and a silence that could kill a lion.

'I'm here too,' I say eventually. 'But I have only half an hour before I have to leave for work.'

'OK, I'll start,' he says. 'I have no idea why you went off on one last night. I was late for dinner, OK, and for that I apologise.' He lifts his hands and presents his palms to me. Is he trying to show me he doesn't have a gun? If so, he's playing a role in a very different movie from mine. I'm in a re-make of Roman Polanski's *Repulsion* where I'm Catherine Deneuve playing a mentally ill woman who is repulsed by men and sits alone in an apartment while her mind unspools into madness and hallucinations; he's Eliot Gould in the noir thriller *The Long Goodbye,* adrift in a self-obsessed society where lives can be thrown away without a backward glance and notions of friendship and loyalty are meaningless. He puts his hands flat on the table. 'But I don't get why you were so hysterical. What the hell have I done to make you go off on one like that?' He slightly shakes his head completely unaware we're in such divergent genres we couldn't even lip synch into the same conversation. I don't know where to begin.

'For a start, I wasn't hysterical, I was angry. You calling me hysterical proves you think this is all down to me. Well it isn't. You need to bloody grow up, see your side of things and take responsibility.'

He stares at me across a gulf so wide I can't see any viaduct, cantilever, arch or suspension bridge spanning it. 'One thing's for sure,' he says, 'if you want a conversation with me, you'll have to stop coming on so fucking superior and self-righteous.'

'That's rich coming from someone with narcissistic Oedipal fantasies so deluded he imagines he's some kind of omnipotent sex-god. And if you think I am going to pander to such deranged arrogance, you're very much mistaken.'

He spins right around and back to face me. 'What the fuck are you on about? You're talking absolute crap.' He leans on the table, his face close to mine. 'Your fancy long words mean nothing to me. And let me inform you, Lizzie Loughran, you will never manage to control me in a million years.' He stares at me. I stare back. He pulls away. 'This is going fucking nowhere. I'm out of here.'

He seems to be in a soap opera spitting out an exit line as the theme tune kicks in and the end credits roll. In my film we're teetering on the edge of a chasm and about to fall down a sheer rock face with no ropes.

DAN

I arrive back at Lizzie's and she goes haywire all over again for no reason, going on about Oedipal omnipotent fantasies and deranged narcissistic arrogance. I haven't a clue what she's on about except she goes on about it as if I've murdered a kitten. She's crazy. I want to turn around, get my coat and leave. She breathes out a long sigh of resignation, despair, impatience, sadness... I've no idea. I scratch my chin and wait for whatever's going to come flying at me.

'I know I went off on one. I was very upset,' she says.

'OK,' I say. A tension in my neck softens, a tiny release, like a single bubble rising in a glass of sparkling water, not so anyone would notice. But I remain on guard; she's not finished.

'We had an arrangement and I made a meal, but you didn't seem to care and just got off on having fun with the woman who drove you home. You came in all smiles and so pleased with yourself it was as if I didn't matter at all. I felt insignificant and abandoned.'

At least she's not throwing poisonous darts at me and there are tears in her eyes. I'll try to explain and smooth things over.

'It's true, I wasn't really thinking of you or what we'd arranged but that wasn't because I don't care about you. It was just that I was where I was, you know, in the moment and all that.'

'Cut the Zen crap about being in the here and now - you're not the Dalai fucking Lama!'

'OK, Lizzie, OK.' This is where I need a horse whisperer, someone who knows what to say and how to say it. I always get it wrong and send the horses bolting in a blind gallop. 'I get that you were hurt, but that wasn't my intention. Yes, I fancied Bethany, but I'm here now aren't I?' I manage to bite back saying, of course I fancied her, she's beautiful and sexy. Even I know that's not something to blurt out here. 'Can't we just forget it and relax?'

I have no idea what Lizzie wants or what's going on. I just want it to stop. I love her - why isn't that enough?

LIZZIE

We face each other across the table. A mug with a sunflower on one side is half filled with coffee that's gone cold. The crust of my toast and marmalade is covering a design of daisies on a plate. There are rings on the pine wood from hot drinks that have sat on this table waiting to be drunk while I've opened mail, read newspapers, marked homework, written letters, sent birthday cards to friends all over the world and now I'm sitting here, opposite someone I love more than I have ever loved anyone before, who probably has to leave because this love is hurting us beyond our pain thresholds. Yet Dan just wants to 'forget it and relax', pretend nothing's happened. He hopes this fight is just a freak wave in a calm sea. Well I know rogue waves like these can smash surfers to smithereens and drown even ancient mariners with maps of the depths carved into their bones. He thinks he can surf any wave, even monster waves, and because he loves me, that's enough, love can cure everything. But he doesn't know the darkness of those depths where there's not a photon of sunlight. I do. And I've fallen into that darkness all over again. I try to fight back the tears that are threatening to fall but they have a life of their own. The words tumble out of me in a rush.

'When you didn't arrive, I thought you'd had an accident, then maybe that you'd forgotten, then I saw you kiss that woman with the hair, and I thought you wanted to be with her more than with me.' I wish I could stop my tears but they roll down my cheeks as a torrent of feeling pours out of the black hole inside me. 'I might appear to you to be together, someone who can surf tsunamis without drowning, but that's just an act. Really I'm a broken, spread-eagled catastrophe spiralling out of control. In fact I'm so fucked up you'd better leave before I drag you down with me and we both drown. A broken person like me could never be with someone like you, someone with life and warmth, ok not perfect but not a shameful existential mistake like me.' I wipe my tears with my hands and spread streaks of mascara over my face. 'I really loved you, Dan. And now I have to say goodbye. I've flown too close to the sun and have fallen into the sea. And now I'm drowning.' I sob like I'm bleeding to death.

DAN

Lizzie's gone from an icy hatred verging on the near absolute zero of the Boomerang Nebula, through the indifference of a dead flat fish lying on a fishmonger's marble slab, to a semi-psychotic breakdown. On the one hand she says I'm a psychopath, on the other, I'm way out of her league and it's over between us. I've no bloody idea what's going on. This is verging on psychiatric territory, not remotely within the expertise of a drummer. She's bent over pouring out a river of snot and tears. Who'd have thought we have so much water in us? She talks about drowning and, yes, it looks like she's drowning in herself.

I want to reach out and take her in my arms but she's so unpredictable and crazy she might as easily sink her teeth into me as let me hold her. I compromise and go to the kitchen to get her the kitchen roll to help mop up her tears. I tear off a piece and pass it to her. She takes it. 'Thank you,' she says. I sit there not knowing what to say and so say nothing.

LIZZIE

I look up and see Dan staring at me with concern. I see his blue eyes flecked with grey. I see his hands flat on his thighs. I see his blonde hair, falling over his left eye. I see him brush it away, perhaps out of habit, perhaps to see me better. I see the brown and red aliveness in his skin. I see the small scar on his cheek from a fall off a horse as a child. I see his chest rise and fall as he breathes. I see the fear in his eyes that I've gone crazy. He's maybe thinking I need an ambulance to cart me off to an asylum, or at least a psychiatrist to obtain a prescription for anti-psychotic medication.

When we first met, Dan invited me to fly with him into the heat and light of the sun. I tried to warn him, if he stayed with me, he'd have to swim down into the cold black waters of the deep ocean. But you can't swim to those depths without knowing how to drown. I've drowned enough times to know drowning in these dark waters is not necessarily the tragedy it appears. It can be a liberation from the heaviness of gravity and a release from all striving. It can be a floating lightness with no more struggles to remain upright nor weary muscles from climbing the ladders of status and achievement. It can be a drifting freedom to travel in three dimensions supported on all sides by water that turns out to be a friend, not an enemy. Dan can fly because he's not afraid to crash land; I can dive deep because I'm not afraid to drown. I see the fear in his eyes and want to reassure him, don't be afraid, you can't go with the flow if you always hold onto the firm solidity of land and you can't swim to the depths without knowing how to drown - this is not a catastrophic drowning in darkness, it's me falling into the depths of myself. But I can't. These understandings swim in my psyche like tadpoles that have not yet evolved into frogs with legs and lungs who can hop onto land and croak, and so remain unsaid. Besides, you can't reassure someone there's no need to be afraid when you yourself are afraid - especially when what you're afraid of *is* yourself.

DAN

Lizzie blows her nose and looks at me. She looks devastated, a wreck, gone into territory I've never been to and can't say I want to. At least her sobs have subsided.

'Have you got anything to say?' She looks at me with her head slightly tilted and a little of the old Lizzie in her eyes. I'm wary I might set her off again.

'I don't know what to say. I might say the wrong thing and I don't want to hurt you more than you are already hurting.'

'Just tell me if you don't want to be with me any more. I'd rather know.'

'Of course I want to be with you. I am sorry if anything I've done has hurt you but...' I reach around my mind trying to find words that will explain I need my freedom though in a way that won't hurt her any more than she seems to be already. 'It's complicated,' I end up saying.

LIZZIE

I push my hair away from my face. Dan's looking at me with a worried frown, anxious he's with a woman on the edge of a nervous breakdown. 'Maybe if you've been ship-wrecked and smashed to smithereens on hard rocks then to drown is not a tragedy, it's an escape. I mean maybe not being alright is alright, maybe feeling fucked up is not fucked up.' I run my fingers through my hair. 'Oh I don't know what I mean.' We're both lost. Neither of us knows what to do or how to be in this situation. And there are no answers anywhere I can see. But then if there were we'd learn the ten million commandments on how to live life alongside the times tables. There are no rules. Though I keep trying to find them. It seems we have to feel our way through the labyrinth of our humanity blind. Like when you drown, you end up on the bottom of the ocean among the creatures that live in the midnight zone, the ones who swim completely blind except for whatever faint bioluminescence they've created themselves. That's us, all of us. We're all stumbling about in the dark with only the bioluminescence we've created for ourselves to shed any kind of light on this thing called life.

DAN

I'm lost here. Lizzie seems to be trying to say her tears are nothing to be afraid of but that's not how it looks to me. All I can think to do is reach out and hold her hand. She doesn't pull away.

'Maybe I should go for therapy but I'm not sure talking about any of this will change anything,' she says. She leans back and sighs. 'And right now I have to go teach drama to children who'd rather be playing football or running free in the fields.'

I've had enough drama to last me years, but I don't say so. 'I don't know what you need, Lizzie, but I do know you're funny, intelligent, beautiful, creative and kind. Your friends love you and so do I. Every now and then some demon gets into you and beats you to a pulp. I can't understand it, but I do love you.' She leans into me. I stroke her hair. 'How about we do something together this evening? Maybe go to the new Star Wars movie.' I hope I come across as caring and not just trying to escape. She gives me a slight smile. 'Yes, I'd like that.'

In every group the bass and the drummer need a deep rapport, else there's no foundation. The lead singer, lead guitar and rhythm guitar, they give you the melody and are the front men on the stage. They take you high, play the riffs, and carry the tune you sing along to, but the bassist and the drummer, they're elemental. Without their grounding, nothing will fly and the band goes nowhere. The electrifying primal performances of the front guys totally depend on the drum and bass giving out the pulse and groove that hold the whole show together. Aston Barret, the bass player with Bob Marley and the Wailers, described it, 'The drum, it's the heartbeat, and the bass, it's the backbone.' Lizzie's the front woman.

She's got the charisma that can telegraph every nuance of a song, mesmerise an audience into following her even into silence, can reach for notes that aren't there and still she sings them. I love this about her, but I'm also wary. She's angry and the whole house shakes, she laughs and the stars brighten, she cries and rivers burst their banks. Such brilliance casts deep shadows. I'm standing in those shadows. Perhaps I have to love her like I love my drums, love her enough that I'm content to be at the back, eclipsed by the front men who strut their stuff in the limelight. Because I know, even if no one else does, without me this show goes nowhere.

LIZZIE

One summer I went to Italy with an Italian boyfriend. In Tuscany we walked hand in hand along the moonlit beaches of Follonica Beach, in Florence we gazed at Botticelli's Birth of Venus in the Uffizi Gallery, and in Venice we kissed in a gondola under the Bridge of Sighs. Full of the beauties of Italian culture and the careless innocence of young love, he took me to a C17th villa. 'È una casa di famiglia,' he said. 'You'll love it.' I did. Complete with balconies, towers, stone steps, terraces and courtyards, sweeping stairs and wide halls that led into elegant rooms with marble floors, antique chandeliers, gold mirrors and beautifully faded colours on the walls, it overlooked Lago Maggiore and the Alps. The palatial dining room, lit by radiant moonlight shining in from the lake under ceilings that depicted gods and angels in their heavenly glory, could not have been a more magnificent setting for our first fight.

He accused me of flirting with his cousin. It was 'un attacco alla sua mascolinità e un tradimento dell'onore dell'amore,' he said. I told him he was a male chauvinist who objectified women and wanted to control me. He stood up full of menace and tight rage, and shook his fist in my face. I glared back, my lip curled with threat. Suddenly we were in vicious territory, fighting with claws and teeth to rip flesh and draw blood. Under all that romantic sweetness had lain a raw anarchy that erupted in our fight and proved even lovers who've walked hand in hand under an Italian moon and kissed under the Bridge of Sighs do not escape the law of the jungle, kill or be killed.

Golden mirrors reflected a thousand points of light from chandeliers onto gods painted on the ceiling. They looked down on the struggling and confused mortals below with a serene indifference, perhaps mildly entertained by the spectacle of these human creatures and their strange passions. But whatever those gods thought, something changed under their gaze and a defiance rose in me. Maybe it was Lorenzo's lack of conviction in his machismo posturing. A few days earlier he'd cried when we witnessed a donkey being beaten for moving too slowly, its back bent under a load of firewood. Maybe it was the humanist spirit of the Renaissance itself that ordered me to defy those sneering immortals, after all, who created those mighty gods in the first place? Or maybe my period was due and I was angry at any hint of the patriarchy. But whatever was behind it, I was going to exact revenge on even those old masters of the art, the ancient gods. And I knew exactly how.

Their might and power can shock and awe, kill with impunity, create and destroy worlds on a whim, but they're impotent when it comes to making love.

You don't need love when you're already perfect. You don't need anything. A bit of adoration and worship might not go amiss, possibly a few prayers, but that's not love is it? Only we frail mortals, with our imperfections, insecurities, needs and inadequacies, our awful mistakes, our dreadful anxieties about death and annihilation, only we can make love, can create the love that brings all things to life. I reached out to Lorenzo and under the marble-hard gaze of those old gods we walked through the palatial windows onto the balcony without a backward glance, lay under the stars and made love. The kind of love only weak, frail and frightened mortals know, a love so raw, exposed and naked, nothing can hide in it, yet so potent it makes even the gods jealous. Because in the depths of our humanity, with all its frailties and imperfections, we can make a love with such power and glory it turns those immortal gods green with envy. Why else would they drive us mad and then destroy us?

Chapter 5   Music Feeds the Love

DAN

I'd invited Lizzie to one of our gigs. I'd been putting it off because it was one of those make or break situations. If she didn't like our music, that'd be it. But by then we had a small following and I fancied her seeing me in my elemental role as frenzied drummer to screaming fans. Actually they didn't scream that much, they shouted out requests in between knocking back pints. We could handle classic rock or a punk/reggae mix no problem, heavy metallers were tougher to please. Though even a ballad can sound heavy if you give out a few blast beats and split four strokes between the hands and the feet. But really we fancied ourselves as part of the alt rock scene, think REM and early Talking Heads. The New York Times described alt rock as, 'hard-edged rock distinguished by brittle, '70s-inspired guitar riffing and singers agonising over their problems until they take on epic proportions.' I could run with that. I hoped Lizzie could too.

LIZZIE

I'm home around 4.30pm. It's cold. I turn up the heating, peel off my school uniform, blouse, skirt and tights and step into the shower. The water runs down my hair, face, arms and body, washing off the thirty or so kids who'd not wanted to act in the coming of age drama I'd planned for them until I changed it into a sci-fi war between dinosaurs and aliens. I wrap one towel around my waist and the other around my hair and wander into the kitchen. I wonder if Dan has noticed he never sees me naked, that I always slide into bed sideways, that while he emerges from the shower and wanders around making breakfast stark naked, I hide the evidence of my past with a towel wrapped around me.

I light a cigarette. I'm nervous about this evening. I'm going to see Dan gig at The Swan. I haven't seen him play before and know it's a big thing for him. It is for me too. What if his band mates don't like me and freeze me out? What if surrounded by adoring fans he realises he wants to play the field rather than stay with me? What if I don't rate Obsidian's music at all? Maybe I could pretend to like it even if I didn't. Except I know where pretence goes, spiralling into an alternative reality that requires constant vigilance to maintain. It's like keeping a hundred plates spinning on sticks, only worse because if one falls the whole lot crashes. So I'm trying to keep it real with Dan even though my habit is to seek the refuge of lies. Though, lies are more brittle than reality, like it's easier to wake a person truly asleep than someone pretending to be asleep, so maybe in the end it's reality that offers the real refuge. But if we're seeking refuge because reality is so harsh, what kind of refuge is that? My mind can swerve down paths that lead to the edge of a cliff. I need another cigarette.

I reach for my cigarette packet. I pull one out and put it between my lips. I feel for the matches among the debris on the sofa, strike one and hold the flame to the tip. I breathe in as the tobacco catches light. The nicotine travels via my lungs into my bloodstream and I give myself over to that first sweet hit with its seductive promise of deliverance from the existential angst of our human condition. I lean back into the cushions and gaze at the glowing tip that's going to save me from further forays down the wormhole of myself. Maybe it's not the nicotine that is addictive, it's that glowing red tip on the end of your cigarette so there's always at least this tiny light in the pitch black of whatever dark night of the soul is upon you in that moment.

I sit by the fire and dry my hair while I wait for Jan and Michelle. I've asked them to come with me because I need support. I pull on a scoop line T-shirt and my new tight parachute pants. I rub Vaseline into my hair to give it a shine. I spice up my eye shadow with neon purple and green. I'm pretty much ready for a night getting down on the dance floor to Dan's band when the doorbell rings. It's Jan and Michelle. They've brought flowers. There's always a reason when your lesbian mates bring you flowers for no reason. These two are going to ask or tell me something they think I won't want to hear.

'It's cold. I need a drink of something. What have you got?' Jan shrugs off her coat, reaches for Michelle's, and hangs them on the back of the door. She's gone straight to the kitchen without waiting for an answer. She's been here often and knows the lay of the land. They both do. Jan sits next to me, Michelle on the chair facing us. 'OK, tell us about this guy Dan you've been seeing,' says Jan. 'We've hardly seen you since you took up with him,' says Michelle.

I could tell them about his drumming, his sheep shearing, his kindness, his laughter, his smiling blue eyes, how he holds me in his arms with a warmth that melts resistance like butter in the midday sun, how he touches me with a gentle invitation to feel parts of my skin I've not visited since I was a baby, how when we make love rivers run uphill, fish fly and the sun shines at night, or I could just give it to them straight. These two have been my friends since early feminist days. We've seen each other rise and fall through many levels of consciousness and hemlines, marched alongside each other to reclaim the night, protest about Miss World and demand abortion-rights. They are the only ones who know some of my darker secrets and even in the relentless self-revelation required during deep consciousness raising they've never betrayed me. They deserve the full story. I give it to them.

'I love him.'

They glance at each other and nod. It's as they thought.

'You mean 'love him' as in you are lusting after each other and enjoy nights of passion together, or 'love him' as in, he's your soul-mate?'

'I don't know,' I say. 'But this one's different.' I look at them in turn. 'I think it's the real thing.'

Jan purses her lips. 'If that's the case then he'd better be worth you.'

Michelle gets to her feet. 'OK, we'll see him tonight and give you our verdict later.'

DAN

I've tuned the drums, drunk a pint and am twirling my drumsticks at the back of the room while the place fills up. Chris is in the final straits of a meandering anecdote that involves a sandwich, a truck and a dog with three legs when Lizzie arrives. She takes off her hat and shakes down her hair. Rainbows fly through the room. She looks for me and her green eyes shine out from behind her fringe. I'm not the only one who looks at how her body shimmers when she moves in her low T-shirt and tight pants.

She sees me and gestures that she's going to the bar to get a drink. I pretend to be listening to the final act of Chris's story but really I'm keeping an eye on Lizzie. She's met Matt before as he was her friend Carole's boyfriend a while back, but I want to introduce her to the rest of the band. You only introduce babes to your band when you're having more than a few nights of fun with them. It's a rite of passage not unlike it used to be when you introduced girlfriends to your parents. This is more risky though. Oumar has already stopped fingering his keyboard and begun to smile at the green-eyed beauty as she approaches. I step between them before he can come onto her with his sexy black keyboard-player vibe. I hug her. Her hair smells of bluebells and summer. I keep my arm around her shoulders as I turn her to face the band. 'Guys, this is Lizzie. Lizzie, this is Obsidian.'

'Pleased to meet you,' says Oumar, with a grin that lets her know he's up for a lot more pleasing if she has a mind that way.

Lizzie smiles. A Californian sun shines down on this band of brothers who don't own a surfboard between them. 'Pleased to meet you all,' she says, 'I've heard so much about you.' Though she speaks with a cool sexy vibe not the polite straightness of a wife meeting her husband's work colleagues. She puts her arm around my waist as she speaks. I shift slightly so Oumar can see how the land lies. He nods to me. Loyalty to your band mates usually takes precedence over following your energy with a band member's woman. Though that loyalty only goes so far and you need to keep your guard up. Especially when your lady's beauty is well capable of bending loyalties in several directions. It's time to climb the stage, or rather walk to the floor area marked out for us, and give out the tunes. I kiss Lizzie, a long lingering kiss, and not only for Oumar's sake.

LIZZIE

Jan and Michelle are eyeing up Dan from their vantage point by the bar. Their verdict shouldn't matter but it will. Jan and Michelle are sisters from the first days of the Women's Liberation Movement, way back when women were supposed to be content being sisters, girl-friends, mothers, daughters, wives, muses, honorary blokes... Until the glaring absence became apparent, not even 'me too', just 'me'. That kind of sisterhood creates a bond you can't argue with. Or rather you *can* argue but it makes no difference, you're still sisters. Life will be easier if they give Dan their seal of approval; I'll be able to moan to them when he gives me grief without the two of them dishing out relentless lesbian compassion for someone stuck with an agent of the patriarchy. And we've done plenty of moaning about the patriarchy. It first began when we went to a pub after a meeting to plot the downfall of western capitalism and were told this pub didn't serve women. The brothers had swaggered about, waving their roll ups and suggested we wait demurely for them outside while they supped their pints. They thought it was hilarious. We didn't. We began our own meetings.

Our comrades were not pleased. They tried to talk us out of our bourgeois individualism and told us feminism was a divisive capitalist plot to undermine the solidarity needed for the class struggle. But we just stared at them with a new look, one eyebrow raised, a knowing smile and fuck-you drags on the fags. 'Back up boys, you're breathing our air!' They soon came round. Most of them realised pretty quickly, if they wanted to get up close and personal with the sisters in future, they had to take feminism seriously.

Meetings like ours sprang up all over the place. Within a year Marxist Feminists, Radical Feminists, Socialist Feminists, Libertarian Lesbians, Anarchist Feminist Separatists and other species evolved. We'd often end up fighting each other about which was worse, patriarchy, racism, capitalism, organised religion, global corporate greed destroying the environment or the new VAT on unnecessary items like sanitary towels. Patriarchy was no pushover, we needed to organise ourselves. About a hundred of us, the whole feminist contingent in Manchester at the time, including the Northern Lesbians, an elemental force rather than a faction, congregated in a church hall to organise ourselves into consciousness-raising groups. Jan, Michelle and I joined up with three others and we decided to meet at Jan's because she had two sofas.

Our group met on those two sofas every Monday for the next five years. They saw us through many risings and fallings of consciousness and didn't creak even when we threw ourselves about in the throes of sharing the wounds caused by patriarchy's brutal oppression and those bastard Marxist men we'd tried to turn on with our sexy dancing but who insisted on seeing us as sex objects so we'd had to turn them down. It wasn't all bread and roses being a hard-core feminist in those pioneer days. We had to struggle with the complex demands of being a woman, a cook, a sex goddess, a washer of nappies, a cool counter-cultural chick, a dirty dancer, as well as a self-determining sexual being unafraid to fight for the liberation of all sentient beings, even men, from the oppressions of patriarchy. Plus the day job. Some of us while breastfeeding. All without the support of the sisterhood because we were still creating it. Films at the time still had mostly roles for women as heroic nuns or beautiful desirable sex objects who were bitchy to each other while fighting over men.

We began each meeting sharing anything significant that had happened that week. When one of us was in a crisis such as a broken heart, homeless, no money, or the realisation we'd never again be a size 10, then obviously we'd focus on that, otherwise we'd explore particular subjects we'd planned in advance. Frequent topics were sexuality, motherhood, and what on earth has this thing called love got to do with anything except that it seemed to have something to do with everything. And there is more than one kind of love as Jan and Michelle discovered when they fell in love over the biscuits during a tea break between realising fat is a feminist issue therefore eating chocolate is a political imperative, and we didn't need to define womanhood because it was anything we said it was – because we were women. Obvious after you said it. Jan and Michelle have been together ever since. Dan has his band of brothers,

I have my circle of sisters. I hope Jan and Michelle will give him the OK. Though as lesbians they're unlikely to get off on the same things that do it for me.

DAN

Behind a drum kit you forget everything but the beat. I can't see Lizzie but know she's out there and that intensifies things as the sounds pulse through my blood and I fall into the zone. I have my fans. 'Dan's the man!' they shout. It's the cue for my drum solo while the front guys take a break. I lead into it slowly building the pace, bringing the people with me, turning up the intensity and keeping us together until we hit the ferocity. Just when we're crawling on the floor in a savage slavery to the beat, Matt returns with the bass, Oumar arrives with his chords and we're back together, tighter than ever, making music that flies. Eventually we return to Earth, sweaty, wrung out and nodding to each other because it's all cool.

We pack up. I can't see Lizzie. She must be waiting outside. I hope her friends have gone. They seemed rather heavy to me, as if they'd give me the evil eye if I dropped some phrase that revealed a lack of solidarity with whatever struggle was their thing, racism, sexism, classism, speciesism, ageism, whatever. I've been in trouble before now for using a word or phrase that revealed my low level of political consciousness. It doesn't help when I try to explain, words are not my thing, music, energy, instincts, they're more my realm of play. That just reveals my consciousness is even lower than they'd thought. I want to walk back with just Lizzie. We can wander through the park arm in arm and she can tell me how she adored our tunes, especially my drumming. And if she's going to tell me she didn't, I'd prefer to walk away into the night to gaze at stars alone without witnesses to my angst.

Geoff passes over the fifty quid and we step into the cold night. Chris has picked up a couple of fans, sweet smiling girls who've probably lied to their parents they're doing homework together. He invites us all back to his place but I've seen Lizzie standing at the corner. 'Thanks man, not tonight,' I say. I walk towards her and hug her. She laughs in my ear. 'So the drum-shaman wants to come home with me.' Which lets me know things are cool. I pull her arm through mine and put my hands in my pocket. We walk home like The Freewheelin' Bob Dylan album cover. Up close and in love.

LIZZIE

We walk home through a cold Manchester, but we aren't cold. We lean into each other and I tell him Obsidian's performance was way tighter than I imagined. I don't tell him that when there were shouts 'Dan's the man!' I'd allowed myself a private smile the magician knocking out those primal rhythms would be sighing in my arms later. Dan's happy I enjoyed his drumming. He's laughing, and his warmth spins a magic around us. I squeeze his arm. He's seen how I can fall into a primitive private darkness yet still he's here. This man is going to make me happy.

When we get home, we don't say much. We smile and climb into bed to sing the body electric and play a different kind of music. I lie in Dan's arms. He's gently snoring. Perhaps it's not Dan who holds the magic, it's love. But can love work its magic on someone as broken as me?

Moonlight shines through the window and casts the pale shadows in which ghosts like to hide. They shimmer in the half-light and whisper, 'nothing can save anyone, not even love, because there's no escape from suffering except through the living of it and that's no escape.' Their soft voices insinuate their warnings into my brain. 'And if you don't suffer your darkness, someone else will have to instead and further down the line you'll have to redeem that too.' Dan murmurs in his sleep. I curl closer into his comforting smell and warmth. Maybe the power of love is not that it eases anguish and takes away pain, it's that it gives us the courage to suffer reality so totally there's no karma left to burn a hole in anyone's heart ever again. Though what kind of hope is that?

Chapter 6　　The Ties That Bind

DAN

I wasn't going to tell Lizzie but she saw the invitation in the bin.

'What's this?' She pulls out the card, its gold embossed lettering smeared with tomato ketchup. 'You are invited to the wedding of Sarah Brewin and Charles St John-Stevens on June 21st at Chatterton Hall.' She put her head on one side. 'Is this Sarah that's your sister? If so, why on earth did you put this in the bin?'

I put down my toast and marmalade. I have some explaining to do.

'Well, you see, Lizzie…' I pause. She's not going to get it but I'll try. 'I don't want to go.'

'Why not?'

'I just don't want to, that's why.'

'But why not? Why do you not want to go to your sister's wedding? Won't your family be upset if you're not there?'

'It's not what you think.'

'You don't know what I think, I've not told you yet.'

'Well for a start, my family's not like yours.'

'If they're not like mine that's a reason to go, not one to stay away!'

'You don't understand.'

'What do you mean?'

I stand up. 'I mean Lizzie that I don't want to go and that's that. Let it go.'

But I know Lizzie; she won't let it go. She'll go on and on about it until I tell her more and still she won't get it. I've never met anyone who did. I put my unfinished toast in the bin and the plate in the sink. I stare out the window at two robins fighting. I turn around.

'OK Lizzie sit down. I haven't told you the truth about my family. They're not just well off, they're loaded. I mean they have serious money, shit loads of it. So much they don't know how much they have. They have their people to take care of that stuff.'

I can see Lizzie doesn't understand, how can she? I've not told her much about my family other than I have two sisters, Sarah and Emma, a brother, James, and my father and mother don't get on but pretend in public they do, and I am very different from any of them. So different it's like a dolphin swimming with sharks.

I pull out a chair and sit facing Lizzie with my hands palm down on the table.

'Lizzie, they're not just messed up like most families are, they're completely dysfunctional. And this is the thing, they think they're amazing and superior and classy while the reality is they're so beyond dysfunctional, they're in the realm of totally fucking delusional. Yet they have so much money, they get away with it. They're a bunch of sharks who'd sell their souls in an instant for a quick profit on a deal or a feature in Hello magazine. Except that none of them has a soul to bargain with anymore, they sold them all to the devil a long time ago.' I hit the table. 'And that, Lizzie, is what makes my family truly fucking insane and best avoided at all costs.'

LIZZIE

Dan resists but I don't give way. A wedding is a celebration of love even if the family is a nightmare. Besides, I want to meet his family. What finally clinches it is when I tell him, I need to meet them if only to know I never want to meet them again.

We drive to Hampshire in our smartest clothes. I take extra care with my hair and eye make-up, and even though my dress is from C&A and my bag from Littlewoods, I look stunning. I can tell in the way Dan smiles at me that despite his extreme reluctance to go on this trip, he's proud for his family to see the kind of woman he lives with. And I'm pretty sure, despite Dan's dire warnings of venomous snakes, ruthless vultures and cold-hearted sharks, I'll be able to hold my own. I smile at Dan briefly and turn back to the road as I navigate traffic on the A34. We turn left onto a B road. Two miles further Dan tells me to turn right onto a narrow leafy lane that twists through the Hampshire countryside.

'It's round the next corner,' he says.

We drive through large wrought iron gates onto a gravel driveway through an avenue of lime trees. I see the house and abruptly brake. This is not the large detached house Dan described, it's a manor house with enough bedrooms to house a whole council block. Maybe you can even pay money to walk through rooms and gawp at antiques and oil paintings of ancestors on the walls. I turn to Dan and stare at him with my eyebrows raised and my mouth open in mock surprise. Except it's not mock. Dan shrugs. 'I tried to warn you,' he says. He points to where I should park. We climb out of the car and stretch our legs. Our feet crunch the gravel as we retrieve our bags from the boot and I try not to feel like a heroine in a Jane Austen novel. One relief, there's not an animal predator in sight.

A tall man with even blonder hair than Dan comes out to greet us. 'Hi brother! Welcome.' He clasps Dan in a bear hug. This must be James. Dan has already told me about James, his elder brother, who is taller, better at cricket and more ruthless with a vicious streak that'd kick someone on crutches out the way to save himself the hassle of walking round him. Once he and some mates burned a load of fifty-pound notes in front of a homeless guy just for the fun of it. When Dan asked, how could you? He'd laughed and said, yes I know, like a sixties car park, wrong on so many levels.

James slides towards me. 'Ah, this must be the gorgeous Elizabeth.' I expect a kiss on the cheek but he embraces me in a hug with pelvis moves more bodice ripper territory than a Jane Austen novel. He pulls back, bends over my hand and kisses it. 'Welcome to our humble abode,' he says, with a one-sided smile and an eyebrow raised to show he knows he's being a prick. 'I've heard so much about you.' He can't have. Dan hardly ever speaks to any of them. He pulls my arm through his as we walk into the house. 'I think I'm going to enjoy getting to know you, Elizabeth,' he says. 'Lizzie,' I say. This predator's charm may work on Sloane Rangers who sip Moët and nibble at caviar while Daddy's American Express pays for a trip to the Maldives to discover themselves on a yoga retreat, but it does nothing for me. I turn round to Dan behind us and roll my eyes.

We gather for drinks on the terrace. A barman is making cocktails. I order a Manhattan. James arrives at my side as I'm asking for it to be served on the rocks in a lowball glass rather than traditionally in a cocktail glass with a maraschino cherry. I know my cocktails. I was a cocktail shaker in a bar in Germany.

'I see you are a woman who knows what she wants,' he says.

'I know what I like,' I say. 'What I want is more complex.'

'You can't always get what you want,' he says.

Before he can tell me but if you try sometimes you might find you get what you need, I tell him, 'I'd rather find what I truly long for than merely get what I think I want.'

'And what might that be?' He nods to the bartender to make him a drink like mine.

'Not knowing is an invitation into the experience of the longing which itself may be what we're seeking.' I gaze at him with wide open eyes he can interpret however he likes.

He sips his Manhattan. 'Clearly Dan's gone for a deep one this time,' he says. He runs his finger round the rim of the glass. 'Tell me, what do you make of this?'

'Well it's too heavy on the Angostura bitters and perhaps a Rob Roy would have been more appropriate here with Scotch whiskey instead of rye. But it's all a matter of taste I'm sure you'd agree?' I give him a smile, one of my radioactive ones that promise voyages to somewhere dangerous. Perhaps he imagines I'm flirting with him rather than warning him because he says, 'I'd love to discuss the relative merits of different cocktails with you, perhaps later in the rose garden, but I was meaning this.' He gestures around him at the house and garden and the gathering on the terrace. 'What do you make of all this?' Before I can reply a woman in a pale green linen dress and a cashmere shawl slips her arm through James's. She nods to me. 'James, you have to come with me. Daddy wants the family to have a toast to Sarah and Rupert in the library.'

'Ok.' He holds his arm out to me. 'Are you coming?' 'Just the family,' says the woman. 'Oh but she's almost family. She's Dan's woman. Let me introduce you. Lizzie, Emma, Emma, Lizzie.'

'Oh hello Lizzie. You look charming. Now come on James I know Daddy doesn't like waiting.' She pulls James away with her into the house.

'I'll be back,' says James over his shoulder.

DAN

It went exactly how I knew it would. My mother blanked Lizzie, turning away when Lizzie spoke and not replying even when Lizzie said goodbye. My father was polite, condescending and remote, but then he's like that with everyone. Sarah, in role as royal princess bride, glanced at Lizzie's shoes with a gracious smile and barely disguised pity. Emma looked over Lizzie's dress and jewellery, before rushing off to more important matters in her Lacroix gown and diamonds. James was attentive and engaging, very attentive and engaging. There's nothing he'd like more than to seduce my woman and discard her, looking back at me with a smirk as he strode off. Fortunately he was being watched and just as James was asking Lizzie if she'd like to see his paintings, stroll with him through the rose gardens or go for a spin in his Porsche, Frances, his wife turned up with a brittle smile and insisted he accompany her to somewhere else. As far as I was concerned, we couldn't leave soon enough.

LIZZIE

We're in the car driving home.

'Are you OK Dan? You've said nothing since we left. What's up?'

'Nothing's up. I'm fine. Watch that truck, you came in too soon. You should be paying attention to your driving not going on at me.'

'There was plenty of room. And I'm not going on at you.' I look sideways at him. He's a ball of tension hunched over himself.

'Change gear,' he tells me, 'you're in third.'

'That's because we're climbing, I'll go up a gear when we level off.' Half a minute later later the road flattens and I change gear. 'What's got into you?'

'Nothing's got into me. What are you on about?'

'Well you're in a foul mood and have been ever since we got in the car.'

'No I'm not. Though you can talk. You've been parading around displaying yourself to all and sundry, flirting with anyone who came your way and continually making eyes at James.'

'What are you talking about? I've been doing nothing of the sort.'

'Oh yes? Then why were you laughing with that pompous twit Rupert? Why did you dance with George - twice? And why did you welcome James' smarmy approaches with such eagerness?'

'Don't be ridiculous Dan. Of course I was friendly to people. It was a wedding for goodness sake!'

'I shouldn't have come. It's your fault. You forced me. You often sound like you know what you're talking about when really you haven't a fucking clue and this was another of those times. I'll never listen to you again.'

'Well I'm glad we went. Seeing your family home and the extravagant luxury displayed in all directions, I now understand why you have hardly any possessions and are so critical of frivolous consumerism. The money your family spent on drink alone could pay the national debt of a small country and your sisters wore dresses that cost more than whole towns spend on welfare.' I turn and smile at him. 'Besides, I didn't force you, Dan, I persuaded you. You could have refused. You're a free man.'

DAN

I'm as free as a fox who gnaws off his foot to escape a trap or a prisoner who can choose to look at the bars or his chains. 'Don't give me your fucking analysis of who and what I am! You don't know me. You only think you do.' I'm tight lipped with a fury I don't understand.

'I know some things, Dan,' she says. 'You're like Diogenes who lived in a barrel and told Alexander the Great to stop trying to conquer Persia and instead come live next to him in a barrel. Alexander said, 'Thank you for your wise advice but later, after I've conquered Persia. Though I'm rich and powerful, ask for anything you want and I'll give it to you.' Diogenes thought for a while then said, 'Can you move a bit to the left? Your shadow's blocking the sun.' That's you, Dan. You're Diogenes.' She laughs. 'Having seen the scene of the crime, I now get why you wear clothes until the holes take over, sift through the bin to find paper you can reuse for shopping lists and recycle tea bags by taking out the tea for compost before chucking the bag into the bin.'

She turns to see if I'm smiling. I'm not. This is no laughing matter.

'No, Lizzie, you *don't* get it. If you did you wouldn't laugh. You've absolutely no idea whatsoever about my family. You've just experienced them for one weekend, I've had them my whole fucking life. So don't start thinking you know things when you don't.' I grit my teeth and refuse to look at her.

'Hey, hold on Dan. There's no need to go off on one. It could be a lot worse.' She laughs again. 'You could have remained in the bosom of your family, worn red trousers, gone to regattas in a striped blazer, and driven to polo matches in an ancient Range Rover with dog hairs everywhere saying 'carpe vinum' while swigging Moet from a Fortnum and Mason hamper. A fate worse than being the drummer in a band that plays only ballads, except for the Moet.' She turns and smiles, one of her killer 'come into my parlour' ones. This time I see a spider, not a goddess.

'Let me tell you, Lizzie.' I poke my finger at her for emphasis. 'My life is not a joke for your amusement. Far from it. And if you carry on as if you know what you're talking about when you haven't a fucking clue, you'll fucking regret it.'

LIZZIE

Dan's doing his head in over nothing. Except it has everything to do with the family we just left.

'Oh, so I'm not allowed to make fun of your precious ego? I'm supposed to bow to your innate superiority and bite my tongue because I'm in the presence of someone who must never be laughed at even when he's being a total arsehole - is that it?'

'Ah so that's why you went out of your way to flirt with every fucking guy who spoke to you. You were stupidly compensating for feeling inferior. You've just proved it.' He sneers.

'Look, Dan, you're attacking me because you're full of complex conflicting feelings about your family, which you're projecting onto me and then fighting me. That's what's stupid, not me.'

'Look who's being superior now! Well you can take your fucking psychoanalytical bullshit and stuff it up your arse. I am not going to stay in this car being insulted by you for a moment longer. Stop the car, I'm getting out!'

'Don't be ridiculous, Dan, we're miles from anywhere. You're acting out like an angry teenager. Talk with me about it instead of digging yourself deeper into the hole of whatever solipsistic mind-fuck you think is reality.'

'Shut the fuck up! You just spout psycho-bullshit that's utter crap. Well, you can fuck the fuck off because I'm not going to take that shit from you any more!'

DAN

I clench my jaw and stare out the window. I'm not making sense even to myself and even as the words come out of my mouth I hear the portcullis open and the trundle of cannons as Lizzie's weaponed up army rides out to slaughter me. She takes a deep breath.

'There's so much here I don't know where to begin. Let's start with your mother, a Machiavellian matriarch who thinks you belong to her, 'my darling' as she calls you, who completely fucking ignored me. Which, by the way, I take as a compliment as that means she sees me as a threat to take away her beloved Dan, the boy she uses as a substitute lover in the place of your cold arrogant father so giving you the Oedipal delusion that you are greater than what made you, your parents' relationship. I know now why you have an overblown omnipotent fantasy and believe you are so fucking amazing you don't need to ever do anything, you know, like actual work. And I can see this clearly now because, Dan, while you imagined I was flirting with all and sundry, what I was actually doing was watching your family, and I saw in glorious detail the pathological shit going down in all directions.'

'And what are you? I'll tell you, a demanding bitch who tries to escape herself through laying shit on me. And if you don't fucking shut up I'll make you. No one messes with me so you can keep your mind-fucking analyses to yourself. I'm not fucking interested.' I kick the dashboard in frustration.

She tightens her grip on the steering wheel. I knew this would happen. She's about to go for the jugular in full Kali jihad. 'OK, Dan, here it is. You bang a drum and imagine the world is going to fall at your feet when really you're just an entitled posh boy with a god delusion. You think you're living beyond an empty materialist consumerism when the truth is your arrogant superiority is nothing but a puerile escape from your responsibilities. You wank on about Zen detachment and following your energy when that's nothing more than an excuse to have others do your dirty work for you while you swan about dreaming of a record deal and supporting the Stones on a tour of the States.' She pauses for breath, but only briefly. She's back on the case in no time. 'You've been ruined by a delusional class superiority and sense of entitlement that has kept you sucking on the shitty tit of privilege so you've never grown up and the only thing you care about is yourself. You're a boy not a man!'

I knew it. Lizzie has revealed herself in her true colours as a psycho-assassin on a mission to destroy me. I'm not going to say any more. She'll just twist my words and use them against me, making them mean things I don't mean at all. I want to smash my fist through the windscreen and rip out the dashboard. Anything to shut her up.

'And you're a fucking bitch who is about to lose the best thing that's ever happened to her!'

I yank open the door and jump out.

Chapter 7   War or Peace

LIZZIE

I screech to a halt by the side of the A34 and climb out onto the hard shoulder. Dan is limping away. I call to him, 'Dan! Get back in the car!' He ignores me and continues to stagger along the grass verge in the dark. I want to drive off and leave Dan to find his own way home, but the threatening headlights of indifferent trucks roar past me. I can't leave him so perilously close to this danger, not in this rain, not in his state. I run after him. He's clutching his leg. We stare at each other, two creatures far from where we belong.

'I've hurt my knee,' he says.'

'It looks like it. Come back to the car.'

He turns and heads back to where I've parked the car and without saying anything climbs back in. We drive with just the sound of windscreen wipers and the swish of traffic. This heavy silence is a quicksand going nowhere but deeper into the mire.

DAN

I'm going to sit here in silence and may never speak again. Not to Lizzie, not to anyone. Everyone can fuck the fuck off and go to hell and leave me alone.

LIZZIE

We're approaching Swindon. 'Do you want to talk?' I glance sideways. He's staring ahead with folded arms. Around Coventry I try again. 'Are we ever going to speak again or are we going to continue like this forever?' The only sign he's heard me is his clenched jaw. Near Stoke-on-Trent I have one more go. 'Shall we see if we can sort this out?' He looks out the window.

'I don't trust you,' he says.

'That's part of what we need to talk about,' I say.

'I used to trust you, but not now.'

'Well that was your mistake then wasn't it, you can't blame me,' is what I nearly say, but bite it back. I don't want a deadly radioactive silence past Manchester and all the way up to the arctic. 'OK you don't trust me. We've hurt each other. What do we do now? '

Headlights flash into the car. Street lights reflect off the wet road. The windscreen wipers squeak.

'I don't know,' he says.

'How about we each speak for five minutes and the other doesn't interrupt or say anything until it's their turn to speak.' I keep my eyes on the road. 'And we just keep going until some kind of resolution shows itself.'

He's thinking about it.

DAN

I spent the journey from Stoke to Stockport banging on, in five minute bursts, fuck the fuck off, no one owns me, I'll never be controlled and I'll never give in so quit trying to fucking change me, I'm me, I belong to nobody and don't you forget it you. This was followed by five minutes staring fixedly through the windscreen while Lizzie took her turn to tell me, I blocked intimacy, was terrified of being vulnerable, defended myself with a psychopathic attack, was a narcissistic puer aeternus, whatever that is, with a delusional sense of entitlement and other things I can't remember. To be honest, I didn't really listen.

Most of what she said simply made me determined to stay separate and cut off from her. I can't therefore say how things changed. It's like when a discordant sound clash gradually finds the beat that gives it meaning and the jarring chords are revealed as a tune, you don't always know how it happened. I think it was when we were driving through Wilmslow. One moment Lizzie's on a jihad to convert me to my total failure as a human being, the next she's saying, 'I felt hurt by what you said about me.' It was like the aluminium snares had backed off and the hidden beat on the soft sound ring began to come through the noise.

LIZZIE

It's an old dilemma, do you refuse to lay down your arms until the other makes the first move or do you risk it because you want to resolve the conflict more than you want to win. Or do you work out the odds and decide you're going to lose so fold before the costs mount?

'I felt hurt by what you threw at me,' I say but don't look at him.

'I felt hurt by what *you* said.'

'But I only said those things because you were gunning for me.'

'But you were coming onto me weaponed up to the eyeballs in a full-on assault, of course I'm going to protect myself. I'd be a fool not to.'

'Not necessarily by beating up on me though.'

'And you don't think you were beating up on me?'

All peace comes at a price. I take a step back from the fight. 'But remember, Dan, with all that drumming, you can beat way harder than me.'

DAN

A slight smile appears at the corners of her mouth, so slight you'd miss it unless you were looking for it. I was. The change of key gives me hope we might emerge from this war eventually, even if neither of us would be victorious. But then no one ever truly wins a war.

'OK,' I say, 'but what about the vicious words you threw at me like knives, do you think they didn't hurt?'

'But you have to admit there was some truth in what I said.'

'I don't have to admit to anything.'

'Even if you won't admit it, it can still be true.'

In a truce between warring tribes if each side keeps their weapons to hand, the war can kick off again at any moment. I don't want that. Being trapped in this fight in a car with Lizzie is like being incarcerated in a metal prison with no escape from crushing accusations you don't understand.

'Look Lizzie, I'm sorry if I hurt you, it's just that...' But I don't know why I'm fighting like a cornered wild animal. That's part of my rage, I can't explain myself.

'*If* you hurt me? You did.' She pauses. I wait with no idea which way the wind will blow. 'And I'm sorry too for throwing words like knives at you,' she says.

By the time we turn into the home stretch of this long ride, I'm admitting that the fight was more about my family than her. 'I always feel I'm being judged, blamed and condemned for not living the life they want me to. It's as if they can't forgive me for what they think is some kind of betrayal. But how is trying to be me a betrayal of my family?'

'You're asking me? Look at me and my family.'

She parks the car and turns off the engine. We sit and stare through the windscreen into the night. She puts her hand on my thigh. 'I must admit, Dan, I hadn't realised until today, your family is almost as much of a nightmare as mine.'

We unlock the door and walk in. It's late. We undress and climb into bed. Without the words that like a surgeon's knife can wound as well as heal, we reach out to each other in the dark. After all, love may not be all we need, but we all need love.

Chapter 8   What About Me?

LIZZIE

It's summer. I've left my teaching job and now run psychodrama workshops. Obsidian plays gigs regularly in various venues where they're paid a lot more than the £50 they got at The Swan and they've begun to write their own songs. Dan says it's tough for a drummer to get song-writing credit. Even if you create a crucial groove that makes the whole song memorable, you only get your name on the credits if you write chords, melody and lyrics. So he's begun to write lyrics. I'm hoping he'll come up with a few poetic love songs but so far it's been all foreboding angst ridden themes of alienation and meaninglessness.

I sit on the patio surrounded by the evening chorus of thrushes, sparrows, robins and blackbirds. I wander through the garden, back into the house and back into the garden. I can't sit still. I'm waiting for Dan with news I'm longing to share with him. I've bought champagne and planned to open it when I told him but I pull the bottle from the fridge, pop the cork and pour myself a glass.

I hear Dan arrive. 'Hang your coat here and I'll get us drinks,' he says to someone. He walks through the living room to the kitchen and sees me on the patio. 'Hi Lizzie,' he calls and comes through the French windows to where I'm sitting. He leans over and kisses me on the top of my head. 'I've brought Oumar back for dinner, I hope that's OK.' 'Sure,' I say. He smiles and kisses me again, this time on the mouth. 'Hey, what's this? You're drinking champagne!' I smile. 'Yes,' I say. He goes back inside. I call out, 'The bottle's in the fridge.' I sit back in my chair as the dusk deepens. A thrush sings in the lilac tree. A blackbird squawks a warning and flies low across the lawn. The red deepens in the clouds. I hug my news to myself a while longer.

Oumar joins me on the patio while Dan fetches drinks before we eat. 'This is a lovely place you have here,' he says. 'Yes,' I say. 'It's a good home for us.'

Dan brings the bottle and two glasses to the table. He pours the champagne. 'Cheers,' he says, raising his glass. He leans back in his chair. 'Something to celebrate?' He gestures to the bottle. I sip the champagne and peer at Dan over the glass. 'I had an amazing offer today,' I say. 'Ken Loach called and asked me to come work with him on his next film.' 'What!' Oumar leaps out of his chair. 'Ken Loach! I love that man! Poor Cow, Family Life and of course Kes.' He falls back into his chair. 'Wow, Lizzie, this is amazing.' 'What does he want you for?' asks Dan. 'He wants more improv in this film. Improvisation,' I explain. 'And he wants to meet me to see if I can use psychodrama to help the actors enrich the spontaneity of their unscripted performances.' 'Shit man, this is brilliant.' Oumar shakes his head, reaches for the champagne and refills our glasses. 'Let's have a toast. To you, Lizzie, and your future career as… now what are drama therapists called on the credits, psycho-consultants, drama-gofers, executive spontaneity producers? Whatever, here's to you.' He raises his glass and drinks it in one go.

Dan's response is more muted. 'That's good news, Lizzie. How did it happen?' 'One of his researchers did a course with me a while back. Ken was wondering about psychodrama, she remembered me and told him.' Dan raises an eyebrow. 'So it's Ken now is it?' Maybe he's playing it cool until Oumar has gone. 'I'm off to meet the man himself next week in Helmsley, where they're filming,' I say. 'I guess this means our planned trip to Arnside's off,' says Dan.

I turn my head slowly and look at him. 'Are you serious?'

DAN

We'd been jamming in Matt's basement all day in a musical heaven. With no audience to please and no score to follow, you freewheel through the tunes and rhythms, vamp on songs and chord progressions, and focus purely on the groove. In jamming sessions, you don't just indulge yourself and go crazy, they're where you commune with god, Jah, the cosmos, and the high spreads through the whole field. I walk home with Oumar. Some fresh Afghani black has arrived in town and he's scoring from a mate near me. We sample it and expand further into the wonders of being alive and being us. I invite him for dinner. The high does not last.

There's an open bottle of champagne in the fridge. Champagne? I'm wary. Lizzie can drink to the point she goes into free-fall and I can't catch her, neither catch up with her nor catch her to save her. She insists she doesn't need saving but she doesn't know as much about herself as she thinks she does. She throws out such a bright light, folk don't see Lizzie's frailty, and neither, mostly, does she - but I do. I've seen her strung out with a howling wind blowing her to pieces weeping that she wants to die. It makes me more cautious than perhaps I need to be but all the same, I have to watch out for her. She explains the champagne. She's been invited by Ken Loach to work with the actors on his next film.

I see Lizzie shooting off down the motorway into fame and celebrity while I'm left standing on the hard shoulder, a pathetic wannabe drummer with just his sticks and his empty dreams. My first thought - what does this mean for me? I'm not proud of that. I tell myself, get a grip, man, this is her dream, don't shatter it, you're supposed to love her no matter what, not wallow in self-pity. But I can't shake this shit off. I try hard to get off on a scenario in which Lizzie jets off into the bright lights of fame and I'm left behind in a mundane existence being ordinary. Oumar's rolling with it, having fun with Lizzie playing out dramas of fame and fortune, why can't I? Of course I want the best for Lizzie and this is a fantastic opportunity for her, it's just... I can't help it... what about me?

LIZZIE

Dan is in the kitchen. Oumar is offering me celebrity advice. 'You know you're A-list famous when mad people pretend to be you so what you need to do, Lizzie, is pretend to be a mad person, which is mad, and then pretend to be yourself, which makes you famous. Then you can get into Club 57 with me as your trophy boyfriend.' We preen ourselves in our super-cool New York fantasy. 'You'll also need to get fancy with your riders, Lizzie.' He grins. 'I know one singer has a person employed solely to take her used chewing gum and get rid of it. And I know another who insists her toilet seat is destroyed after the show so it doesn't end up being sold as something that's been touched by her arse. I've heard of another one who...' Dan returns with plates of food 'Let's eat this before this gets cold,' he said. After an evening walking imaginary red carpets and playing about with dreams of fame and fortune, two of us anyway, Oumar leaves. The door closes. I stare at Dan, 'We need to talk.'

He walks slowly and sits heavily down on the sofa.

'Dan, what's going on? Has something happened? Why are you upset?'

'I'm not upset. I'm fine.'

'We both know that's not true. But I've no idea what *is* going on. You'll have to tell me.'

'Look, I know I should be delighted you've got this opportunity but...' He trails off. 'It's just...' He runs his hands through his hair. 'I don't know.' He stands up. 'I need to get out of here for a walk.'

'That is *not* what you need. You need to sit down and tell me what's going on. Are you upset that I'm off to Yorkshire next week? If so, what's that about?'

'I don't know, OK?' But it's not OK. He paces around the room. 'I think it's better you leave me alone.'

'But if I leave you alone this will just fester. And that's not good for either of us.'

'If you don't leave me alone I might say something that *definitely* won't be good for either of us.'

I don't like where this is heading. 'What do you mean? What would you say? What are you on about? Dan, you have to tell me.'

'I don't *have* to do anything,' he says. He grabs his coat ready to leave.

I leap up and stand in front of the door to block his exit.

'Don't go. Let's sort this out.'

'Get out of my way, Lizzie. Otherwise you'll regret it.'

'Please stay. I'm begging you.'

'I'm warning you.'

His threat hangs heavy in the air between us and crushes the happiness out of me. I'm suddenly furious that what should have been a celebration has turned into a fight. 'I'm not moving,' I say.

He stands over me, a pillar of tension and threat. 'I'm asking you one more time, Lizzie, get out of my way.'

'No. I won't. You'll have to make me.'

He pushes me to the side with a swipe of his arm. I stagger and grasp the hall table to stop myself falling. He's out the door and gone.

DAN

I had to get away from Lizzie before I said or did something that would lead to more trouble. My mind is spinning out of control into multiple scenarios where a glowing Lizzie is surrounded by admirers and I'm a boring non-entity who's ignored. I try to rein in my thoughts but they fly at me like crows pecking into my brain. A murder of crows, that's about right. The shit show going down inside me proves I am exactly the failure I try so hard not to be. Now, on a night when I could be loved up and laughing with Lizzie, celebrating her good fortune, I'm pounding the streets of Manchester, adrenalised into a rage and wanting to release it in a furious freedom of punches and kicks on the first person who crosses me. Hours later my head aches, my feet hurt and I'm exhausted. I turn around and head home. It's 3 am. I quietly open the door. I take off my shoes and look into the bedroom. Lizzie is asleep. I don't disturb her and lie down on the sofa and hope I'm a better man in the morning.

I wake to the sounds of a kettle boiling. I get up off the sofa, run my fingers through my hair and straighten my T-shirt. I walk into the kitchen where Lizzie is making breakfast. I lean into the doorframe with a smile that's a lie. 'Hi,' I say. 'Hi,' she says. She doesn't smile. 'Do you want a coffee?' 'Yes,' I say. I sit down and she hands me a mug. She faces me with her hands around her mug. 'Do you have anything you want to say to me?' I have the sense she wants me to say sorry but there's a thicket of shame and guilt between me and her that I don't understand. Do I have to cut these brambles down, slashing my way through the thorns to reach the sleeping beauty? Or do I stay where I am, unscratched, invulnerable and, like the hanged man in the tarot, upside down and stuck?

'I wish I could have been different with you last night, Lizzie, been like Oumar and just celebrated with you. It's just…' I scratch my head. The words are not coming easily. 'It's just… I just couldn't,' I finish lamely.

'Is that so?' she says and goes to the sink with her back to me. Before I have time to tell her anything more, she's washed her mug, put on her coat and is about to leave.

'Lizzie, please, can we try again.'

'OK, go ahead,' she says, with a coolness threatening a deep freeze that leaves me wishing I'd stayed away in warmer climes. I'm not sure how willing she really is to listen because she keeps her coat on and remains standing. I have to come up with the goods else she'll be gone. Again, I can't. I don't know why. I just can't say sorry.

'You can't do it can you?' she says. 'You just can't say it. Or rather you won't. Because to say sorry is to admit that you behaved like a complete arsehole last night and in your narcissistic universe it's never your responsibility when you act like shit. It's always someone else's fault, never yours.'

She turns to leave. I leap up and grab her arm. She stares at me with blazing eyes.

'How dare you! Leave me alone! I don't want to stay a moment longer with a man who's so in love with his own miserable reflection he can't even celebrate my success and instead undermines it with self obsessed mind-fucks about his own pathetic existence. Well let me inform you, Dan, I have a life to lead. An interesting, rich, and creative life, far more fulfilling than the cul-de-sac your narcissistic resentment has led you down, where your mean-spirited envy has turned you into a psycho-spiritual pigmy eaten up with jealousy.'

I refuse to let go of her arm and squeeze it tighter.

'Stop it! You're hurting me! Let go, you bloody idiot.'

'I'll fucking let you go when you apologise for speaking to me like that.'

'What the fuck! Are you crazy? You need to apologise to me, not me to you! Let go of my arm.'

She wrenches her arm away from me and I let it go. I sit down with my head in my hands. I have probably fucked it up with Lizzie forever. Ten whirling dervishes are spinning inside me, each swirling in its own volatile unhinged chaos. I remain with my head in my hands and can't speak or even look at Lizzie. To my surprise she sits down.

'Dan, we're plummeting in a spiral deep into a quagmire. We have to sort this out.' She stands up, walks into the living room and sits on the sofa. 'Are you coming or not?'

I follow her to the sofa.

Chapter 9   The Law of the Jungle

LIZZIE

There's one kind of love, where you gaze into each other's eyes, murmur sweet nothings, share intimate secrets and make love. There's another love that grows between comrades, fellow travellers and teammates, where you work side by side for a common goal. Dan and I have made plenty of the intimate love; this is about the other. Do we have a common goal? What is this relationship about for him? Is it the same for me? I pull a chair from the table and turn it to face us on the sofa.

'Imagine a wise person is sitting there, someone who's seen it all. We speak to them and say whatever we want to without checking or censoring ourselves.'

I glance sideways. Dan's hands are spread out on his thighs, his jaw is clenched, his stare fixed forward. I plough on. 'We can say whatever we feel about anything whatsoever, all we have to do is refer to each other as 'he' and 'she', 'Dan' and 'Lizzie'. This is something we do in psychodrama, to take the sting out of a full frontal attack on each other.'

I'm aiming to sound like a comrade in arms but fear I'm coming across like a teacher speaking to a pupil with learning difficulties.

DAN

I stare at the empty chair. I've no idea what's meant to happen here. I feel trapped and want to fight my way out. My arms want to beat something, anything. My legs want to run. Voices in my head tell me to get out, quit while you can and don't look back. Lizzie has no idea how hard it is for me to sit with her and speak like this. She might if she were behind a drum kit with an audience looking up at her expecting a Purdie shuffle with a 16th note groove and she's holding those beaters and frozen. But I know I have to stay if I want Lizzie in my life. I hear her breathing. I see the sun coming through the window onto the low table in front of us. I rub my cheeks, full of things I need to say but don't know how. I try to imagine I'm in front of a wise person but see only an empty chair. The only thing I can do is not leave.

LIZZIE

Dan is silent. 'OK, I'll start,' I say. I turn to the chair. 'I don't think Dan understands how serious it is that he went for me on a night that should have been a celebration. I'm angry but I also want to get through this. Whether we can or not, I don't know. But I'm not going to let him mess this up for me.'

Dan scratches his head and shifts in his seat.

'First of all, Lizzie's used to this kind of thing and I'm not. Plus she's better with words. So I'm not very trusting of how this is going to pan out. All I know is she can hurt me with her words and here we are in the realm of words. And she thinks because I started it that means she's not responsible for the shit she dishes out.'

'Well he did start it. I'd never do to him what he did to me. If Obsidian took off I'd be delighted for him. I'd celebrate his success and never be the mean spirited bastard he was last night.'

'There she goes again. Going at me. She's supposed to be a great psychodrama therapist so how about she tries to understand me instead of going on about how pathetic I am.'

'Of course I want to know what's going on, that's what this is about, to find out what is really going on so we can deal with it instead of fighting about it. I'd like to know exactly what upset Dan about me working with Ken Loach.'

I sit back and fold my arms. I need to hear what Dan has to say about all this.

DAN

I feel a pressure to speak but don't know what to say. I rub my forehead. This is hard. I gaze across the room and out the window. There's just a bird in a tree, no answers.

'I don't know what to say.'

'Well you have to find out,' she says.

'Don't tell me what to do. And don't talk to me - talk to that.' I stab my finger at whatever is facing us. 'It's is your fucking thing to do this after all.' I'm shouting.

'It's not my 'fucking thing'. I'm trying to find a way through the shit you're flinging at me.' She's shouting too.

'And you're not doing that? Bullshit! You're as bad as me but won't admit it as then you have to come down from your ivory tower where you arrogantly think you know how I should be, what I should be doing and what's supposed to happen in a relationship. Well fuck that, because you don't.'

I fold myself into a stubborn refusal. I'll sit here and wait like a statue that can stand defiant for centuries even as the city around it falls into ruins. I may not be good with words but I can wait. When you're living on the road there's a lot of standing about doing nothing and in this kind of waiting game I can be as patient as a snake. Sand boas bury themselves in dirt, copperhead snakes hide in leaves, gopher snakes change colour for camouflage, anacondas lie submerged with only their eyes and nose above water, but one thing they have in common, they are masters of the art of doing nothing while they wait. They lie at the entrance to caves used by bats, next to ripening fruit attractive to birds, near rocks where lizards sun themselves, and there they wait for as long as it takes. Some, like the ball python, the rat snake and the diamondback rattlesnake can wait for years. Though in the second year they begin to digest their own hearts to stave off starvation.

I've learned from snakes how to sit and do nothing, to wait and listen for the rustle of leaves, watch for the flash of movement, alert to subtle shifts in temperature, the sudden shadow, the squeak, the smell, the change of light that indicates something's on the move. And here I am again waiting for what I don't yet know to happen, waiting for Lizzie, waiting for myself... I hope I don't have to eat my own heart to stave off death.

LIZZIE

A fury swirls around me trying to land on my heart. I want it to. Dan dishes out more hurt than I know how to handle. I want hatred to seep into every chamber of my heart and freeze the love out of it so this will all be over. Dan, me, our love... over and out, and he'll never be able to hurt me again. I hate him. I love him. I hate him. I love him. I could pick the petals off a daisy for hours and still not know which petal I want to find is the last. Yet, though I don't want to admit it, for love to reach the wounds in us that need it most, the hard shells protecting those raw places must be first cracked open - and that's going to hurt. It's written into the script that the lover who invites us to meet them in the depths is the same one who forces their way into the places where we hide our primal hurts, keeping them secret even from ourselves.

How else are those dark primitive places that never see the sun to be prised open?

Dan says nothing. He sits beside me as unmoving as a statue.

OK, the kind of love that heals the wounds of history, calms ancient terrors and mends broken hearts is not a sweet play of moonlight, roses and romance, it's a fierce beast that grabs you by the neck, bites into your jugular and refuses to let go until you've given up all your hiding places. But I'm already devastated; do I need more of this open heart surgery without anaesthetic?

I'm remembering other fights I've had, ones I'd rather forget.

It had been another day of fighting. I was fighting that I had to be home from the Catholic youth club too early and so missed out the best bit, when after singing about living for Jesus we hang out together outside and explore living for ourselves. I was fighting about going to Mass without having eaten or drunk anything since midnight to be pure for the Holy Sacrament and each week teenage girls slid onto the floor in a faint and were carried off white-faced to sit at the back with our heads between our legs considering ourselves lucky if we weren't carted away by one of the men who helped us come round by opening our legs and touching us. I was fighting about the stupidities and cruelties in a dysfunctional Irish Catholic family even though my struggle made no difference. But I was fighting anyway because if I didn't I'd die.

I didn't even care any more about the crazy punishments, wearing scratchy string under your vest tight around your waist, having your dinner cold, sitting upright and not allowed to lean back on any chair not even the sofa for weeks. Once I'd had to clean the garden path with a toothbrush. A neighbour asked what I was doing. Instead of saying what I knew I should, 'I'm playing', I told her, 'I'm being punished for saying Pius XII was a fascist.' Not being a

Catholic or a political historian, she looked blank and turned back to weed her flower bed with a shrug. My punishment for revealing something to an outsider: I must throw my favourite doll on the fire and sleep for a week in a bed full of toy bricks. The wooden cubes had sharp edges that cut into my sleep and covered me with lines of thin blue bruises.

I waved my arms with its badges of harm accusingly at my parents risking further punishment. They took no notice. These punishments were necessary mortifications of the flesh in order to pull me out of the clutches of the devil and save me from hell; it would have been a grave dereliction of their parental duty not to beat my wickedness out of me. I was fighting for my wickedness, my freedom and my life.

I'm still fighting. Now I'm fighting to keep the love between Dan and me alive because I so desperately need it.

DAN

How does silence become sound? What changes anything into something it was not? What makes one moment different from another? I don't know. But I'm sitting next to Lizzie waiting, alert, listening.

'I love you and I hate you, Dan. I need you and I want to hurt you. I'm afraid to lose you and I want you gone.' She turns and faces me. I sense a shift in pulse-rate so slight it's only a possibility, not yet real. 'Perhaps it's always this way when the animal instincts of sex are involved. It may be different on Mars or Venus but we're not there are we? The fact of life on this planet is eat or be eaten, kill or be killed.' She sighs. 'And however much we love someone they remain 'other' and dangerous.'

I can't see where the hell Lizzie's going with this. I may be fucked up and afraid of intimacy, as she so often tells me, but I've no plans whatsoever to kill and eat her. She's not finished.

'So whenever we need someone, that vulnerability makes us afraid. And we tense up with an array of defences ready to protect ourselves with ways to control, manipulate, distract, bully, seduce or eradicate the intrinsic threat of the other.'

'If you mean I'll hurt you to stop you hurting me, you're dead right. Just like you'll hurt me to stop me hurting you. So don't pretend you're beyond the fray.'

'That's exactly what I'm not doing,' she says.

'What do you mean then?'

'I mean any creature without an evolved protection system would have been eaten to extinction long ago. And, however civilised we humans like to think we are, we're also animals with instincts that have millennia of evolution in their design. Let me count the ways. Play dead. Camouflage and hide. Puff up to look bigger. Spit poison. Curl up inside a hard shell. Fly up high and far away.'

This I can follow.

'I get it,' I say. 'Deceive. Distract then run. Overpower. Undermine. Weave webs that entrap. Stick out sharp spines in all directions. Pretend to be harmless until the other is vulnerable then strike. Freeze so you're not seen and the threat goes away. Play dead until they're close then jump them. Creep up silently and kill from behind.'

I'm not sure if we were still in a fight or brokering a peace but something has shifted. One moment we were beating out furious blast beats and smashing down on the foot pedal of the bass drum breaking things up, the next we're sliding into a soft shuffle groove caressing the melody and a new rhythm is coming through. The new tune is hardly here, so faint you can't be sure it isn't the sound of your own heartbeat, but you go with it all the same because if you don't, the show goes dead. It's like stroking a wild tigress until she lies down and purrs; yet on every out-breath she breathes a raw pungent tiger-ness over you and curls her lip to show her blood-stained teeth. Eradicate her danger and you've killed her. Jump over the drum frenzy and the tune loses its timbre. Avoid the fights and your love becomes a pale shadow of itself.

'I'm sorry,' I say. I'm not sure if I'm sorry for the fight, the things we'd both said, the universal human predicament in which our anarchic animal instincts are continually at war with our human longing for peace and harmony, or just for being me.

'I'm sorry too,' she says.

I reach across the divide between us, the same that separates night from day, war from peace, predator from prey, as wide the divide between me from all that is not-me - that's everything, and take her hand. I love her. Despite that sometimes I wish I didn't. Despite that nobody warned me love could be this hard. Though when you think about it, without the raw terribleness of war and its painful aftermath, peace is at best a bloodless compromise, at worst an anaemic indifference. After all when WW2 ended the world came together in a way it never had before. Even if that war was not, as was hoped, the war to end all wars.

I hold Lizzie's hand as I weep. 'I'm so sorry, Lizzie.'

My tears fall all the way down to the ground. This time I know what I'm sorry for - all of it, the whole damn show.

Chapter 10   Playing Away

LIZZIE

Dan and I drifted through the week after the fight in a spreading quiet as if floating in a clear lake with just the lapping of waves, the soft croaks of frogs and the calls of wading birds. One warm night, we climbed into the park and wandered through the smells of honeysuckle, jasmine, tobacco plant and lavender. Dan bent and picked a four-leaved clover. 'How on earth did you see that?' I said. He drew me to him, stroked it against my cheek and whispered into my hair, 'You're teaching me to see in the dark.' We lay under an oak tree among creatures rustling in the undergrowth and owls hooting in the trees. With naked limbs wrapped around each other in the moonlight, we laughed and picked twigs and dead leaves from our hair, an Adam and Eve before the fall. A week later I packed my suitcase and Dan drove me to Manchester Victoria for my train.

There might be fifty ways to leave a lover but none of them are easy. It's even harder when you're resting in the sweet eye of a storm of such savagery it almost killed your love stone dead.

On the platform waiting for the train to York, we hug and breathe in the smells of each other to fix our togetherness inside us. I climb into the carriage and lean out the window for one last kiss. The whistle blows, Dan stands back and I'm off.

At York a man at the ticket barrier holds a placard with 'Pete, Mike and Lizzie' scrawled in blue felt tip. He leads us to a car. Pete, a sound engineer, and Mike, a lighting man, climb into the back, I sit in front. Andy, the driver, explains his Audi Sport Quatro with four-wheel drive can manoeuver rough terrain like the Yorkshire Moors, no problem. Pete and Mike have worked together before and are gossiping about previous shoots so it falls to me to appreciate the 2,144 cc engine with turbocharger and intercooler that meant we could go from 0 to 62 mph in 7 seconds. I'm more impressed by the electric windows. Pete and Mike smoke continually and when I can't find the winder to let in some fresh air, Andy swings his arm across me and points to a switch that winds the windows down electronically. We arrive at Helmsley and into a whirlwind.

DAN

I've just said goodbye to Lizzie. I sit in the garden with a mug of tea and stare at the uneven paving slabs of the patio. I know it's only for two weeks but two weeks in the glamorous world of a film crew on location in the wilds of Yorkshire is not a fortnight with an aunt in Bournemouth. I finish my tea and wander through our flat, or rather Lizzie's flat. I've been living here for four years but however much she insists it's my home too, I still feel a visitor en route to somewhere else, though I don't know where. Everything reminds me of her, the neatly folded towels, the flowers in vases, the clean and organised kitchen, unlikely to remain that way for long. I made a mental checklist of what I must do, keep stuff tidy, hang out the laundry, do the washing up regularly, clean the bath and make the bed neatly. That way, on her return, there'll be no plates of mouldy food, unwashed coffee cups or dirty T-shirts lying around among a mess of takeaway food cartons to prove beyond doubt my irresponsible lack of maturity.

One thing I know for sure, she's eager for her new adventure and not thinking of me at all, while I'm moping about her flat and already missing her.

My determination to be a practical householder lasts until the afternoon. It's just not my thing. I'm off to Matt's to practice some syncopation and second line rhythms. At least the drum is never seduced by the bright promises of movie-land, vacuous attractions of fame and preening trips down a red carpet.

LIZZIE

I meet the great man at the centre of all the activity in a bar at his hotel. 'Hi Lizzie, lovely to meet you.' He reaches over and shakes my hand with a firm grip. 'Glad you could come at such short notice. Do you want a coffee?' He beckons to a waiter. 'Or would you prefer tea?' 'Coffee thanks,' I say. Even before the drinks arrive we're straight into the meat of this meeting. 'What kind of contribution do you see psychodrama can make, Lizzie?' He smiles and leans back, nodding to encourage me. 'Well my primary focus will be to help the actors connect with aspects of themselves that are unfamiliar to them, to enrich the energies they bring to their performances.' I'm about to explain further how psychodrama can unlock our potential for spontaneity and expression but he smiles again. 'Great. That's exactly what I'm looking for.' The drinks have arrived and while sipping the coffee we gossip about walking the Cleveland Way, the beehive querns from the Iron Age found nearby and how half of Helmsley is in the North Yorkshire Moors National Park and the other half isn't. I imagined this meeting would be some kind of interview but Ken seems to have made up his mind on the basis of my single sentence. He turns to a tall thin woman with long grey hair. 'Sally, make sure Lizzie has what she needs for a session at around 10am tomorrow. And let the cast for the factory floor scene know to be there. Later we'll timetable more when we know what kind of time we're likely to need.' Sally and Ken smile together at me. 'Let me show you around,' says Sally. 'I'll introduce you to a few people.' 'Thanks,' I say. 'Great.'

The next days are a blur of meeting people whose names I don't remember, getting lost until I learn my way around so no longer turn up in the make up trailer when I'm supposed to be helping move lighting gear, and coming to grips with the timetables of meetings, informal get-togethers, meal times and the continually changing schedule of actual filming so I'm not taking time out for a fag when I'm expected at an impromptu meeting about the change to next day's programme.

I can't believe how friendly everyone is. I'm loving it.

DAN

I limp through the week not doing too badly, though I have to bite my lip when Lizzie tells me how much fun she's having. Mending a dripping tap and hoovering the living room carpet doesn't compare with hanging out in hotel bars playing poker with the cool dudes of Ken's entourage. Then she tells me she's staying another week. Fuck this! I'm off to Matt's.

There's just Matt and me but I don't care. I'm a beast of a drummer jiving off my own improvisations. I'm heavy, groovy and intense. I'm John Bonham playing Heartbreaker on Led Zeppelin's 1971 European tour, the one that ended when hundreds of tear-gas wielding riot police charged into the stadium in Milan injuring many fans and damaging the group's equipment. And if Lizzie phones this evening, I'm not there to take her call.

Oumar arrives just as I've come down from the heavy rock scene and become Ringo, the king of feel, an underrated drummer who sits in the song with his own feel. That's because I'm sensitive and subtle as well as heavy and intense. Take that Lizzie.

In the pub afterwards Oumar says he's off to Reading Festival, 'Do you fancy it? We might get to gig in one of the tents if we take our gear. What do you reckon?' It's a no brainer.

LIZZIE

I quickly get the hang of film set etiquette. Rule 1: Don't get in the way. These are professional crews who have honed what they do to a smooth operation and they don't want a rookie novice messing with their slick procedure. Rule 2: Wear comfortable clothes not stylish outfits that restrict your ability to move promptly and get out of the way fast. And wear dark clothes not bright white outfits that bounce the lighting into a glare. Rule 3: It takes an army to create a film and don't forget you are merely one cog in this military machine, and not a very important one at that. Rule 4: Be relentlessly up-beat, positive and encouraging without fail, all the time, with absolutely everyone.

The first evening I call Dan from the phone box outside the B&B. I tell him I've been drinking with famous actors in the hotel bar. He tells me he's mended the leaking bathroom tap and hung out the laundry but it rained. We don't speak for long. There's not much to talk about when one is tipsy and excited and the other is stone cold sober after an evening wondering what the first one's been up to.

The psychodrama goes well. Having read the skeleton script, I have a few things planned. I ask each of the actors in this scene to write the names they'd been called from early childhood onwards, nicknames, pet-names, insulting names, formal names, baby names, sweetheart names, harsh names from authority figures, whatever they can remember, and act as if at a party in the character of a positive name, then as one of a negative name. Usually when I do this it's light fun and warms people up for deeper explorations later, here we are immediately into intense territory, laughing, squaring up as if to fight, banging the table in frustration, flashing invitations with seductive smiles, storming off with dramatic exit lines. Of course, these are professional actors. I throw out my plans and we go straight into scenes of conflict from their childhoods, one of the themes of the film. Two hours later we've finished. Ken is standing by the door. He steps forward. 'Thank you, Lizzie. This has been extremely helpful,' he says. Everyone applauds me. Not what usually happens at the end of one of my sessions. I'm loving it here.

DAN

Seven of us pile into Lizzie's Renault 4, literally, we're on top of each other. I'm free from the pile-up because I'm driving. Oumar, the canny bugger, is in the front passenger seat and has manoeuvred the wild and beautiful Bethany onto his lap. Matt and Steve are in the van with the tents and gear. We drive in convoy and head for Reading.

We stagger through the entrance carrying guitars, drums, all the gear and pieces of equipment that make up a band, and into another world. I love this festival vibe. You dress how you feel, in costumes, half-naked or in the same T-shirt for the whole three days. You wander around drinking in the scene. You plan what DJ's to watch for, what bands to see and how to get a slot to play your own music. You find a place to pitch your tent. You roll a joint or maybe go deeper with acid or mushrooms. You're cool and don't stare at the weird and wonderful happenings all around you, not blatantly anyway. You have meandering conversations with people in the queue for the toilets, some interesting, some boring, others just totally off the planet and weird. And you dance to the music coming at you from all directions. I'm in my element, man.

The Main Stage is for the major rock, indie and metal bands. The NME stage is where you find the less well-known acts not quite yet headliners and the Lock UP Stage is for underground hard-core acts. Then there's the Festival Republic stage where less known and breakthrough acts can gig, that's where we hope we're in with a chance. Plus the dance tents, the DJ sets and the comedy and cabaret acts. It's a whole world in here, with a lot of fun to be had. Though it can get heavy too. And I don't just mean the comedowns from whatever high you've been on.

One year, Bonnie Tyler was pelted with bottles and turf, though she stoically finished her set. Meatloaf was the headliner later that day and he berated the audience over their treatment of his friend Bonnie. The punters did not take kindly to this and chucked burgers and bottles at him. Meatloaf stormed off. He returned and shouted at the crowd, 'Do you want rock 'n roll or do you wanna throw stuff?' A full 2 litre cider bottle was thrown and struck him in the face. Meatloaf left the stage and didn't return. Canning is always a danger with the heavy metal fans. They don't like ballads, nor being lectured to, and they're not too keen on the hippy peace and love vibe either. But today, this festival is mine, man. This is my scene and I'm loving it.

LIZZIE

We become a world unto ourselves, like a family. Perhaps this is inevitable on a film set where the intensity of feeling and focus required in the creation of a film spills into relationships between members of the cast and crew. Director, executive producers, actors, assistant producers, line manager, first and second assistant directors, script supervisor, director of photography, location manager, camera operators, sound mixers, boom operator, key grip gaffer, wrangler who cares for the horses and dogs, art director, best boy, props master, makeup artist, costume designer, gang boss, or even those on the fringe of things like me, we're all in it together. My relationship with Dan is trickier. Our conversations take place in a phone box after I've been having fun with the crew in the bar. A few knock on the phone box as they walk by urging me to join them for more fun in the lounge at the B&B. Then there's Keith, a camera operator I'm spending time with and we're having a lot of fun. It takes a week before the fun moves onto another level. Drinks in the hotel bar, a spliff back at the B&B, a stagger upstairs, and we're in bed together.

My phone calls with Dan become less frequent, shorter, and full of awkward silences. I'm asked to extend my stay for another week and the silence when I tell Dan is so long I think he's put the phone down. They cease altogether after he tells me he's off to Reading for a music festival. In the pre-mobile phone era, this means we're out of contact completely. 'I hope you have a great time,' I said. 'Yes, I hope so too,' he said.

DAN

Matt, Oumar and Chris meet me outside the tent where D J Bubba is mixing tunes. They have broad grins across their faces. Either it's the dope or they've won a raffle. 'Do you want the good news first or the bad?' asks Oumar. I'm like, 'Come on guys, give it to me straight, whatever it is.' Matt does a jig. 'We've got a gig tomorrow on the Festival Republic stage!' 'Wow. That is seriously good news,' I say. 'What's the bad?' 'We're on at 11 am,' says Oumar. 'Ok, not the best time,' I say, 'but hey, this is great. We must find Steve and come up with a set list.'

Later that night high on alcohol, drugs and dreams of a record deal after our staggering performance tomorrow morning, I fall in with Bethany. We stroll through the tents trying to find our aldehuela, our caserio, nuestro pequeño pueblo. Why I'm suddenly speaking Spanish escapes me. It must be the combination of highs, the promise of a serious gig tomorrow and hanging out with the sexy Bethany; it's doing something to my brain. And not just my brain. We're at a festival so naturally Bethany and I go with it. And a lovely going with it it was too. A night of love and delight that made me forget myself. And Lizzie.

Next morning we somehow managed to arrive at the tent at 10:30 with guitars, keyboards, drums and the rest of the gear intact. We've also managed to organise ourselves into a crew that appears less wrecked and dishevelled than we are. We climb onstage, tune in and nod to each other. There's a lot riding on this, we're not just playing a gig, this is a perfect chance to trade our wares and get Obsidian's name out there. This is what we've been waiting for, man.

It takes a while to get the crowd cheering and dancing with us. And it isn't really a crowd, more a group of dishevelled partygoers from the night before to begin with. But neither is it a crash and burn disaster. By the third song the energy is growing and the field is forming and once that energy field builds, you're on your way. It begins to happen. The crowd cheers us, drawing more towards this Obsidian happening in the Festival Republic tent until it's not just us on stage performing, everyone's playing this gig. We're stamping and sweating, our hearts are beating in synchrony with the beat and we're hitting the groove like there's no tomorrow. Chris and Steve hit the riffs like machine guns. Oumar is cruising with the gods on his keyboard. The bass pounds out the speakers, shaking the Kundalini up our spines until the body electric comes through. Matt and I are the brotherhood keeping it super-cool and tight on the beat. The fire feeds the fire of this synergy until there's a crazy rush taking us high right out to where it all begins and ends. And then it's done.

We're breathing heavily, guitars hanging off our shoulders, holding the sticks in one hand, bowing to the crowd. They want more but we're not big names who can go in for encores, we're on a strict timetable and have to move over for the next wannabe headliners to showcase their stuff.

No one from NME rushes over to interview us, neither does a guy from a record company seek us out, but somehow it doesn't matter, at least not when luxuriating in our post-gig high a while longer.

LIZZIE

The intrigues, dramas and love affairs on set are as intense and dramatic as the narrative of the film itself and the one that blossoms between Keith and me is sweet and fun. I'm not experienced in the etiquette of love on a film set but I'm street-wise enough to know that part of our affair's sweetness is we both have commitments elsewhere and what happens on a film set stays on the film set.

After the wrap party we leave and Helmsley returns to its markets on Thursday and Saturday, walkers setting off on the Cleveland Way and tea shops selling Yorkshire Tea Loaf, all signs of the recent occupying army gone. On the train back to Manchester I shapeshift back into the Lizzie who lives with and loves Dan, other loves forgotten. OK, a small part of me remains in the glamour and energy of that world and the fun with Keith. Everyone knows that's how it goes. It'll fade in time.

Dan is on the station platform waiting for me. I run to him and we hug. He winces. With the light shining so brightly in my eyes I haven't seen his arm is in a sling and his hand in plaster. 'What's this?' I ask. 'I'll tell you later,' he says with a smile I can interpret in fifty ways. It seems I'm not the only one who's been having adventures.

DAN

This was my greatest festival ever - and not only because strangers kept coming up to me and offering me a toke on their spliff or a swig from their Newcastle Brown. 'Man, that was some set you played.' 'You guys were great.' 'Obsidian, I'll keep an eye out for your future gigs.' OK not yet a rock star but at least standing on the first rungs of that stairway to heaven.

Then there was the lovely Bethany. It was fun hanging out with her and the energy flowed between us both nights. Though I felt a bit flat afterwards. I didn't want to admit it but something was missing. The dissolved togetherness and soul-melting I knew with Lizzie wasn't there. But thank you Bethany all the same, you're lovely and beautiful.

The final morning I was unofficially jamming with a bunch of rastas and punks playing a fusion of reggae and street punk. We were joined by some heavy-duty metallers. They took the groove up several notches and though I wasn't playing my own drums, I was kicking out a hefty rhythm. Another crowd formed. We were going for it but sometimes the field is only half there. I worked to feed the energy but it was not quite happening. I smashed down harder, faster – whack! I played a rimshot and caught my fingers between the stick and the drum. It hurt but I kept playing. Later my forefinger swelled. And it hurt more. I didn't have access to ice or arnica gel so for the rest of the festival I held it close to me so no one could knock my finger and send spikes of red-hot throbbing pain through my whole body.

We drove back in the typical low energy of post-festival come down that is usually because the drugs are wearing off and we're facing a return to work the next day. I felt a little awkward with Bethany. She's beautiful but what happens in a festival stays in the festival, that's my take on it. I hoped she was cool with that. Though I also felt slightly guilty. I don't see why, it's not as if Lizzie and I are married or anything, and I'd bet she'd been up to a few things on her swanky film set. But it was hard to concentrate on anything with a finger pulsing in so much agony I could hardly change gear. It was so painful I dropped everyone off at Matt's and went to A&E. My finger was X-rayed. It was broken. And now, instead of Lizzie returning to a swaggering nearly rock star, she finds a drummer with a broken finger.

We meet, both of us with guilty half-smiles that confess all. Despite my hand not functioning, other parts do, and it's as beautiful as ever to make love with Lizzie and melt into her. Maybe there was nothing to worry about in the first place because we are and always were each other's destiny. I don't know, but it was a sweet surprise to find each other again, and with a new note coming through I hadn't heard before.

Chapter 11   A Conference of Birds

DAN

We're driving across the Pennines. Shadows of clouds race across the moors of the Peak District. Lambs gather along the edge of fields. They've lost their trembling innocence and have become woolly hooligans squaring up to dive bomb each other before they run across the skyline in pursuit of whatever happiness gangs of lambs seek in summer grass. We're on our way to Hull where Lizzie's parents live. She's been resisting introducing me to them for years but it's her mother's birthday and her sister has planned a party. She wasn't going to go but I kept reminding her I'd given way to her insistence she meet my family and now it was her turn to suffer. I smile at her.

'I'm looking forward to meeting your family.'

Lizzie snorts. 'If you think this is going to be fun, you'd better prepare yourself.'

'OK', I say. I glance sideways at her with a grin. 'But it can't be that bad – look at you.' She shakes her head.

'You've no idea,' she says.

The wind blows her hair into her eyes and she brushes it away. She's beautiful.

LIZZIE

I want to tell Dan about the dysfunctional insanity of my family but don't know where to begin. One brother, Kevin, is an alcoholic who loves nothing more, apart from his beer, to draw you into a labyrinth of conspiracies and counter-conspiracies so complex even the conspirators lose the thread which somehow proves they were right. My other brother, Stephen, is a financial advisor. If you want to compare interest rates, endowment mortgages and indemnity insurance, he's your man - anything else, forget it. If Dan tells him he's a drummer in a band, he won't ask about the music, he'll want to know the percentage their manager gets and how Dan fills out his self-assessment tax forms. Meanwhile my sister, Mary, has diagnosed herself as suffering from depression, anorexia, agoraphobia, obsessive-compulsive anxiety, bi-polar disorder and panic attacks. Though really it's her family who suffer more than she does. To warn him, I tell Dan the bare bones.

'At least hanging out with your crazy mob sounds more fun than being compressed into the Brewin bourgeois box of my lot,' he says.

I want to explain that the craziness of my brothers and sister is just a surface fault-line; the deeper geology of my family is a history where obliterated hopes, bitter disappointments and devastating loss are the only landmarks. I'd like to tell him that when your mother is a granite rock of petrified hardness and your father has a personality disorder the size of an island, except that he has no personality, then you are scattered to the four winds with no centre to hold you together and no way back home except through the terror you're running from. But I can't. I haven't let myself know enough of the story yet, let alone share it with another.

I shake my head. 'You've no idea.'

DAN

A flock of starlings flies over us. Hundreds of birds swoop and dive in flawless synchronicity. They fly in a tight swoosh towards us. Suddenly they bank away, turn sharply together then veer towards us again.

'That's a murmuration of starlings,' I tell Lizzie.

'Do you know about such things?' She brushes her hair off her face. 'Tell me,' she says.

I search the sky looking for how to say the things I know but can't express. That my heart soars when I watch birds fly. That I fly with them towards a blue vanishing where everything drops away and all that's left is freedom. That they then fly further into the singing emptiness while I fall back to Earth with a sense of having lost something so precious I hardly know what it is. I wind down the window to let in a cooling breeze.

'When I was ten, I shot a robin.' She stares at me. 'I'd been given an air rifle for my birthday and from my bedroom window had seen the robin singing in a bush. I took aim and fired. The song ceased. The dead robin fell onto the lawn, its little legs pointing skywards silently accusing me of treachery. Horrified at what I'd done, I swapped my rifle for binoculars and vowed never to kill another bird again.' I glance at Lizzie's to see how she's taking this. She's listening. 'I never became a fully fledged twitcher, the ones constantly on message who ride across the country on Harley Davidsons to tick off on their list a little brown bird from Bulgaria, but I was a true birder, definitely not a stringer. They're the ones who string you along thinking they've seen a Ring Ouzel when all they've really spotted is a female blackbird.'

She laughs. 'I've never even heard of a Ring Ouzel. I guess you have to be a proper bird spotter to know one.'

'Never refer to a birder as a bird-spotter, Lizzie. Watching birds is as far from train spotting as John Bonham, whose genius drum rhythms make you want to fling yourself off a cliff, is from vague tambourine tapping, which makes you want to jump off for a different reason. Watching birds is complex. You note their size, colour, species and location of course, but you also pay attention to their behaviour. You want to know why they do things, like for example, why they fly in flocks.'

'Because they like to hang out and gossip about who has the longest tail feathers or what's the latest cool sky-dive move?' I give her as long a sideways glance as you can when driving. 'Go on,' she urges, 'really, I want to know.'

'Well for a start, birds can protect themselves better in a flock. A hawk can easily pick up a lone bird but will avoid a plunge into a crowd for fear of injuring itself in a collision. And while they feed, doze and groom, there'll always be a few on the alert for passing predators.' I look to check she's still listening. I can become so absorbed in one of my obsessions I lose my listener - great when playing the drums, you get lost in the grooves and riffs and take your audience with you, but an intense triple stroke roll and a shovel groove is one thing, banging on about birds is something else. My audience might be bored stiff and I wouldn't notice. She leans over and kisses my cheek. 'This is amazing, Dan.' I'm not sure whether she means the facts or that I know them.

I pull the car to the side of the road and turn off the engine.

'Yes, birds really are amazing, Lizzie. For example, when a flock flies over oceans with no landmarks, tiny adjustments are continually made by individual birds and these finely tune the magnetic precision required for navigation during migrations. Plus the leaders constantly rotate so the burden is shared. The stronger the bird, the more time it flies in front, while weaker birds can relax in the wind-stream produced by those ahead. The whole thing is beautifully and organically balanced.'

'Wow,' says Lizzie, 'they're natural Marxists, eco-socialists.'

We gaze at the magnificence of the murmuration as it swerves and turns around itself, a shape-shifting creature of many parts, each bird spinning along an invisible highway in perfect harmony with the rest until each wheels away into its separate existence in the centre of its own ever-widening sky circle.

LIZZIE

Dan is telling me about birds. I'm fascinated. I've been reading Michael Ignatieff who says modern culture is a society of alienated strangers no longer bound together by a sense of community, and theatre and drama can explore this tension, the conflict between the freedom of the individual and the responsibilities of community, in ways politics can't. It seems birds have this conflict worked out in a way we haven't. Maybe I can play with this in a psychodrama workshop. Dan points to the magnificent display overhead.

'There's a great mystery here,' he says, 'one that even biologists with massive research grants can't solve.'

'Tell me! I love that there are still such mysteries beyond the reach of science,' I say.

'Any individual bird can initiate a movement of the whole flock by a flick, which sends a wave through the flock radiating out from that bird. These 'manoeuver waves' as they are called, can move in any direction and spread through a flock almost instantaneously. They spread with a speed of less than 15 milliseconds. That's way quicker than a starling's average reaction time of 80 milliseconds.' He glances to see if I'm still with him. I am. 'Mind-blowing when you think our human reaction time is between 200 to 300 milliseconds.'

I look out at the birds, the clouds, the blue vastness of the sky, all of it a mystery, and shake my head. When we recognised the significance of each individual, we may have found freedom but lost something equally precious, our belonging to each other and our home in the cosmic mystery. I stretch my arm out the window and feel the wind. 'Those birds have what we've lost,

Dan. They've found a home in the sky, in their flight, in each other.' I watch the last starlings disappear over the horizon into their sky-freedoms and wonder if I too can find a home in homelessness. The warm wind swirls through the car and blows my hair into my eyes.

DAN

The moors turn into fields with dry stone walls. We begin our descent back into civilisation and leave flying to the birds. Suddenly I feel able to express what I've always known but never been able to articulate.

'You know when drum rhythms pound in your blood and the drum, the beat, the dance, you, me, and we're all in the zone and one with everything, maybe that's the body remembering what our minds have forgotten.' I reach across and hold her hand, thinking as I speak. 'Maybe we haven't lost what those birds have, Lizzie. The unconscious is not an ethereal entity invented by Freud that vaguely dangles in the ether, it's the living breathing reality of the body and its instincts. Our glorious instinctual heritage isn't lost, it lives on in the unconscious energy of our bodies, in the tidal ebb and flow of our hormones, in the sparks of our neural networks, in the metronomic beat of our hearts, in the kinaesthetic memory of our muscles.' I stretch my arm out the window and feel the wind as it blows by us and swirls into the car. 'The body is not a 'thing', an object, it's a flow of energy, an unfolding process, a living mystery. And our beautiful animal bodies have never forgotten what those birds know, that we belong to life more than to ourselves.'

I'm turning into a genius! I don't know why Lizzie has this effect on me but I like it. It makes me love her even more. I turn to her. 'I love you, Lizzie.' 'I love you too,' she says. But her hand is limp and she doesn't smile. She stares out the window. She flicks ash off her skirt, fiddles with her hair and lights another cigarette. That's her third on this journey, not counting the joint.

LIZZIE

Dan hums softly and taps his fingers on the steering wheel. He turns to me periodically and smiles. I don't smile back. I can give out psycho-spiritual theory until the cows come home about the existential conflict of freedom and belonging but it doesn't help me. I'm neither free to be myself nor do I belong anywhere. I don't even belong to myself. I wish I knew what blights my happiness. Perhaps its power over me would weaken if I could name the beast. But I can't. I should tell Dan some of my history but I'm afraid he'd pull away. After all, what happened must be my fault, a fated generational curse, a shameful misalignment within my DNA or a shadowy wrongness that wormed itself into me like a virus and now lies coiled in my lungs, something so dreadful it can never be named. I light another cigarette and breathe the smoke deep into my lungs. I hope it will smother and choke the evil away.

I look out at rows of houses with their neat front gardens and closed front doors, and remember things I'd rather forget.

It's a rainy Saturday. We four children are squabbling over whose turn it is to clean the shoes. Mary sticks her legs out and Mark trips over them on his way to seize the cricket bat Stephen's been swiping through the air hitting imaginary balls over boundaries. Mum yells from the kitchen to stop messing about. It's a small house for four children to be growing into themselves, especially when it rains and we can't escape outside. Stephen, furious that Mark has taken his cricket bat, pulls my hair. I squeal and retreat under the table. My father ignores us while reading his newspaper. He reads something that makes his eyes bulge and his face turn crimson. He shakes the paper at us. 'Communists and homosexuals should be put up against a wall and shot!' He bangs his fist on the table and knocks a cup to the floor. I'm under the table trying to read my Bunty comic, pretending I'm somewhere else. The hot tea falls on me. 'Ow!' I shout. 'Look what you've done!' But I'm not angry about the tea. I'm angry about the desolate dysfunctional deranged dynamics of my family surrounding me in all directions. I couldn't have named it; I just knew I hated it. I scream from under the table. 'Communists and homosexuals are not the ones going to hell! It's a far worse sin than anything they've done to shoot a communist dead for trying to create a fairer society or a gay person for trying to find love where they can. You're going to hell, not them!'

My father grabs me by my hair and pulls me out from under the table. He wrenches the cricket bat from Mark and hits me with it. I scream. He hits me again. And again. His eyes glaze over and his face contorts into a red fury and like the wooden puppet Punch I'd watched on the beach beat Judy, his arm rising and falling pulled by strings I can't see. I scream and try to protect my head with my arms while the bat beats down on me. My brothers and sister are frozen in terror. My mother watches from the kitchen. When my screams subside because I am blacking out she says, 'Arthur, stop it. She'll have learned her lesson by now.' He yanks me up off the floor and yells at me to go to my bedroom. I stagger up the stairs and pull a chest of drawers in front of the door so he can't get in. I think my mother might come to see if I'm alright but she doesn't. No one comes. Hours later my sister Mary whispers through the door, 'They say we can't speak to you. Sorry.' She stays for a while and scratches at the door so I'd know she was there. I know how brave *this is of her because I've seen how my fights with our parents terrify her. I love her for this small rebellion.*

Chapter 12   Nuclear Winter

DAN

We drive into Lizzie's parents' neighbourhood. Terraced houses are squeezed into rows with few trees or open spaces. I can't imagine Lizzie growing up here. A grim miasma from the C19th seems to hang over the streets and linger on the pavements. People walk bowed over as if forced into a grey resignation by the relentless harsh winds off the North Sea. We turn into a street indistinguishable from hundreds of the others. 'This is it,' Lizzie says. I park and we walk up to number 61, its green door opening straight onto the street. She knocks. The door opens. 'Hey, Lizzie! You must be Dan. Come in.' It's her sister Mary.

We enter a dark hallway. Straight ahead are steep stairs and a narrow passage with swirly wallpaper, different swirls on the carpets and more swirls in the plaster on the ceiling. People wander through small rooms crowded with furniture holding paper plates of sandwiches, crisps and sausage rolls, all talking at once, holding several conversations in parallel, yelling comments across the room, up the stairs or through the hatch from the kitchen. It confuses me until I realise you don't have to actually say anything meaningful, random comments on the weather, last nights TV, the latest news on next door's cat, almost anything seem fine. I much prefer this chaos to the stultifying politeness of my family and dive in. While in the kitchen picking up my second sausage roll, I encounter Stephen, the accountant. He doesn't bore me with tax advice, he entertains me instead with tales of the dangers of endowment mortgages. I peer out at the garden. Kevin notes my interest and points out the assorted statues of hedgehogs, birds, pigs and ducks, and a small fountain, in the compact backyard of a Victorian Terrace. 'Dad's a gardener,' he explains. 'Here, let me introduce you.' He takes me to meet a grey haired man in the corner of the living room.

'Dad, this is Dan, Lizzie's boyfriend.' 'Good afternoon, sir, I hope life is treating you well,' he says. I'm about to tell him how much I love his daughter when he disappears into the garden, perhaps to do some weeding, rearrange the statues or creosote a fence. I shrug and wander back into the dining room where a woman stands with her back to me. Perhaps sensing someone behind her, she turns and stares at me. They say if you want to know what a woman will be like when she's old, look at her mother. If I believed that, I'd turn around and walk out of Lizzie's life immediately; I can't see the slightest similarity between them. I hold out my hand. 'Hello Mrs Loughran, I'm Dan, Lizzie's boyfriend.'

Despite years of work to overlay the upper class accent of my family with an Aussie twang, in socially awkward situations I have an embarrassing tendency to revert to those cut glass vowels. Unfortunately I do so now. Maybe that's why I'm left holding a hand out to empty air. 'Oh so you're Lizzie's new boyfriend,' she says. She may once have been the sun around which this family orbited but she seems to me to be more like a dead star whose inner fire has died.

The contrast between my family and Lizzie's is as stark as that between classical harp and punk improvised drumming. At Brewin family gatherings you comment on the state of the economy or international politics and pretend to listen while really you hear only the sound of your own voice. In Lizzie's family, everyone speaks at once, doesn't even pretend to listen, yet manages to hear a sentence in a conversation from the next room. I like that Lizzie's family seem to be simply themselves without dressing it up with the fancy packaging and posturing my family go in for. Soon I'm swimming with the herd, flying with the pack and running with the flock like the rest of them. Periodically I emerge, take a breath and dive back in for another round of recipes, bargains and T.V. soaps. I even offer a few contributions of my own; one in particular goes down well: the only difference between branded groceries and the Co-op's own brand is the packaging. I don't explain how I've come by this knowledge, because my family's firm makes the boxes for both.

After going with the flow for half an hour or a whole afternoon, maybe longer, it's hard to judge in timeless conditions like these with conversations on endless repeat, Lizzie finds me, grabs my arm and hisses in my ear, 'Time to go.'

LIZZIE

I can't stand it a moment longer. We're supposed to stay the night but I 'remember' I'm teaching the next day, standing in for someone who's sick. Dan is still in the mix but I stare hard at him. He doesn't get it until I fetch our coats and thrust his jacket at him.

I kiss my mother on the cheek. 'Happy birthday, mum, take care, see you later.' It's like kissing a statue. Dan comes over smiling and shakes her hand. 'Thank you for having me, Mrs Loughran. Rest assured I will take care of your daughter.' He bends over her hand in what is not really a bow, more of a lean, but I've noticed before that in awkward situations Dan can come out with degenerate Jane Austen. He looks surprised when his Darcy impression receives the dead-stone look I'm so familiar with. My father reappears, ignores me, but shakes Dan's hand. 'Pleased to have met you, Sir. Godspeed.' If I didn't know the sinister meaning in the lines around his eyes and hadn't read the contours of fear and rage at the corners of his mouth, I'd imagine he's simply an old man eager to return to his plants.

DAN

Lizzie shoves my coat at me and, after a general good-bye to the gathering, we head for the door. There are none of the prolonged handshakes and 'let's do lunch next time you're in the city' or 'will we be seeing you in Tuscany this summer?' that my family go in for. We climb into the car and drive off. I get the bends from surfacing so quickly from a total body immersion in a world unlike any I've encountered before. I take deep breaths to stabilise myself. How on earth did such a gorgeous, funny, beautiful, intelligent, sexy creature like Lizzie emerge from that?

We drive over the moors back home. Except Lizzie doesn't come home. She's gone. Gone to where I can't find her and don't know where to begin looking.

LIZZIE

I stare out the window as we drive back to Manchester. It's midsummer and the sky is blue but a fog descends on me that blocks out the sun and turns the world grey. Birds, clouds, sheep, stone walls and stunted oak trees move by me; nothing moves me. That night I cling to Dan like a rat who's left a sinking ship and must grab onto any bit of flotsam she can find else drown in the black water all around her. Dan is bewildered. 'Where have you gone Lizzie? Come back.' I can hear him but can't reply because I've slipped away from even the temporary mooring he offers and am sinking to the bottom of the sea with a mile of ocean on top of me.

Dan falls asleep and gently snores. I stare at shadows on the ceiling and ponder how much better it would be for everyone if I simply ceased to exist.

In the morning Dan asks how I am. 'I'm feeling better now,' I tell him. I'm lying. Relieved, he puts on his coat, kisses me on the cheek and leaves for a session with Obsidian. As soon as the door clicks shut, a familiar toxic cloud of misery and shame invades my arms and legs, crawls into my lungs and curls into my heart. Hello darkness my old friend.

DAN

We were jamming all day experimenting with 12 bar blues and inverted doubles. On the way home I bought flowers for Lizzie from the local corner shop. Straggly carnations and daisies rather than orchids and roses but something to let her know I loved her. The night before she'd drifted over a bleak horizon into a cold world far away where I couldn't reach her.

I hang my coat and go into the living room. Lizzie looks up without a smile. This is not the woman I know, full of laughter and passion. It's like an invisible force has squeezed her into a two-dimensional shell of a person. I hand her the flowers. 'These are for you,' I say. 'Thank you,' she says, and places them on the table without looking at them. I take them into the kitchen, fill a vase with water and stick them in it. I return to the living room and put them on the table. 'You look like you need a treat. How about a take-away Indian?' She shakes her head. 'Perhaps a movie?' Silence. This is going nowhere. 'Look if you're not going to communicate with me I may as well get on with things myself.' She shrugs. 'Do what you want,' she says. The lack of life in her voice infuriates me. I run my fingers through my hair. 'Look Lizzie, I've no idea what's going on but if you're not going to talk I'm never going to find out am I?' She shrugs, glances at me with flat eyes and picks fluff off her cardigan. I stand up. 'I've got better things to do than hang around here trying to get you to speak when you don't want to.' I pace in tight circles in a room that has become a cage trapping us both. I look out the window. Trees sway in the wind. The sky calls me. I turn back to Lizzie one more time and hold out my arms. 'Anything?' Nothing. I fetch my coat. 'See you later,' I say, and walk out.

Oumar went to London last week and bought a load of US and Jamaican imports at Rough Trade in Notting Hill. We'll get stoned and listen to those new tunes. I feel in my pocket for my beaters. I'll experiment with the new riffs and patterns we hear.

LIZZIE

The phone rings. I let it ring. The answer machine clicks in. 'Hi, Lizzie, it's Jan and Michelle. We've something to tell you. Let us know when we can pop round.' I don't want to see anyone, not even my best friends. I feel sick. I've ingested poison and the toxin is myself. There's only one way out. Virginia Woolf loaded her pockets with stones and walked out into a river. Sylvia Plath put her head in a gas oven. Diane Arbus slashed her wrists. But I'm too cowardly to go for that ultimate freedom, the only one that liberates you from the prison of yourself.

However brainsick you are, you still have to pee. On my way back to the sofa the phone rings again. I listen to the answer machine. It's Michelle. 'We're nearby. Are you there Lizzie?' I pick up the phone. 'Oh you *are* there,' she says. 'Can we come by now?' They'll demand an explanation if I say no. 'OK,' I say. I claim I want to be alone yet pick up the phone - I can't even be honest with myself.

Jan and Michelle arrive. They see the discarded tissues and my tear stained face and sit either side of me on the sofa. Several cups of tea later, I remember they have news to tell me. I've given them my news, I'm a broken mistake of a person who'd be better gone from existence, and ask them for theirs. 'I'm not sure now is the right time,' says Jan. 'No, tell me,' I say. 'It sounded like good news. It might help me crawl out of the mire.' They look at each other. Jan nods. 'OK, we're going to have a baby.' I blow my nose and sit up. 'Well that's…' I pause. How do you describe the news that your dyke friends are pregnant, at a time before IVF was freely available to anyone let alone lesbians? 'Fantastic.' I cup my hands around my mug and sip the Darjeeling. 'OK, confess, which of you has done the deed? I presume no angel announced god had done it.' 'I am,' says Michelle. 'Pete helped.' I smile. 'Helped as in… you know… did it?' 'Yup,' they say together. 'Well this calls for a celebration,' I say. I go to the fridge and return with a bottle. I pull out the cork. 'Though only a sip for you Michelle.'

When Dan returns, Jan and Michelle have gone. I appear, on the surface at least, to be a saner person than the one he left. He takes tentative steps towards me, sees me smile and bounds over to sit next to me on the sofa. He tells me in a relieved rush of Oumar's adventures in London and his chance meeting with Sledge Hammer Sounds of Jamaica in Portobello Market. I'm as interested in Oumar's exploits as Dan is in the fact Jan and Michelle are pregnant, but I have something else to tell him. After the visit to my family and now this news from Jan and Michelle, I am at the point where I must tell Dan the thing I've been avoiding telling him ever since we first made love.

DAN

When I got home, Lizzie had colour in her cheeks and was no longer the pale insipid version of Lizzie I'd left. She tells me Jan and Michelle had been for what I imagine was an intense 'moan about men' session. Whatever. I was relieved things were returning to normal. I leaned back, breathed more easily and told her about Oumar's London trip. Normal service was resuming.

I was as wrong as a drunk insisting it's the line that's askew, he's walking as straight as a ruler.

Chapter 13   Cry Baby Cry

LIZZIE

Another milestone in my relationship with Dan has arrived. I'm about to tell him what I haven't shared with even my best friends. I'm not sure if this is a betrayal of the sisterhood or a deepening of my intimacy with Dan.

'I've something I need to tell you,' I say.

He looks wary of another meltdown.

'OK,' he says.

'I had a baby when I was young.'

Dan's eyes widen but he doesn't look away.

'I gave him up for adoption.'

Dan slightly moves towards me. Not away.

One day I'll tell him how much this almost imperceptible movement meant to me.

DAN

Lizzie says she's something to tell me.

'OK,' I say. I hope I'm not going to be hit by another burst of craziness.

'I had a child when I was young.'

I stare at her.

'I gave him away.'

She's trembling. I move closer to her and hold her hands in mine.

'He's a teenager now.'

Nothing I think to say seems right so I say nothing. I put my arm around her. She leans into me and I hold her. A thousand questions run through my mind but there'll be plenty of time to talk later. I stroke her hair.

LIZZIE

I've never told anyone the whole story before, only dished out fragments when the situation demanded it. But if not now, when? And if not Dan, who?

I describe my convent school where the nuns insisted we wear skirts low enough to hide our knees, we must not run or wave our arms, nor we must ever talk to a boy, not even our brother, when wearing school uniform. Sex was seeping out of every pore of us teenage girls but, I tell Dan, except for dire warnings of its evil, our sexuality was completely denied. We were supposed to be inspired by martyrs who chose death with beatific smiles rather than impurity. A favourite was St Maria Goretti who was stabbed to death when she refused to submit to her cousin's advances. However we wouldn't all take the high road and become a bride of Christ and the lesser evil was to marry a Catholic boy. Which is why each year we had a Christmas party with the boys' school run by Jesuits, where we danced the waltz and foxtrot with ladylike decorum, hands resting lightly on our partners' shoulders and no other part of our anatomy closer than 18 inches to any part of theirs. But patrolling nuns with rulers had no hope of controlling teenage girls who'd just heard a new kind of music, music with a rhythmic beat that made you want to twist and shout well outside the routines of strictly ballroom.

In the heart of the crush on the dance floor, we moved closer, touched each other and danced in moves never seen in a Loreto Convent before. A boy held me in his arms, bent down and kissed me. He put his tongue in my mouth. A flood of feeling made me nearly faint. I would have fallen but he held me tightly in the crush. I fell anyway. The list of sins in my prayer book to help jog my memory before confession included one that informed me to kiss with an open mouth for longer than five seconds was a mortal sin. If I died before confessing and doing penance for this, I'd burn in the flames of hell for eternity.

'I was burning anyway,' I tell Dan. 'The flames of hell, the heat of desire, the melting of my petrified life, they all ran into each other. And I came in from the cold.'

DAN

I'm wondering where all this is going but I guess Lizzie has to approach this in her own way so I listen without interruptions or questions. She tells me how she got drunk at parties, drank black coffee, smoked French cigarettes, pretended to be an existentialist at the Sorbonne, and as the night wore on, got up close and personal with the boys. I smiled. We'd all gone through versions of that. Though I'd never been a French intellectual, I was a roadie for the Rolling Stones. But I understood completely when she told me that despite the priests and nuns trying to teach them sex was something dirty and corrupt, the tidal pull of that powerful undertow carried them towards each other with a current you couldn't swim against even if you'd wanted to. I too remembered how the force rushed through you, knocking you sideways so you fell into the pleasures of sex in cars, under trees, in fields, having fun like young people do all over the world when given the chance. But my fear was about being fumblingly inept or being found out, not any shame about the delights and pleasures of sex itself. Lizzie seemed to have been grappling with something else, something darker and deeper.

LIZZIE

There was always a point where I'd draw a line and pull back, but as the glacier melted and more of me came in from the cold, the line moved. The day came when that line of desire was irrevocably crossed. My boyfriend and I lay in the fields on the banks of the Humber Estuary and among bluebells, buttercups and lilac blossom, between an oak and an ash in full leaf, under a cloudless blue sky that promised the earth, I was baptised into the one true religion. 'This very body, the Buddha, this very Earth, the Lotus Paradise!'

A month later I was on the toilet staring at another piece of toilet roll with no sign of blood. I put my head in my hands. Abortion was illegal. The Catholic Church condemned unmarried mothers as fallen women who were headed for hell. An unholy sick feeling of dread sat in my stomach like a poisonous toad. My parents were going to kill me.

DAN

I listened while Lizzie told me of her teenage pregnancy and the cruelty that surrounded her. How the Parish priest, the nuns and her parents all told her she was a sinner and a whore. Who on earth would subject a young innocent girl to such abuse when all she's done is have some natural fun with her boy friend and been unlucky enough to end up pregnant? I thought this kind of thing had gone out centuries ago and was astounded that religion did such things to its people. I was beginning to see why Lizzie is so adamant religion is worse than capitalism. I've always argued capitalism is worse because I couldn't see how a bunch of people kneeling down, singing hymns and splashing holy water about was remotely comparable to the grinding daily sweat and labour of employees at my family's firm making riches for my family and not for their own. Though, as Lizzie points out, the Roman Catholic Church is the oldest and richest institution on the planet and you don't get to keep all that money and power for thousands of years without dishing out some heavy shit down the centuries.

When Lizzie could no longer hide the growing bump she told her parents she was pregnant. They reacted, as she'd known they would, with condemnation and judgement. After consultations with the parish priest and the nuns they packed her off to a mother and baby home run by a different cabal of nuns, The Sisters of Mercy, but without the mercy. It was like a prison sentence. She was stripped of most personal possessions and given a bed in a dormitory. It got worse. No one from their families was allowed to be with the girls when they were in labour, just the hospital staff. Not that Lizzie wanted her righteous parents anywhere near her while breathing through her contractions; it was bad enough knowing the nuns were praying for her. There was no celebration of the miracle of birth, no loving hugs or congratulations, no flowers and chocolates, just labour pains, the birth, and a lonely mother and baby saying hello to each other for the first time. Soon the little one would be gone anyway.

LIZZIE

Dan is holding my hand. No one held my hand at any time during my pregnancy or during my labour. And there was no hug, no hand on my arm, not even a compassionate smile, on the day I gave my baby away. It was a pragmatic operation like a trade deal. Though what I was getting in this exchange was nothing. A clean break was considered best for everyone. That way adoptive parents could rest secure in the knowledge they were the baby's only parents, the unwed mothers could get back to their schooling and the little child would never know he or she had been born in sin. Perhaps because I have so few memories I cling to the ones I have.

130

I remember the first contractions of labour as I swept the floor of the dining room after dinner. I remember being driven to the hospital and lying on the narrow bed, sweating, breathing hard, and swearing when I was supposed to be saying the rosary. I remember being swept aside by an elemental force that rushed through me and began waves of pushing. I remember a baby's head appearing between my legs. I remember reaching down to touch this delicate, blue, slippery, velvet head and stroking his little helpless body. He yawned, his small fingers moving like seaweed, his open mouth searching blindly in a vast new world for my breast. I placed my nipple between his tiny lips and he fastened on. I knew he'd never be mine, but I wanted to hold him and keep him safe forever.

DAN

Lizzie tells me she insisted on breastfeeding her baby for the two weeks they were together even though it was frowned upon and the nuns disapproved. They warned her, 'It'll make it all the harder for you when you come to give him away.' But Lizzie had said she wanted to give him as much of her as she could before he left her forever.

'Why did you not keep him?' I ask. Though I keep hold of her hand to let her know I'm not judging her or anything like that.

She shrugs. 'You just didn't. There were good Catholic families lined up to adopt them. And we were told again and again, 'your baby will have a far better life with them than with you'. We just went with it. We'd already proved we were sinners who'd shamed our families and the Church. It was taken for granted we'd be lousy mothers. I don't remember any of us questioning it.'

I stare at her. This was mediaeval.

'I guess, when you get down to it, we were all depressed, anxious and confused. We were lost really, still children. I was fifteen, some were thirteen, one girl was only twelve. We had no idea what was what. Except what we'd been told, that we were fallen and wicked.'

She'd been allowed to name the baby herself, though it had to be a saint's name, not Jaydon or Kylie or anything like that. She'd gone for Joseph.

'I called him Joey, little Joey. Though the nuns said the new parents would probably change it.'

I can think of nothing to say and hold Lizzie's hand in silence.

LIZZIE

Two weeks after I'd given birth, I gave Joey his last breast-feed in a quiet corner of the dormitory. I stroked his cheek, kissed his little body all over and told him, 'I'll never forget you and will pray for you every single day of my life until I die. Goodbye little Joey. Have a beautiful life.' I wrapped him in the blanket I'd knitted and gave him to the nuns. I thanked them, for what I'm not sure, picked up my suitcase and left.

I went back to school as if nothing had happened. The nuns regularly ignored the absence of certain girls who disappeared and four months or so later re-appeared. Only the observant might have noticed we'd changed. Sometimes we were quieter and more withdrawn than before, sometimes louder and more rebellious. We stopped running like young colts around the playground. We gazed out the window during maths and forgot to do our history homework. We avoided netball and hockey in case someone saw our stretch marks in the showers. We congregated in guilty solidarity round the back of the bike shed, a shameful sisterhood who'd smoke and talk of boyfriends and plans for the future but never of the secret thing that marked us out and bonded us. We talked of that to no one, not even to each other.

Dan hasn't moved. 'And now you know why I try to hide my stretch marks, can't give Jan and Michelle the support they want from me, and turn away pretending to be busy when people coo over babies.' Dan reaches across, strokes my cheek and brings my chin up so he can look at me. His eyes are moist. 'I'm so sorry this happened to you, Lizzie.' I wonder if he's expecting me to cry but I'm frozen. 'It's hard to speak about it, even now,' I say. 'At home I was forbidden to speak of it to anyone. My parents didn't even want to know his name.' I'm speaking one step removed in the flat voice of a witness to a crime rather than the victim. 'I felt it was probably a sin to hold the secret of Joey so close when he didn't belong to me but I didn't confess this sin in confession. Nor did I admit I selfishly wished I could have kept him.' I've been staring at the floor but now lift my eyes to look at Dan. 'But even though I know nothing about Joey and he knows nothing about me, I couldn't abandon him a second time by pretending he didn't exist, could I?'

Dan listens with the silence of an oak tree. I've told him more than I've ever told anyone. He strokes my hand with his thumb. 'No,' he says. 'And now he's part of my life too.' His response is as far from that of my parents as a birthday gift of flowers is from a cruise missile. I start to cry. Dan passes me a tissue from his pocket. It is torn and a bit dirty but means more to me than all the prayers and masses my parents said for me to help me repent and learn the error of my ways. I dry my eyes.

I don't mention that when adopted people reach the age of 18 they now have the right to see their original birth certificate. On it is the name of their birth mother. One day, if he wants to, Joey will be able to find me.

Chapter 14   War Games

LIZZIE

I wouldn't have known if Dan hadn't left the card on the draining board. He'd obviously planned to bin it and then been distracted. I hold it by its corner and walk through to the living room. I wave it in front of him.

'You weren't going to tell me were you?'

He sighs.

'Look, we've been though all this before, Lizzie, read my lips. I do not want to go anywhere near my family and I do not want to go to my father's 60th birthday party.' He picks up NME and starts to read an interview with Kate Bush. I stand in front of him continuing to wave the card. He glares at me. 'I said, Lizzie, just drop it.'

I stare at this man with the child in his eyes.

'But he's your father. He's not going to be around forever. Perhaps there's a chance you can ease things between you. You don't want him to die and then be faced with a terrible regret that you did nothing.'

'Lizzie, you don't understand.'

DAN

Lizzie sees a family as something that when broken needs mending. I see families as dangerous swamps to be avoided at all costs. We're going to fight over this. Though I have a sinking feeling the battle is already over and she's won. Lizzie thinks I always get my way; she has no idea how potent she is at getting hers. And yes, we're soon driving to my parents' house for the party.

The first leaves are turning red and remind us autumn is on its way. Swallows fly about us, their high-pitched liquid chirps and gurgles filling the air. They will soon be gone for winter. Already they're twittering in lines on telegraph poles preparing for their long journey south. Lizzie and I stop for a break and watch them swoop low over the fields catching flies, crickets, grasshoppers, dragonflies, beetles, moths and other flying insects.

'I was in Swallow Patrol in the girl guides, but I know very little about them,' says Lizzie. She leans back and puts her feet up on the dashboard. 'You're a birder, tell me about them.'

'Ah, Lizzie, these little birds are amazing creatures. Each autumn they migrate through Europe, up and over the Pyrenees, across the Mediterranean, high over the Moroccan mountains, down through Africa, across the equator, all the way down to South Africa. Six months later they fly 6,000 miles back again to the same nesting site and have another brood of young to hatch, feed and teach to fly. The next autumn the whole family makes the same arduous return journey all over again.' I want to share with her the magnificence of these beautiful birds and the remarkable miracles of nature they are. 'They're so small yet have to survive multiple hazards. If you think about it, their migration routes took millions of years to evolve but now there are skyscrapers, TV aerials, radio masts and power lines disrupting their flights and killing thousands. That's not all, they have to survive the heat of the Sahara, now wider than ever before. The burning flares on floating oil and gas platforms attract them, they fly towards the light and are killed in the flames. They have to cope with hunger, exhaustion and the ever-present threat of predators such as hawks, falcons and the great African buzzards. They also have to survive hunters who every year shoot thousands of them, blasting these wonderful birds out of the sky just for fun. After surviving all this, they reach their destination and often find it has been destroyed, an old barn has been renovated, a field has become a housing estate, a wood felled. And frequently there's little food because modern insecticides and pesticides have killed too many of the insects they feed on and they starve to death.'

'Oh how dreadful!' Lizzie says.

'And yet here they are. In fact they live for about eight years.' I squeeze her arm. 'And they mate for life. Not only that but their young will select a nesting site within half a mile of where they were born. A family of swallows remains close and migrates together. Perhaps that's why a group of swallows is called a flight of swallows; a swallow family that flies together stays together.'

'What happens if a swallow loses his or her family? Do they perish?'

'I don't know. Though we're adrift from our families and we're managing to survive.' I reach out for her hand. 'More than survive wouldn't you say?' I want her to smile and say, 'Yes!' but she's silent.

'Yes,' she says eventually. She's looking out the window, probably thinking of my reluctance to visit my parents, of the arguments we had until I capitulated, and of what I've warned her might unfold at a birthday party of hyenas and sharks.

LIZZIE

Dan thinks I am thinking of him and me and how we're alienated from our families. I'm not. I'm thinking of my little family that broke completely apart and didn't stay together and migrate like swallows for even one season. I don't even know if Joey and I are in the same country. But now is not the time to dwell on that because we're on our way to a party to celebrate Dan's father's 60th.

We drive through the avenue of lime trees. To be forewarned is to be forearmed and it's less of a shock this time when wealth and privilege assault us on all sides. I'm weaponed up to meet it and my armour is shiny and bright. My hair gleams with highlights from a rare visit to the hairdressers. I have funny stories to tell of my adventures on location with famous actors. And I'm wearing a Max Mara dress with the latest Nike Dunks to prove I'm both successful and cool.

We're drinking cocktails before dinner. Family, friends, neighbours, local dignitaries and outsider, that's me, enquire about each other's health, offer weather forecasts, tell stories of holidays in the French Riviera, and murmur appreciation of the charming interior decor, the marvellous herbaceous border and the remarkable vista from the window. It's like the first scene of an Agatha Christie play where one of us is going to be murdered and any one of us could be the killer.

'We call this the pink room,' says James, who's appeared at my shoulder while I'm sipping my Negroni, 'for obvious reasons. Maybe you saw that design competition on TV, 'Mansion Makeover' or whatever it was called. The pair who did this went on to win.'

James puts his arm through mine and helpfully points out the flamboyant wallpaper along one wall, wild strawberry pink and deep pink, the painted ornamental plaster ceiling, baby pink, salmon pink and cerise, and the turquoise sofas piped in hot pink. 'It's certainly... different,' I say. The oil paintings of ancestors on horses and under trees with dogs and small children, and a couple of ships on stormy seas were possibly not part of the TV show because, in the culture clash between old classic and bold modern, the paintings look merely dark and old and the dramatic colour looks like a tacky window display. But the rich are different and maybe this is on the cutting edge of design and a mere peasant like myself can't possibly appreciate it.

'Perhaps you saw this room,' he pronounces it 'rorm', 'in that Jane Austen film, can't remember the name of it, but they're all pretty much the same aren't they? Handsome lord of the manor with dodgy friend meets charming vicar's daughter at a ball. Many prejudices and persuasions later she realises she's not in love with dodgy friend after all but with the rich chap who seems indifferent until she falls off a horse and he carries her to safety and it turns out he's been in love with her all along and reader, I married him and all that. You're into drama aren't you, Lizzie, feel free to use my compelling script as you wish.' He takes my hand, brings it to his lips and kisses it. Fortunately Dan doesn't see this. He's in the corner with the local vicar discussing repairs to the church roof and the summer fete.

The gong for dinner sounds and we walk through to the dining room. The long table is covered with a mile of white tablecloth. Hydrangeas and sea grass flowers are in a line of vases between silver candlesticks. Crystal glasses, silver cutlery and white china with the family crest in gold are aligned in perfect order under the chandeliers. Antique mahogany carved dining chairs are around the table and more oily pictures line the walls. Maybe Dan's family goes in for posh bake-off competitions as well as interior design ones.

Dan manages to slip away from learning about the trials of organising regular choir practice, finding enough bell ringers and the challenging architecture of a C14th country village church, and appears at my side. He pulls out a chair for me and whispers, 'Are you OK?' 'I'm fine,' I whisper back, 'how about you?' He turns down the sides of his mouth, 'Surviving – just about.' His attention is demanded by a woman on the other side of him who taps him on his arm. 'Now tell me what you've been up to Daniel. I hear you play in a pop group. Have you been on that programme, what's it called? Top of the Pops I think.' I leave Dan to entertain a woman who's like an aunt out of P G Wodehouse complete with pearls the size of pigeon eggs and a loud voice that drowns out any other point of view than hers.

The Agatha Christie/Jane Austen/Wodehouse mash-up continues through dinner and back into the drawing room where coffee is served while someone plays the Steinway grand piano softly in the background. I'm just thinking this is when one of us keels over and Poirot is called for when Dan's mother, Margaret, makes an announcement.

'Apparently the other day Christie's sold a painting of sunflowers by Van Gogh for nearly £25 million. How ridiculous!' She waves her cigarette about. A long tube of ash is about to fall off it. At the last minute a thin man next to her grabs an ashtray from the table in front of them and holds it under her cigarette. 'Thank you, dear,' she says and flicks the ash onto it from a height. Some of it misses and lands on the man's trousers. He flicks it off but continues to hold the ashtray following the movements of the cigarette. 'I mean it's not as if it's a painting of horses or royalty, nor even of roses or lilies, I mean, a bunch of sunflowers.' She curls her lip with a disdain that would wither a whole herbaceous border and flicks her ash without looking to check if the ashtray is in place. It is.

'Think of the insurance you'd have to cough up for a thing like that,' says Charles, Dan's father.

'As well as the security you'd have to hire.' This is the thin man still assiduously attending to his ashtray duties.

'What I can't work out is how on earth would looking at a painting of sunflowers ever give you a pleasure worth £25 mill?' says James. 'I mean think what you could do with all that. I'd enjoy myself for at least a year, even if I bought everything I wanted.' He looks at me. 'Or anyone.' He smiles. I'm reminded of crocodiles.

'It's as Warhol pointed out, big-time art *is* big-time money.' Twenty pairs of eyes swivel in my direction. 'You may not agree with him, that art is a business and nothing to do with transcendence or truth, but when he bluntly printed the dollar sign as a sign for art, he was definitely reflecting a reality of modern culture, however controversial, that art has become a form of wealth rather than just art.' I wave to the paintings on the wall. 'Maybe it always was.'

'Go girly,' says James.

I blink at him. 'What?'

'Go get 'em,' he smirks. 'I love it.' He turns to Emma on his right. 'I told you she was a deep one.' He leans forwards and stares at Dan. 'You'd better watch out bro, a stunning psycho-philosopher knocking about with a drummer, can't see it myself.'

Dan bends towards me. 'Take no bloody notice of him,' he says. But he clenches his jaw and frowns.

'The problem with young people today is that they've not had the discipline required in the armed forces.' This must be Colonel Mustard perhaps about to do one of us in with the lead piping in the library. 'I said so at the time and I'll say it again, one of our great nation's biggest mistakes was ending National Service. And now look what we have, long haired layabouts who haven't done a day's work between them!'

I grab my napkin and hold it over my mouth to pretend I'm choking on a fish bone.

'How does that relate to sunflowers I wonder.' James doesn't hide that he's laughing. 'I mean I was in the CCF at school and we crawled through fields up close and intimate with a fair few daisies growing out of cow shit but I can't remember an assault course through a field of sunflowers.'

'Don't be silly, James,' says Sarah. 'Mummy, I think it's time for a toast to Daddy, don't you?'

The Mother stubs out her cigarette in the obliging ashtray and rises like an empress heavy with reluctance yet no fear of criticism. 'I would like to thank everyone for coming tonight. It is lovely to see all my children here as well as our neighbours and friends. Thank you too to Dine at Home, the caterers. I'm sure we all agree they created a marvellous feast.' We turn to the staff standing around the edges of the room and clap. 'Dan, darling, bring me my bag will you. It's over there.' She points to a chair on the far side of the room from where Dan is standing next to me. Dan drops my hand and does her bidding. 'I feel very fortunate that I'm able to invite family and friends into my lovely home and share its beauty with you. It is a wonderful thing to be able to give so much pleasure to others. And now a toast to us all.' She lifts her glass. Despite that this is an Oscar acceptance speech not a birthday toast we obediently raise our glasses and swig the Dom Perignon.

We reconfigure ourselves on an assortment of sofas and chairs. I'm between Dan and his sister Sarah.

'I say, Dan, are you going to see Arabella while you're down.' She says 'dine' which confuses me briefly.

'I hadn't planned to. Why?'

'You may not have heard, she's been living in Tuscany since you and she split up but she's come into an inheritance recently. She's looking for a pied-a-terre in London and a place around here. She'd love to see you. Even if only for old time's sake. After all, you two did have an intense and passionate time together. I remember…'

'Thank you, Sarah, but we have to be back. Lizzie has work on Monday. She's very much in demand and worked with Ken Loach on a film recently, didn't you Lizzie.'

'That's a shame. Maybe another time.' She moves on.

Emma beckons Dan over to where she's standing with some friends. Dan stands and reaches for my hand. He wants me to follow him. I shake my head. I can hear them speaking about a holiday on Rupert's yacht. This is not going to involve me.

'Dan, wouldn't it be great if we all took off for a cruise around the Med. You know how much you love Majorca. I'm sure your Obsolete, Obsession, Obstreperous, whatever, can manage without you for a few weeks. How about it?' Emma leans with her elbow on Dan's shoulders and peers around to look him in the eyes with a smile of triumph.

'I don't...' says Dan.

'We can drop in on Antonia and Hans in Calle d'Or. It'll be fab.' She turns to a tall dark haired man with a cravat. 'And Rupert you will adore their place. They have one of those pools with a vanishing edge so you swim with nothing between you and the mountains. It's awfully good fun.'

'Emma, you've convinced me.' Rupert leans over and kisses her on the cheek.

She puts her finger in her champagne glass and sprinkles him as if with holy water. 'Naughty,' she says and laughs. 'That's settled then.'

'No it's not,' says Dan.

Emma raises an eyebrow and turns to stare at me on the sofa. I stare back and raise two eyebrows. Is this a game of poker?

Once a boyfriend and I worked on a farm in Montana. Winter temperatures are way below zero and remain there. We were gearing up for the long cold. Douglas Firs had been felled in spring and chain sawed into logs. Jake, the boyfriend, and I were to split them further and stack them in the woodshed. Jake up-ended one of the logs and showed me how to find a crack to work in the wedge. He demonstrated how to lift the maul and let it fall so that its weight, gravity and the inner structure of the wood worked together to crack the log right through with minimum effort. 'Here, you try,' he said. I held up the maul and let it fall to the point Jake had shown me. There was a cracking sound as the log split from top to bottom that sounded like the fabric of reality was tearing. I never lost the deep satisfaction of hearing that crack when the log split. It proved I was a real person doing real work of the kind humans have been doing ever since we discovered fire. This is a satisfaction none of the Brewin family will have in relation to Dan and me.

Each one has tried to find the crack to slip in the wedge and split the relationship apart. Though Dan's father plays more of a lone hand and just ignores me. We're playing for high stakes. They, to get Dan back into the bosom of the family where he belongs, me, to keep him with me. But all the cards have been dealt and they've failed. I've won because I love Dan, and while his family may want him, they do not love him.

Sarah links arms with Dan. 'Let's go for a walk on the terrace in the moonlight,' she says. She turns to me and holds out her other arm. 'Lizzie, do you want to join us?'

I should have known a family like this wouldn't give up easily. I may have won the poker game but not the war. I suspect the next game will be to seduce me into thinking there is no game, we're friends. Well I'm ready for that game too. I smile and the three of us walk out into the night and gaze up at the splendour of the Milky Way.

Chapter 15 The Crazy Wisdom of Flies

DAN

I don't know which is more excruciating, that I'm stuck here and can't get away, that they all live in a family solidarity that excludes me, that no one gets me in the slightest or even wants to, or that Lizzie is laughing and having fun with them. They're starting to appreciate her, or at least include her. You'd have thought I'd be pleased but I preferred it when they thought she was beneath them. When they were mean to her, she and I at least had a kind of us-against-them solidarity. But I know them, they still think she should be employed as their cleaner rather than on the arm of one of the family, however they've discovered, despite her inferiority, she's witty, intelligent and fun. I'm angry that Lizzie seems to have gone over to the dark side and is on her way to play tennis with Emma, James and Rupert. She's borrowed a tennis dress from Emma and is swinging her racket in a carefree manner that makes me want to yank it out of her hands and throw it out the window. She walks by me swaying that lovely ass of hers.

'Come with me for a walk,' I mutter as she draws level with me. She stops.

'Are you alright, Dan? You look a bit upset.'

'A bit! Bloody hell Lizzie. I need to talk to you.'

'But I've arranged to play tennis and they're waiting for me.'

'Well let them wait. I'm more important than them.'

'Of course you are but we're playing mixed doubles and without me they'll have to find someone else which might be tricky. Most of the others have either gone to the Church for Sunday service or are hanging out in the library hoping drinks will arrive.'

'Oh forget it.' I turn about to stamp off.

Lizzie catches my arm. 'Is it important, Dan, or can it wait?'

'It can wait,' I mutter.

'OK, see you later,' she says.

She walks away, still swinging the bloody racket as if all's right with the world. Which it isn't. She walks through the French windows to meet the others and skips down the steps onto the terrace without a backwards glance.

I go upstairs to our room and lie on the bed. The yellow room. Yes, it's decorated with lemon and buttercup, though I'd call it, jaundice and yellow fever.

James is calling out, 'thirty love', 'deuce,' 'game.' They are laughing and shouting to each other, 'It's mine, I've got it!' 'Oh god, sorry!' 'Great serve!' I bang the window shut. I lie back on the bed and stare at the ceiling. Three flies zig-zag around the lamp hanging over the bed. Each flies in a line that ends with an abrupt about turn into another line until there's another sudden turn into another line. There's no rhythm or pattern that I can see, just the endlessly repeating ritual meaninglessness that flies all over the world go in for. The only imaginable function of this weird obsession they have to zig-zag around a ceiling light in a manner that gets them absolutely nowhere is to mesmerise the humans who lie on beds and stare at them into an even deeper frenzy of despair than the one that led them to lie on beds and look at flies in the first place. Maybe it's revenge for all those insecticide sprays and sticky fly papers. I gaze at the trio of ninja-flies above me. Do they ever get bored? Do they ever go crazy and break out into circles and spirals?

I've closed the windows but can still hear the faint shouts of James, Emma, Sarah and Lizzie enjoying themselves on the tennis court. Why am I not out there with them, serving an ace, executing a killer drop shot and smashing a volley right on the baseline, followed by handshakes and back slaps at the net showing what good sports we are before wandering onto the lawn to sip a Pimms and eat strawberries while being witty and saying 'marvellous' and 'jolly' a lot? They're my family. How can you hate your family? Doesn't that mean you hate yourself? And anyway why do I hate them? Because money is their only measure of worth? Because in a narrow blind patriotism my family right or wrong is the only law and there's no room for any other consideration? I don't fucking know. I stare at the flies. They're a fly version of the Brewin family cohabiting the same small space, dancing around each other in a series of random lines that never intersect. I feel trapped in meaningless thoughts like a fly trapped inside its random series of straight lines. I haven't even got my drums with me to beat them so hard I beat this shit out of me. There's just three flies, me and my thoughts buzzing around in this room going nowhere. It's like a quintet of three kazoos, a mouth organ and a theremin with no harmony or sweet spot of any kind, just noise.

I shouldn't be left alone with only my kind of mind for company. I end up falling down the rabbit hole of myself and getting lost.

One time James and I were out with our air rifles shooting rabbits. We were young. I was ten and James, twelve. We crawled through gorse and brambles pretending to be big game hunters on the Serengeti. The sun was coming up in the east and the new moon was low in the west, perfect conditions to hunt rabbits as in a full moon they feed at night and are back in their burrows by the time the sun comes up. The rabbits were feeding in the early sun. They have extremely keen eyesight with eyes positioned to give them a far wider angle of vision than we have. You don't want to be a silhouette against the skyline, they'll see you and run back underground. We approached them stealthily with the sun behind us to blind them.

Our morning began well. At least 'well' if you're thinking like a hunter and not an empathic sensitive type. A rabbit was sunning itself on a small mound. A short stalk through the gorse, a sightline, a shot and the first one was in the bag. We then had to wait for a while as a shot will always send even hungry rabbits running back down their burrows. We were crawling low down quietly through long grass with a hedge to our right. That's when I saw her, a roe deer caught in a snare trap. Her beautiful rusty brown body was writhing in terror and agony with the snare caught around her abdomen. The more she struggled, the more the metal wire tightened and cut into her flesh. She was dying slowly in prolonged and excruciating pain.

The snare is a cruel and primitive trap. A metal noose is positioned on an animal track where an animal will walk into it. Any animal walking by can be trapped, caught by their leg, abdomen or neck and die a slow painful death. Hundreds of foxes, badgers, deer, birds, hares, otters, cats and dogs are caught, maimed and killed in snares every year. I could see from the churned up grass and ground around her that this deer had been trying for some time to scramble her way out of the trap, fighting the metal noose around her. All this had done was move the snare so it was around her abdomen. And the more she struggled the more it tightened and sliced into her. Her baby fawn was near-by, terrified, running frantically to and fro in panic. This single piece of wire was going to kill them both.

James and I looked at each other white-faced. 'Stay here and I'll run back to the gun room,' he said. He ran back to the house to get a rifle to put her out of her misery while I sat frozen in horror at the unbearable awfulness of this scene. The cries of the deer as she died. Her panting. The whites of her terrified eyes as her desperate attempt to escape further entrapped her. Her sweat matting her red-brown fur into wet tangles. The wire slicing into her organs and tightening as she struggled to escape. The cloud of flies attracted by her blood. The panicked fawn who didn't know what he was witnessing yet his frantic bleating and terrified running was broadcasting that he knew this was absolutely the worst thing that could be happening. Her cries became weaker as her agony continued. Just when I thought I couldn't cope with this a moment longer James arrived back running and out of breath with the rifle. He held it to her head and killed her, ending her agony and her life. He gestured for me to retreat with him while we waited until the fawn approached its mother. It did, perhaps imagining now the struggle had ended and her cries had gone silent it was safe to approach her. As he nuzzled up to his lifeless but still warm mother, James shot him too. He would have anyway died a long slow death either through starvation, being ripped to pieces by foxes or dogs, or killed like his mother had been in the cruel death of a snare trap.

James and I walked slowly back together through fields still wet with morning dew. Blackbirds, robins and thrushes filled the morning with their song. Cattle were lowing in the fields. A cuckoo sounded in the distance. We didn't speak. We walked in through French windows into the dining room. The family were having breakfast with our father's friends who had arrived for a weekend shoot. James swung his bag and air rifle onto a chair. 'We didn't do too well, I'm afraid. Just bagged the one. We came across a deer in a trap. Had to put her out of her misery of course. But we'll be out early again tomorrow and hopefully bring back a brace of rabbits for a stew.' He went to the sideboard and piled a plate with bacon, eggs, black pudding and fried tomatoes. 'Mmmm, I'm hungry,' he said. I turned around and left.

James went shooting grouse with the men to kill the grouse whose lives had been saved by killing foxes with the snare traps that killed the roe deer and her fawn. What is this thing with killing? Killing beautiful wild creatures in order to save the lives of other creatures who you then kill, not because you're hungry, just for the kill. Killing people for killing people because killing people is wrong. It was never the same with James after that.

At school I organised a petition to make snare traps illegal. Four boys signed but they were scholarship boys from Salisbury, not the 'right sort' and it never went anywhere. Except that Matt was one of those boys and he's become a 'brother' in place of a James I no longer recognised. Snare traps are still legal and each year continue to torture, maim and kill innocent creatures, including cats and dogs, thousands and thousands of them. But I never shot another rabbit, pheasant, grouse, deer, duck, squirrel or hare. Neither did I hunt foxes, crows, pigeons, rooks, jackdaws, magpies, geese or badgers ever again, not even rats.

It wasn't only my relationship with my brother that was fractured that day.

Chapter 16   A Feral Baptism

LIZZIE

'Dan, how can you possibly imagine I'm being brainwashed by your family into thinking they're marvellous and you've got something wrong with you. You're crazy if you think I'd fall for that for even one second.' I've come back from playing tennis to shower and change. Dan is lying on the bed and staring into space. To say he's in a foul mood is an understatement.

'Well I don't know why you're having such a good time with them otherwise.'

'I am not 'having a good time with them' you idiot. I'm playing their game that's all. I'm under no illusion that their apparent friendliness is anything other than an attempt to soften me up before they stick the knife in or slip me some poison about you. It's crystal clear they want you to marry some local toff's daughter, that Arabella for example, after which you return to the bosom of your family where you belong, join the business and the Brewin family continues its march towards ever more wealth and power.' I plump down on the bed next to him and nudge him with my elbow. 'Basically the sooner you get over this drumming madness and throw off that totally unsuitable Lizzie the better.'

I lie on my side and stare at his profile. His nose is bent slightly to the left from a rugby tackle. His hair is thinning at his temples though he won't admit it. I can see the pulse in his neck and the creases in the corner of his eyes. I slide my arm under his. 'But, my dear and wonderful Dan, there is no way that is going to happen. Just watch me.' I squeeze his arm and pull him towards me.

DAN

I'm trying to explain to Lizzie the shit-storm that goes down inside me when I'm with my family for anything longer than ten minutes but I can't. I can't even explain to myself.

'You don't get it Lizzie. They're not like ordinary people. They're even worse than you think they are.'

'Dan, I don't care what they are or what they've done, I just want you to be free from all that history and baggage you drag along behind you.'

'But Lizzie, you don't understand how ruthless, vicious and utterly without morals my family are. I do. That's why my best plan is to stay away from them.' I pull my arm away from her and sit up. My face is hot. There's a fire burning in me I'd put out if I could. 'You should never have forced me to come. I knew I'd end up feeling like shit and I do.'

'Dan, we've been through this before. I didn't force you. OK I went in for a bit of persuasion but you agreed.'

'You mean the kind of persuasion where you stamp about full of resentment and hit me with relentless recrimination until I capitulate. The kind of persuasion that people with any sensitivity or awareness would call bullying. You're a bully just like my family. When things don't go the way you want them to you throw heavy shit at me about how I need therapy for my hostility, need, rage, fear or whatever is your latest theory about what's going on in my unconscious until I give in because it's easier than fighting you.' I get off the bed and walk over to the window. I stare out at the sky with my back to her. 'They say you marry your mother. It's true. You're just like my mother. You use any combination of seduction, threat, promises, enticements and bullying to get your own way.' I turn and face her. 'Well I'm not falling for it any more.'

LIZZIE

I sit up and stare at Dan. He's locked into another rage and I'm getting it even though it's nothing whatsoever to do with me.

'I am not your mother, Dan. Yes at times I go crazy at you about leaving a mess, forgetting arrangements, not paying me enough attention and so on. Yes I might go in for some heavy persuasion now and then but there's one basic difference, she wants you to live exactly the life she wants you to lead because she believes it's your duty, and she will sacrifice you on the altar of your family just like she's sacrificed herself. But I want you to be free and happy to live your own life as yourself. Of course I hope your freedom and happiness includes me. And sure I'll fight to keep you. But I'm not going to force you into anything. In the end, if it's not what you want, I'll let you go. I'm not the kind of person who clings on beyond my sell by date.'

A thought occurs to me that the reason I am not that kind of person is because I always leave them before they can leave me. I file the idea away to be examined later when that kind of insight is perfect fodder for my darker moods. Right now there's a hurt and angry Dan to deal with.

'Perhaps we don't partner up with our mother or father.' It's my turn to lie on the bed and stare at the ceiling. 'Perhaps we just think we do because we project onto our relationship unresolved conflicts from our childhood and that makes me appear like your mother but that's not reality.' I pull myself up and lean on one elbow. 'You think I'm a bully because being bullied was the way of things in your family. I think you don't really love me because I was not loved in mine. It's written into our psychic DNA that this is how it was, is and always will be.'

I get up off the bed and walk over to the window next to him. I touch his arm.

'Please Dan, don't take it out on me that your family don't understand you and lack respect for what you do.' He stares out at the lawn stretching out towards the ha ha and the cows wandering through the fields in the distance. Two crows land and hop on the lawn. 'I know I'm not perfect but I genuinely want what's best for you. I think you're so unfamiliar with having someone on your side, you can't recognise an ally when one is here.' I stroke his arm and hope I'm getting through to him.

He sighs and his arm relaxes some of its resistance to me. 'You might be right,' he says. A gust of wind rustles through the trees. The crows take off and call to each other as they fly away. 'I hope you are, Lizzie, else where's the hope?'

I remember when all the miseries and evils left Pandora's box and flew out over the world the last creature left was hope. Humanity has debated ever since whether hope is one of the evils because it prolongs our torment or is our only hope to save us from despair.

'Let's go for it anyway Dan. Let's go all out for love. Let's not stand on the bank, let's dive into the river. Let's fly, swim, crawl, run, climb, drown or fall to wherever love takes us. Let the deadly seriousness of our love do its worst. Let's not shy away from the dangers of a love that could kill us both with its dark intensity, instead let's make a love so crazy and penetrating, so bright and so dark, so real and so profound, it's a love to die for. And let's laugh even as love kills us, because only the best die this way.'

I want to run with him away from this place steeped in privilege with the toxic entitlement of centuries hanging like a noxious smoke in the corridors, the drawing rooms, the halls, the bedrooms, the dining rooms and the library.

I want to embrace the unknown and run in the direction of the danger, not away from it. I want to dive into the river and swim to freedom, not stay safe with the weight of centuries hanging round my neck like millstones. I grab his hand.

'Instead of having a shower here, let's go to the lake for a swim.'

'But we haven't brought swimming things,' he says.

I laugh. 'Who cares about bathing suits when we're heading for the stars? Besides, it's a private lake, who'll see us?'

DAN

We leave our clothes under the willow trees and dive into the cool water of the lake. Fish are leaping for flies and plopping back into the water leaving concentric overlapping circles on the surface of the water. Two ducks swim towards me and then away back into the reeds. Dragonfly wings are reflecting rainbows. Midges dance in the sun. The water is clear and cold, like vodka on ice, and rushes into my mouth, my nose, my ears. I dive, surface, breathe deep gulps of air and dive down again. Lizzie lies on her back and shouts to the sky. She spins over and dives under me. I am laughing as fish nibble my toes and the water runs through my hair and into my eyes. I swim after her and we grapple with each other in a dance where we fall and keep on falling but there are no hard knocks or bruises, just more splashing and more falling freedom.

We climb out and I help Lizzie over the rocks back onto the bank. Suddenly there is James. I want to stand in front of her to protect her from his stare but she's already facing him. The sun shines through the leaves onto her glowing skin and the rich lustre of her hair. Her golden body is upright and glorious. Her long legs, her bushy pubic hair, her softly rounded belly with its stretch marks, her brown erect nipples, her breasts covered with droplets of water, her heart shaped lips, her green eyes, her hair flowing over her shoulders like a Venus whose beauty makes you shiver in fear and quiver in longing. She laughs. 'Hello James,' she says.

I can see he's hastily trying to come up with a witty remark to put him back on top of this situation. The best he can come up with, 'Are those stretch marks I see before me?' He smirks. Emma and Rupert arrive. Sarah, Charles and my father follow. The only missing one is my mother. But she too now walks down the wood chip path between the oak and ash trees to the small clearing overlooking the lake. A line of my family is staring at Lizzie and me with not a fig leaf on either of us to protect us from their gaze.

LIZZIE

Dan's entire family is staring at me as I stand stark naked in front of them.

'Yes,' I say. 'These stretch marks are from when I had a baby at 15. Though I gave him up for adoption.' My voice is clear and resonant with happiness from the swimming and playing with Dan. 'I have other scars that mark my history if you're interested, but you'll have to come closer to examine them and I'm afraid that will involve getting your feet wet.' I spin round and points to a v-shaped scar on my ass, wriggling a little so they can see how magnificent it is, my ass not the scar. 'A knife did that. Either a gravity knife or switchblade, I don't remember. I was probably out of it on cider and mandies at the time.' I smile at them all as if welcoming them to an evening recital of chamber music. 'And here's another one.' I point to a scar along my arm. 'That was in a fight with a man who tried to rape me. He didn't succeed. When you're living on the street you learn how to take care of yourself.' I smile graciously at the assembled throng. 'But do please excuse me, I can't spend all day conversing with you, Dan and I have other business to attend to.'

Perhaps not my finest hour but, though I say it myself, one of my best.

DAN

My family stare at Lizzie in a dumbfounded silence. I can't help it. I'm grinning from ear to ear. I've never seen my family stuck for words like they are here.

Lizzie walks over to her clothes, bends to pick them up with the grace of a gazelle and throws them over her arm. She shakes her head. Her hair splashes rainbows of water over my family like a feral baptism by the goddess. She smiles at them one more time and turns to walk in her beauty through the bushes and across the lawn, utterly magnificent and resplendent in her nakedness. I dance a few steps of a jig in front of my frozen and thunderstruck family and turn to run after my wonderful Lizzie. I catch up with her and, while my family stands in a line of petrified privilege, she strides across the lawn glorious in her radiant beauty.

'That was amazing, Lizzie! You are a queen and I throw not just my cloak but myself at your feet. Come with me and let's make love so that the ghosts of history are exorcised from my heart and mind forever. Let's make love so the paintings of my ancestors fall off the wall, the antique furniture splinters and the priceless carpets roll up in shame into the corners. Let's make love and have the stone walls howl, the roofs collapse and the glass in all the windows shatter. Lizzie, let's be so crazily in love we become completely free of every insanity in the world!'

We run laughing up to the yellow room. I bow to the flies and their obsessive love of random lines and pull Lizzie onto the bed. In this dark palace of greed, this castle of unhappiness where money is the only thing that breaks your heart, Lizzie and I make love. I fall and keep on falling deeper into Lizzie, into the love. After all, how do birds learn to fly? They fall and fall and fall, until the falling gives them wings. And when I come, birds sing in my throat, roses bloom in my chest and laughter shakes my limbs.

I love you Lizzie with all my heart. You are my Queen of the night, a beautiful sorceress who could have just bewitched me but instead you broke the spell, released me from the curse and cut the umbilical cord tying me to my family. Now I'm free to keep my promise to you to be with you through the perpetual night of the deepest ocean until we've created our own light.

LIZZIE

We're driving home. I slide Rumours into the cassette player. Dan beats out syncopated drum fills on the steering wheel. I wind down the window and sing out into the dark fields as we drive by them. *'For you there'll be no more crying, for you, the sun will be shining, and I feel that when I'm with you it's alright, I know it's right.'* There couldn't be a better soundtrack for Dan and me tonight than this sublime album with all the hurt beauty and sweet violence of love fused into the groove of every song.

Dan slows down as we reach a roundabout. 'You've never told me about living on the streets,' he says. 'And you told me the scar on your arm was an accident.' He holds the wheel with one hand and reaches across the back of my seat. He strokes my hair. 'Not that I mind. You could have lived in a tepee on a slagheap or a barge on the Manchester Ship Canal for all I care. I'm just curious.'

I light a cigarette. I take a long drag and blow the smoke out the window before replying. 'It was after Joey. I just didn't feel the same way about school, home, the Church, anything really. Looking back I guess I was depressed but at the time I just thought I was fucked up and there was something wrong with me. In the end I ran away, trying to escape myself as much as the cold war at home.' I put my feet on the dashboard. 'But before I reveal all, Dan, you must tell me what you meant when you said, 'my family are even worse than you think they are.' Is there more to this story than you've already told me?'

'Ah.' He adjusts the rear-view mirror and runs his fingers through his hair. 'Fair enough I suppose.' He pauses and licks his lips. 'But first you must promise never to speak of it to anyone. No one must ever know what I'm about to tell you.'

'OK. This had better be good after that intro.'

'No it isn't good. Not good at all.' He fingers the neck of his T-shirt. If he wore a tie this is where he'd loosen it and open the top button of his shirt.

DAN

It's my turn to tell Lizzie what I've never told anyone before.

'I was 10. It was a hot summer's day and we were going down to the lake for a swim. Just as we were leaving I realised I'd left my snorkel in my room so ran back up to fetch it. I found it under my bed, stuck it in my bag and ran back down the corridor. I got to the top of the stairs and realised I needed a pee. Rather than go all the way back to my bathroom, I thought I'd pop into nanny's, which was much closer, and pee there. She was off shopping anyway, so she'd said. I may have been whistling when I opened the door, I can't remember, but I do remember I stopped dead in my tracks and froze. There were four feet sticking out from under the duvet. Two, I recognised. They were my father's. The other two were not my mother's. They were nanny's. My father and nanny were in bed together.

'I stood frozen in shock with my mind racing to make sense of what I was seeing. Then I turned and ran down the stairs, over the fields and through the woods. By the time I'd reached the lake I had reconstituted myself and was able to pretend everything was fine. And I never mentioned it to a soul.'

We come to stop in a line of traffic. Car headlights flash by. I let go the wheel and rub my face with my hands.

'Sometimes I feel ashamed that I was a coward and never confronted my father. Or nanny. I simply never spoke of it to anyone.' The cars are moving again. I put my hands back on the wheel, slip into gear and we move along the dual carriageway through the darkness. A slight drizzle mists up the windscreen. I flick on the wipers.

'Dan, you poor thing, this is terrible. Just a child and you've had to live with the burden of that knowledge all alone when it had nothing whatsoever to do with you. I mean, what could you do? If being entangled in the complexities and betrayals of your parents' relationship isn't being caught between a rock and a hard place I don't know what is.'

I pull into a lay-by and switch off the engine. I turn in my seat to face Lizzie directly.

'I never expected you to say that. I thought you'd condemn me for my silence, either that or withdraw from me because I'd been so pathetic to just bury it and never deal with it.'

Lizzie puts one arm across my shoulders and pulls me towards her. 'I am so sorry, Dan, that you had to suffer such a horrible secret for all this time and utterly alone.'

She strokes my hair. I feel her heart beating and her soft breathing as she holds me in her arms. Permafrost in my heart begins to thaw. As the melted ice unfreezes it forms a river of tears that runs unchecked down my face.

LIZZIE

My arm goes to sleep as I hold Dan, but I'm not going to move. What's a numb arm when ancient history is unfreezing in Dan's heart? He sits up and wipes his eyes.

'After that I started messing up at school. I couldn't focus and didn't do my homework. I hated staying inside that house. I spent hours walking around the grounds, anywhere but in there. My school reports, never good at the best of times, plummeted. And we used to get them every month, not once a term. I had to listen to my father go on at me about failing so miserably and all the while I was thinking, 'how dare you of all people criticise me for forgetting the dates of the Battle of Hastings or how to solve quadratic equations when you have so utterly betrayed mother and us, your family?' I just couldn't get my head round any of it.'

I am listening to Dan without words, interruption or interpretation, just as he has held and listened to me so many times. I hope he feels as held by my silence in the same way I have by his.

DAN

A story is uncurling out of me that has lain coiled like a spring inside me for so many years I thought it would always remain there, encrusted with rust and resentment forever.

'One day I was playing with two friends in the woods. We built a fire. It had been a long hot summer and everything was tinder dry. A spark flew onto nearby bracken. It caught alight. We stamped on it and thought we'd managed to put it out. But the fire was creeping through the dry leaf litter and grass on the ground and suddenly there was a crackling sound as fire shot up in four different places through bushes and into the lower branches of trees. We ran around in a panic trying to put the fires out but there was already too much vegetation alight and it was spreading. A breeze had picked up which wasn't helping. There was a cinder path I hoped would act as a firebreak but embers sailed on the wind and another fire broke out on the other side of it. In only minutes it was clear we were not going to prevent this fire spreading. My friends ran home in panic. I ran back to the house shouting, 'Fire, there's a fire,' until my voice was hoarse. I ran to where I knew there was a hose, turned it on and ran towards the fire until it was stretched out to its full length. But it was over a hundred metres from the fire and the arc of water fell forlornly into the field, nowhere near the flames. Which by now were spreading and close to one of our cottages, unfortunately one with a thatched roof. I ran towards the cottage to yell at the Stanmores who lived there to get out. They were running around collecting the dogs, cats and hens to take refuge in the field. Tommy was clutching a goldfish bowl. Two cats were squealing in a box. The dogs were running around, thank goodness afraid of the fire so staying close to us. We could hear the sirens of the fire engines getting closer. There was an almighty whoosh and we watched as the thatched roof caught fire and was engulfed in flames. Mrs Stanmore and Lucy began to cry. More people were coming into the field and staring in horror at the burning wood and cottage. I was frozen in shock. The cottage was gutted. The wood was destroyed. Thousands of insects, birds and animals lost their lives.

'I walked around like a zombie for weeks. No one said anything but I was buried under a mile of unspoken condemnation and judgement. As for myself,

I was worse than even my father and James and had lost even the sliver of moral ground I'd been clinging to.

'One afternoon not long after the fire, everyone was out. I went into the library, put newspaper under the door and lay down in front of the gas fire. I turned it on. I lay there and thought, why not have one last wank before leaving this life forever? I did. Energy rushed through me and I realised no way could I kill myself, life is so absolutely real there must be more to it than this. And I'm going to find it, whatever it takes. I turned off the gas, screwed up the newspaper and threw it away. A week later I went to Salisbury and saw the Cream play. Well, that was it. I was never going back in the cage again. Except the prison wasn't the house but I didn't know that then. I even went to the opposite side of the globe and still couldn't get free of my family.

'Being trapped by your own love in a situation that is destroying you is the worst kind of prison; even your attempts to escape tie in you deeper. Like that deer in the snare trap, each time I tried to cut the ties that bound me, I discovered even deeper ones.' I turn to Lizzie. We're parked in a lay-by and in the flashing lights of passing headlights I can see her beauty and that she's really listening to me. I reach across and stroke her cheek. 'The first cut is not the deepest, Lizzie, it's the final cut. That's the one that can't be reversed, that either releases you or kills you. And you, my beautiful crazy wonderful Lizzie, have just cut through the umbilical cord that has tied me to my family for as long as I can remember. Now I'm at last free to love without the fear that love will entrap me ever again.'

Songbird comes through the speakers. I turn up the volume. '*And I love you, I love you, I love you, like never before.*' For the rest of the drive home, we don't say much. But then silence can say things words can't.

Chapter 17 The Wind Turns

LIZZIE

More winters blew through. With a north wind chill it often felt below freezing for months, but Dan and I weren't cold. We had our love to keep us warm. The winters turned into springs with longer days and leaves emerging on trees with the fresh green of innocence and promise. Birds sang and collected twigs for nests. And then the summers arrived bringing sun and blue skies. This summer is hot and the heat bounces off pavements. People walk bare legged in sandals and shorts. They sit on the grass under shady trees and eat ice cream, have barbecues and sip summer cocktails late into the evening. But I still have the cold of winter in my bones. Nothing warms me, not even nights of loving with Dan. There's a glacier moving into my heart.

The ice has been growing silently underground for months. Like sediment slowly deposits in a river until it dams the flow and the river floods into the fields drowning livestock and villages, this arctic freeze is drowning out our love. For all that Dan says I'm precious to him and he loves me, that's not the reality. His drums are more important to him than I am. He cares more about Obsidian than he does about me. And he loves himself above all else. I could give a list of the ways this manifests but what's the point? He is not going to change. It's who he is. He's warm, generous and loving, until he's asked to extend beyond himself then he cuts off and is gone. I feel an object in this relationship, useful, sometimes precious, but not a person. And now another element has arrived in the mix, or rather two. Celia and Naomi have joined the band as backing singers. And Celia, with her blonde hair, sexy long legs and beautiful voice, is bewitching Dan. Or trying to. Dan insists there's nothing happening, but I've done enough bewitching in my time to recognise those soft smiles, seductive leans in his direction and sensuous hip moves full of invitation. I have sniffed the change in wind direction and though it has yet to come over the horizon, I sense the storm headed our way.

DAN

I come off the phone to Matt and go into the kitchen.

'Great news, Lizzie!' I grab her round the waist and waltz with her around the kitchen. 'We may have got ourselves a manager. A guy called Billy Steele. He wants to meet us at 11.30 today.' I throw on my stone-washed denim jacket over a black T-shirt and Levis, lace up my Reebok trainers, and I'm off. I meet up with Matt, Chris, Steve, and Oumar outside a tall Victorian house in Sackville Street. We ring the bell marked 'Steele Ents.'

'Welcome. I'm Billy and this is Sandra, my PA. Take a seat. Or rather five seats.' He shakes our hands in turn with what looks like a genuine smile - but then he'd have to be able to fake sincerity to be any good at his job. 'Let's get talking and see if we have something here.' He's cool in a Michael Caine kind of way rather than the heavy cool of say Jim Morrison. He explains he saw us at Reading and has kept an eye on us ever since. A few weeks back he saw us play a gig at Club Tropicana, OK only a Tuesday night as we're not names – not yet anyway. 'I liked what I saw both times. You're good. As it happens I have an opening right now for just such a band as you guys. We can sort out the finance and legal stuff later, first let's see how we gel. Any questions?'

Well loads. Where to start?

It turns out he was manager for Granite Dreams and we'd all heard of them. He got them a record contract and steered them through to the next level. They're about to go on a world tour supporting Def Leppard. 'I'm good at getting acts started on the ladder, but if they take off, they need a weightier player than me. Don't get me wrong, I'm good. I've got connections and can get you far better gigs than you're currently organising for yourselves. But I know my limitations. And I have to say, every band that's gone onto greater things has left me with no hard feelings between us.' Sandra comes in and hands him a sheaf of papers. He takes them, glances at them and puts them aside. 'So what do you reckon lads? If you need time to think about it, fine. But I'd like to know by tomorrow as there's another band I'll approach if I'm not your cup of tea.'

We look to Matt. He's not exactly our leader but he's been the main man for decisions so far. I reckon Billy can sense this as most of his talking has been done straight to Matt.

'Can you give us a minute?' says Matt.

'Sure. Take your time. I've got some calls to make so you can stay here.'

He picks up his papers, nods to Sandra to come with him and shuts the door.

We jump up, high five each other and dance around the chairs. It's a no brainer. Of course we're up for it.

'Great lads,' Billy says when five minutes later we tell him we want in.

He gives us copies of the contract to read in case we've any questions and we sign on the dotted line with Sandra and Alice as witnesses. Alice pops out to get us sandwiches, we toast our future success with coffee from the Kardomah round the corner, and that's it. Another round of handshakes and we leave a little taller than when we arrived. We're now officially a proper band, with a manager and our own songs. We've also acquired two backing singers, Celia and Naomi. They're not only fantastic voices and great dancers on stage, they're also fun to have around. Within weeks we have two gigs in

Sheffield, one in Leeds and a booking for WOMAD, an international arts festival that began a few years back, on account of Oumar's African roots and Chris's Moroccan gimbri playing. OK, not yet a recording contract but we have a fire burning in our loins and a hunger in our bellies, and we want it, man.

It is a truth universally acknowledged, however, that just when everything is swimming along nicely, something happens to blow you out the water. The high of realising I was living the dream didn't last long. It never does but I knew it wouldn't anyway because, though I've been trying to pretend otherwise, things are difficult with Lizzie. She's cold, brittle and defensive, and there's a coiled spring of anger in her that lashes out at me at random. As a result I'm spending less time with Lizzie and more with the band. Which, let's face it, is not the best way to nurture things with Lizzie, not with the beautiful and sexy Celia and Naomi in the mix.

LIZZIE

'I'm sick of picking up your clothes. You take them off and just drop them on the floor. I'm not your bloody maid.' I stamp around the bed and point at the pile of socks, T-shirts, jeans and underpants lying all over the floor on Dan's side of the bed.

'Whoa there, Lizzie, calm down. I'm not even awake properly and you're going at me.' Dan blinks the sleep out of his eyes and leans on one shoulder. 'What are you going on about anyway? They're on my side, not yours.' He shakes his head, pumps up his pillow and lies back down.

'Don't tell me to calm down. I care about the place being clean and tidy but if you want to live in a pigsty, go and get your own place.' That jerks him awake. I knew it would.

He sits up and glares at me. 'What the hell's got into you? A few items of clothing are on the floor and you're off on one as if I've smashed the door down and set fire to the mattress; of course I'm going to tell you to calm down. Life is about a lot more than continually tidying clothes like a suburban housewife in the fifties. Chill, Lizzie. Stop being such a control freak.'

'Stop trying to make it about me! This is about you. I'm pissed off how you leave stuff lying around and expect someone else to pick it up for you. You never do the laundry unless I tell you to. You hardly ever empty the rubbish unless I remind you. And you get up from dinner and leave the table to be cleared away by servants. But in case you haven't noticed, we don't have servants. So if *you* don't do the washing up, clear the table, hang out the laundry, sweep the floors, make the beds, do the cooking, clean out the fridge, wash the towels or wipe down the surfaces, guess who else has to. Yes – me! So stop calling me a control freak because I care about the environment we live in while you expect to be waited on hand and foot. Get real, Dan. You no longer live in the lap of luxury and no one is going to clean up your mess, tidy your shit or wipe your bum for you, it's down to you.'

'Oh so you think I don't care about the environment we live in? Well let me tell you, I fucking do.' He leaps out of bed, strides over to me and points his finger at me. 'I don't smoke filthy cigarettes and leave stinking ashtrays lying around full of fag ends. I don't drink to the point of almost falling over like you do at times. I don't buy the ridiculous amount of clothes you do, that you don't need, that waste the earth's resources in their manufacture, that you only wear a few times but bought because you're too brainwashed to resist vacuous consumerist fashion ads.'

'Now who's coming on all righteous with his anti-consumerist puritanism! Well let me inform you, you're way more controlling than me. Like when you try to stop me having fun drinking, refuse a joint because it has tobacco in it, and don't eat chocolate because it's not healthy. I know how to enjoy myself and live. You know only how to bash a few drums and take care of number one, Dan Brewin. But that's not enough. For a start, you spend way too much time with the band and neglect me and our home as if things like your girlfriend and where you live are insignificant details in a life where what really matters is pretending you're a cool dude rock star with adoring fans. Which by the way is a total fantasy as the reality is you're nothing but a self-centred narcissistic arsehole and I'm sick of it.'

DAN

Here we go again. Lizzie is off on a rant with no rhyme or reason. It's like a three-year-old let loose on the drums creating a cacophony of sound that pleases only one person, the one bashing the drums.

'Jesus Christ, woman!' I hit my head in frustration. 'And what are you? A demanding woman who moans continually about anything that doesn't meet her high standards of tidiness, partying, having fun, aesthetics, communication, whatever. And if it doesn't go according to how you want it to, you kick up hell. Clearly you live in an illusion you're perfect. Well I'm telling you, Lizzie Loughran, you're not. You're as much a mess as me.'

'This is typical of you. I try to point out something I'm upset about and you make it all about you. You don't listen. You could have just said, 'I didn't realise my untidiness upset you so much, I'll pick them up in future.' But oh no, you just defend yourself by going at me. Well that's no way to foster dialogue or nurture relationships. In fact it's a shit way to go about things.'

'Oh so it's the same old, you know how relationships should be and I don't. You're attuned to me but I'm not attuned to you. You're trying to make it work and everything I do fucks things up. Well that's crap. And if you can't see that, you're even more cut off from reality than I thought.'

'What do you mean, I'm cut off from reality? I'm trying to communicate something that's important to me and you're absolutely refusing to listen. You should be trying to understand what I'm saying, not dishing out shitty accusations to protect yourself.'

'Look, Lizzie, I'm not perfect. I make mistakes. I make a mess. I don't do it 'right' by you all the time. But you're not perfect either. Yet it's always me that's wrong. Always me that has to apologise for my 'insensitivity, defensiveness, armoured selfish narcissistic deluded fantasies' or whatever is your latest take on my failures and inadequacies. What about what you do?'

'You've just proved my point. You don't listen. You don't care. And you're an ego-centric narcissist who'll defend himself against anything that threatens his self-obsession.'

A fury like a forest fire burns in my stomach. I walk round the bedroom in tight circles,

'This is the fourth time this week you've had a go at me about some minor offence. I left a sock in the tumbler dryer. I forgot to water the plants. I didn't wipe the surfaces after the washing up. But it's not just this last week. This kind of shit has been going down for some time. Despite everything I do to prove it to you, you don't believe I love you. You're suspicious of everyone and don't trust a soul. You babble endlessly with your psycho bullshit yet don't see the goodness in front of your nose. You can't recognise it when someone cares about you and you don't believe it when someone loves you. You wear your pain like armour and no one can get to you, Lizzie, not even when they truly love you.'

She shakes her head and looks away. I stand directly in front of her so she can't avoid me. 'It's not me who's the enemy here, Lizzie, it's what's inside your own head. You help others release their pain and anguish with your psychodrama but what about you? Healer heal thyself, Lizzie. And until you do, you'll keep attacking me for my flawed and fucked up human-ness. You think you're right and I should listen to you, but really you just want me to fill up that bleak emptiness inside you. But nothing can, Lizzie. That black hole inside you will suck everything into it and one day will destroy your life unless you deal with it.'

LIZZIE

A curtain of red descends over my eyes. He's warning *me*! How dare he speak to me like that! I'm not the problem - he's the one who's self-obsessed and refuses to take on the responsibilities of this relationship. I'm sick of it. I pick up the nearest object, a vase of flowers, and throw it at him. He ducks and it misses him. I run towards the kitchen for more weapons to throw. He steps in my way and grabs me by my wrists. I spit at him and scream, 'I hate you!' I fight to release his hold but his drummer's arms hold me in a vice-like grip. I twist and turn to bite him. He's too strong and holds me at bay. He's trying to say things to me but I am screaming and fighting and don't want to listen. I try to head butt him but he dodges. I kick at him and make contact with his legs but it doesn't lessen the force of his hold on me.

DAN

Lizzie's gone crazy, kicking and biting like a wild tiger and spitting out a hatred as deep as hell. I hold her arms tight to keep her from laying into me with whatever she can grab. She pauses, breathing hard, but she's still fighting. She stares at me with the red eyes of a rampaging Kali as if I'm a malignant force for evil.

'Lizzie, this is way out of order. For sure I'm not perfect, but I've given you everything I can. Clearly it's not enough. No one would be enough. I'm sorry, Lizzie, but there's nothing more I can do. I've loved you as much as I can. I'm totally fucking sorry, Lizzie, I really am, I'd do anything for it to be different, but you break the heart of everyone who dares to love you and I've had enough.'

I drop her arms and walk into the living room. I pick up my wallet and put it in my backpack together with a clean T-shirt and my toothbrush. I pull on my jacket. I feel for my keys in my pocket, take one last look around and I'm gone.

Chapter 18   Night Descends

LIZZIE

Dan's left. This time he doesn't slam the door or give out one of his dramatic exit lines. That's it. He's gone from me. I slump on the sofa. A dream has just killed itself.

I call Carole. 'Something's happened. Can you come round?' She must have heard the anguish in my voice because she brings a bottle of Southern Comfort. But when your home is a barren wasteland devoid of love there's no comfort to be found anywhere. She tells me she's seen Dan with Celia. They were drinking together, heads close and laughing. She's not sure she should have told me but I'd rather know. It's as I thought. He's gone from my bed to hers without a backward glance or care in the world. Carole thinks I'm jumping to conclusions but I've seen how the land lies.

That evening Dan returns to collect more clothes and his CDs. It's awkward. He bends over with his back to me while he shoves socks and sweaters into his backpack. I spit at him that he's a shit and Celia's a bitch. He ignores me, though his neck muscles bulge so I know he's working hard not to pay me any attention. He leaves. I cancel my classes, take to my bed and stare at the wall. My shock and grief give way to anger and rage kicks in. Just as well. After a betrayal, rage is a deeper healing than tears.

There's no fury like a woman scorned by someone she loved too much. The anger burns its way into my soul like an underground fire that burns for centuries in ancient peat because it cannot be extinguished. I step into the holy fire and burn. Hatred is the only way to crawl back to yourself when you've loved someone more than you love yourself. The blazing heat ignites the air and a wall of flames rushes towards me.

DAN

There's no point thinking about Lizzie, I'm simply going to live in the moment, one day at a time and get on with my life, my way, without anyone interfering or attacking me. I walk round to Matt's and plan to kip on a spare sofa there for a few nights until I get my bearings. Celia's there. She offers me a spare room at her place and makes it clear I'm welcome to stay as long as I need.

It's comfortable at Celia's. And peaceful. She doesn't make a habit of regularly pointing out my flaws, neither does she hassle me about what I should be doing, shouldn't be doing or should have done but didn't. Plus she's sexy and gorgeous. So when she invites me into her bed that night, let's just say, I'm not reluctant.

LIZZIE

Everywhere are reminders of the life with Dan that's gone. The table where we've had many dinners and almost as many fights, the sofa where we've cuddled and watched films, the bed that's seen enough love and laughter to keep it happy forever. On the mantelpiece is the statue of Kali I gave him when sorry for stamping on his drumsticks in a fury after he'd spent the evening laying down a groove for a new song, forgetting I was waiting for him outside the Gaumont. On the bed is the blanket I knitted during our first winter together when the honeymoon was in full flood and we sailed through calm seas under a romantic strawberry moon. In the back of a drawer is the cashmere sweater he bought me for my birthday, 'as soft as silk and grace and you', he'd said.

Waves of grief and rage fill my nights as well as my days. I dream I'm a billion year old astral travelling shark, the most streamlined killing machine biology can create. I swim across light years seeking victims. Dan has let loose this monstrous creature that will prowl the universe hunting for him - and I always catch my prey. In another dream I'm a witch with long red fingernails and black eyes that flash with venom when I catch sight of Dan. I fly towards him at the speed of light, screeching for revenge, and gouge out his third eye. I curse him. His heart will be smashed into a million tiny pieces, just like mine, and he will burn in a hell of remorse and regret forever, just like me.

I wake and another day of mourning for my ruined life begins.

DAN

I worry about Lizzie. I leave messages on her answer machine but she doesn't call back. I heard she'd cancelled all her workshops. Oumar told me he'd met her in Tesco's but when he asked her how she was she said, 'how do you think I am?' He asked her for a coffee. She said no but he could give me a message which was to fuck off and don't contact her. So even though I worry, I'm not obsessing about her. I focus on our coming gig in Leeds and concentrate on living in the moment. I'm back where I belong, on the road with no responsibilities or claims on me other than whatever is happening in front of me. It's good to be back. Especially as Celia and I are having fun and she makes no demands on me. It suits me to be free like this and I wonder why I ever left this easy living, where there's no need to consider the consequences of your actions because you are responsible only for yourself.

LIZZIE

I lie twisted in my bed of nightmares and tangled sheets. I stare at the ceiling. I turn sideways and stare at the wall. I curl into a ball and close my eyes. I'm in cold turkey from an addiction to the most potent medicine and poison of them all – love.

I guess when love has been your escape from yourself you have to be completely alone to find yourself; it's the only way back home when you've loved others and not yourself. I mean your love has to go somewhere, and if you can't love yourself then it will go to others. But those you love will not love you in the same way - of course not, they love themselves too, usually more than they love you. It's that fatal attraction of opposites. Dan and me, it's an old story.

DAN

Away from Lizzie I'm enjoying myself. Obsidian is on a roll. We are coming up with interesting tunes and our gigs are going great. Celia is fun too. I know I have to get my own place soon, I've no plans to live with another woman, but there are so many things happening now we have a manager hustling for us, it seems simpler to stay at Celia's for the time being. Anyway, we're not in a relationship as such, we're just enjoying each other, no strings attached.

Though I have to admit, on a few occasions I've sensed something is missing, a vague feeling of emptiness and not being met. But then I just switch focus back to the here and now where it all happens anyway. Besides, you can't think too much when you're behind those drums giving out those pulsing rhythms and riding high on the beat.

LIZZIE

I don't know if I'm running towards reality or away from it, penetrating truth or diving into madness, discovering myself or having a nervous breakdown. Time will tell, I can't.

There's a cold wind blowing. Dark clouds threaten rain. I sit on the edge of my bed surrounded by the ruins of what was once my life. I rake through the ashes. Flashes of diamonds glint among the rubble. I look closer. They are sharp piercing truths that burn into me like lasers. I can blame no one but myself. I alone created this devastation. I am the one who laid waste my life. I have fallen into an abyss of my own creation, dreamed impossible dreams and broken my own heart. The awful truth hits me like a tsunami. Love has not betrayed me; I have betrayed love.

No one promised me a rose garden. And even if Dan did, I didn't have to listen. I wanted to. I wanted that ride through the calm seas of the pearly Adriatic with not a ripple of a storm. I wanted that honeymoon that never ended under a full moon that never waned. I wanted that free entry back into paradise where there is continuous dancing, laughter and pleasure, with pain, tears and broken hearts banished forever. But when the angel at the gates with the flaming sword inevitably turned me away, I went into a rage. And there's no fury like a deluded fantasy when reality smashes it to smithereens.

When we sinners rage at angels, however, those seraphims and cherubims turn their flaming swords in our direction and burn us to a crisp. *'Thou art ashes and unto ashes thou wilt return.'* The holy flame that will burn away what is false in me is the heat of my own rage. This is the purifying hell-fire that will bring me out of my fantastical dreams and lead me into reality. Reality was never what I should have been afraid of anyway. The real monsters were my dreams of a paradise where everything I didn't want was banished and incarcerated forever in the dungeons of my unconscious. But sweet dreams like these don't just fade away; they devolve into nightmares. What we exile will one day return and wreak the very havoc we feared. Like the king in the Sufi tale who feared wasps and so ordered them to be exterminated but then was stung to death by scorpions. Or the sheep who spend their lives being terrified of the wolf only to be killed by the shepherd.

Perhaps I should deny my experience has any meaning, medicate myself out of the whole damn show and just take the pills. But you can't escape yourself through drugs, alcohol, pills, sex, parties, shopping, not even meditation. I should know; I've tried them all. None worked. All they did was bring me into a worse nightmare. I'm alone with this, without even the higher power of the recovering alcoholic to help me. That's how dark it is down here.

DAN

When I walked out of my old life with Lizzie, I felt an immediate high at having broken free. I cartwheeled into a different life celebrating I was once again travelling unencumbered, ready for whatever fun and games would come my way. But as time went on I was thinking of Lizzie more and more. Even after making love with Celia or another of the irresistible lovelies who came to say hello after a gig.

A few times, surrounded by an entourage of the cool and beautiful, partying hard after a successful performance with gorgeous women saying hello to me on all sides, when I should have been playing the field and thinking, this is the life man, I've wandered out into the hotel corridor and sat on the floor with my back to the wall. There, thoughts of Lizzie have come to me uninvited, unwanted and unwelcome.

LIZZIE

My friends think I'm having a nervous breakdown and should see a psychiatrist. Yes, I'm in the middle of a breakdown, a breakdown of a way of being that has led me nowhere but into ruin. I tell my friends, I'm a hollow non-person sitting in the ruins of my heart and must release myself from the tyranny of love through the sacred force of rage. That's when they urge me to see a doctor.

I see them from the window as they leave. They shake their heads and speak to each other in low voices. How can you help someone who refuses to be helped? How do you talk with someone who won't listen? I want to shout to them, this breakdown is me being born! This despair is my only hope! This darkness is forcing me to create my own light! But they wouldn't hear me and just see a crazy woman gesticulating through the double-glazing. I must stop staring out the window and look in the mirror. I turn back to more free-diving into a darkness as deep as the Mariana Trench where, like the deep-sea Dragon fish, Goblin Sharks and Sea Devil Anglerfish who live in that eternal night, I must create my own light.

I've read enough self-help books to know I should walk away from the toxicity of my family and never look back. I could then claim victory over circumstance and sing 'I'm a survivor!' But dark histories have their source not only in an individual, they have roots in a family's ancestral soul. I have my mother and father in me, grandparents, great grandparents, and their ancestors too, Irish peasants, forced off their land, allowed to grow only potatoes, forced to live in squalor and starvation, permitted only one pig, crushed by landlords and merchants who made fortunes off the food being shipped to feed the wealthy in England while those who grew the food starved. My anguish hasn't come from an intrinsic evil within my parents but from a society where the rich and privileged maintain their power through oppressing, starving and stealing from the poor. If I don't unearth the true source of the bitter wind that blew through my childhood in this political injustice, I will be forever divided from the love that created me.

Perhaps generations of my family are praying for me to release them from the wastelands of despair where they had to sacrifice all that made life worth living in order to live a little longer in a life that was not therefore worth living. But their hard fight for survival kept the line alive. I owe my very existence to the same hardness that made my childhood so painful. Maybe the repressed hopes and unfulfilled dreams of my ancestors are seeking fulfilment through me. Maybe I am the dream of my ancestors, their love at last free from the continual struggle to survive, after all I've had the freedom to love in ways they couldn't imagine. Maybe my personal liberation will not only release me, it will release them too from an ancient primordial darkness that infects us all.

The politics of experience is as dark and complex as the world.

Do psychiatrists help with this?

DAN

I'm living the dream. Great gigs with adoring fans. Talk of a record deal. Possible support band for REM on their next UK tour. Hanging with mates. Being creative. Fun with the sexy Celia and other beauties. Money arriving in significant quantities. Drink, dope and whatever other substances we fancy arriving as if by magic in our hotel rooms. Yet... something's missing. It's hard to define and I hate to admit it, but with Lizzie there was a meeting, a depth, something elusive, that I haven't found with anyone else. It was just that the intensity of her demands and emotional freak-outs were too much for me. I couldn't handle them. There's something else.

Celia used to be cool and hang loose but recently she's begun to hassle me with questions about where I've been, what I've been doing and who I've been doing it with. A few times she's found me having fun with another lovely and come on heavy. Matt and Oumar laugh and say, 'You should have seen it coming - what did you expect?'

Chapter 19   Familiar Strangers

LIZZIE

The sun comes out from behind the clouds. It shines through the window and casts moving shadows of branches on my bed. I get up and stretch. I step into the shower. The flow of water rinses away months of encrusted grief and I emerge clean and fresh like the first leaves of spring after a bitter winter. I towel dry my hair and smooth moisturiser on my face. I gaze into the eyes of the woman in the mirror. I've felt the sorrow of generations, expressed the grief of my ancestors and released their despair through my rage. I'm no longer frozen petrified in the fearful permafrost of my ancestors and am ready for a new world, where I will live and love for them as well as myself. I thought my love had left me when Dan walked away, but no, my love is always here, with me - it's mine. If love can be defined as the gift of oneself, well I loved Dan and gave myself totally to him - now I'm going to give myself as completely to myself. They say you can't love another until you love yourself; I'm learning the other way round. Through loving another I'm learning to love myself. I put on my coat. I'm going for a walk with my love. We're going to live today for ourselves and no one else.

I spend the morning at a spa where I sweat out the last remnants of my grief in the sauna. I buy a new dress and jacket, one needs a touch of glamour when emerging from a dark night of the soul after all. I have sushi and champagne for lunch. I wander slightly inebriated through the David Hockney exhibition at the Whitworth Art Gallery. I return home with flowers and carrier bags full of my new life.

That night I float in a sea of dreams and am carried by waves so high their crests reach the clouds. There's nothing between me and the stars.

DAN

We're back in Manchester after a tour with R.E.M. The whole experience was amazing and dreadful, both. There were fantastic highs and a great deal of hard partying interspersed with complete exhaustion and long stretches of boredom. Set up, play, tear down, party, fall into bed, sleep, wake, back on the bus, on the road to another town, and round it goes. If you're a headliner with clout it's different. You don't have to carry your own gear and you're whisked off to luxurious hotels. When you're low down the pecking order touring can be tough. So I'm not unhappy to be back. Despite that Celia's been mad at me since we returned to Manchester and I went to Matt's and not hers.

I told her I needed some space. She told me, 'OK spaceman, fuck off.' But the next day she came up to me and said, 'Hello, how's the spaceman doing?' We were in the studio. Matt and Oumar were riffing off each other and I was softly coming in with a reggae groove where the bass drum and snare hold the sweetness and are only played once every four beats. It was all coming together in a thick easy harmony when she and Naomi slid in with the chorus. Celia turned and came onto me full dancehall, with those booty hip moves, as she sang, 'I know you want me, honey, but do *you* know you do?' Of course I smiled and brought in another level of the laid back vibe with the cross-stick on the snare. And that night, well why not? But in the morning it didn't feel so good and I told her it was over. She said, 'It's that Lizzie again isn't it?' Though it wasn't really a question. I told her, no I hadn't seen Lizzie and had no plans to. That was over too. 'Sounds like you're getting over a lot,' she said, 'well get over this as well.' And she threw a cup of coffee over me.

I move in temporarily to Matt's again. The mate was visiting his girlfriend in Greece again. And I'm back where I was all those years ago when I first met Lizzie again. It's disturbing but what's the point in fretting about the past? Especially now we've an album to record and are busy writing tunes and laying down tracks.

LIZZIE

I'm riding my bike through autumn leaves. It's the first day of an autumn cold where you can see your breath. I've pulled my hat down and have a scarf wrapped round my face. I've just ended a sweet love affair. Not for any particular reason, simply because I want more time and space for myself. I've never done that before, just said goodbye and thank you, looking back smiling not with either guilt or regret. I lift my head, swing my legs and feel the wind.

In the distance a man is walking with his hands in his pockets. He's come out without a scarf or hat and is hunched over to keep warm. From here he looks like Dan. I cycle closer. I recognise the coat. It *is* Dan. I ride up to him. He steps sideways out of my way and smiles. It's been years since we saw each other and he doesn't recognise me.

DAN

A woman is riding towards me on a bike with a hat and scarf that hides her face. She reminds me of Lizzie. I haven't seen her since we got back and don't plan to. She's made it clear she wants absolutely nothing to do with me. The last time I called her I expected an answer phone but she picked up. I said, 'Hello, it's Dan.' Without a word, she put the phone down.

The woman stops and unwraps her scarf. She smiles. I stagger. It's Lizzie.

LIZZIE

We go for a coffee in the café in the park. Not my favourite watering hole as it's usually full of pushchairs, babies and breastfeeding, but it's late afternoon and there's just the stragglers of that mummy brigade. I pull off my hat and shake down my hair while Dan buys the coffees. He walks back to our table in a gait that is shockingly familiar yet also not.

What do you talk about in this situation? The weather? The latest Star Wars movie? The holidays we've had since we last met? Or that released from loving Dan, my heartbreak taught me to love myself and redeem the dark history of generations? We take the easy option and talk about work. I tell him my psychodrama is going well and how a few months back I spent a month in Ireland with a film crew. Yes I'd had a love affair there but it was over now. He tells me about his last tour supporting R.E.M. and how it was exactly as you might imagine, wonderful and exhausting. He says they've signed with a label and are in the studio laying down tracks for their album. I hold my coffee cup without a tremor and drink without spilling a drop. I'm not fazed even when he gives me that familiar smile and tells me he's back at Matt's temporarily until he gets his own place. I must be over him. Yet when we hug goodbye we hold on to each other a little longer than two people who are just friends might do.

DAN

We went for a coffee and talked about this and that. It was a bitter-sweet meeting. I was pleased to see Lizzie happy and doing well but, if I'm honest, I was rather disconcerted that she's got over me so completely. I'd have preferred more poignancy and a few rueful smiles of regret. What I got was a laughing Lizzie with a career that's taking off and who's enjoying herself.

It's intense in the studio. Plus we have a gig in a few weeks to try out some of our new songs. I don't have time to think about Lizzie. But I do. I think about her a lot.

LIZZIE

I'm definitely over Dan. I don't wake at night in a torment of longing and loss. I'm not obsessively thinking about him. I don't look back in either anger or regret remembering the past. But I have to admit it's not easy to see posters with details of Obsidian's next gig around the town. Then he calls me. Would I like to go with him to see 'Basic Instinct'? I briefly wonder if this is a coded message but Dan doesn't go in for that kind of elliptical messaging. Even so it doesn't feel quite right. I suggest we meet up for a drink early one evening. I'll make sure I have a dinner date to go to afterwards.

DAN

We meet for drinks. In no time we're laughing and having fun as we once might have done regularly. OK not as lovers but as good friends. I say, let's stay on and eat together. She says, no I'm off to have dinner with Brian. I say, who's Brian? She says, no one you know. I wonder if he's a friend or a lover. I don't ask. Instead I say, let's do this again sometime. She pauses. 'I don't think so,' she says. 'Why not?' I ask. 'It's too intimate,' she says.

LIZZIE

I tell Dan the history between us means we can't be just friends. We need to let each other go. 'Let's thank each other for all the love we've given each other and be on our way,' I say. I put my hands on the table and lean forward towards him. 'Thank you Dan for all you gave me. It was wonderful. It truly was.' I smile. 'And it was what it was.' He doesn't reply.

I gather my things together, put on my coat and stand. Dan reaches out and holds my hand. 'Nothing I say will be enough to thank you, Lizzie. I love you and I always will.' There are tears in his eyes. I smile at him pleased there are none in mine. We hug goodbye.

DAN

I return to Matt's. No one's around which is fine by me because I need to be alone.

I kick off my shoes and lie on the bed. I put my arms behind my head. I look up at the ceiling. I've done everything to get free of Lizzie, tried to beat her out of me with the drums, focused on the moment, diverted myself with whatever was going round on tour, fucked a variety of other women on the road and at home - yet here she is. I masturbate to distract myself but it's the image of Lizzie that takes me to climax and I ejaculate thinking of her again. I just can't get her out of me. I stare at the lampshade. It's slightly askew and hanging at an awkward angle. I have to face it - I have well and truly fucked up. Lizzie, Lizzie, what have I done?

LIZZIE

OK so I shed a few tears that night, just a few into my pillow for old times sake. The next day I was off to run a workshop. I was home by 6pm. The light on the answer machine is flashing. There are seven messages from Dan. Can I call him? He'd like to meet me later. Can he come round? He wants to speak with me urgently. It's one of those fateful moments where you make a choice in one moment and it shapes your life for ever after. Perhaps it isn't a choice. Perhaps I have to discover what a deeper part of me has already decided. I lean back on the sofa. I imagine not calling him and how that feels. I imagine calling him and how that feels. I call him.

'Hello, Dan, it's Lizzie.'

'Lizzie, I've been calling you all day! Can I come and see you?'

I pause and close my eyes. 'OK,' I say.

DAN

I leap into my car and drive round to Lizzie's. Her living room's been decorated but there's still the familiar blue sofa and soft cushions. She brings a bottle of wine from the kitchen, opens it and pours it into glasses, elegant crystal not the old ones we used to have from Woolworth's. She sits on the sofa and pats the cushion next to her for me to join her. Her hair is gleaming. Her skin glows. She smiles and her green eyes look at me with that old familiar suggestion of both promise and warning.

'Here we are,' she says. She leans back on the cushions. 'What a long strange trip it's been.'

'Yes,' I say. I sip the wine. 'Here we are.' I run my finger around the rim of the glass. 'Lizzie,' I pause, not sure how to say this.

'Yes?' she says.

'I want to be with you.'

She puts her head on one side and raises an eyebrow. 'You mean tonight?'

'I mean forever, Lizzie.'

There's a silence like a heavy door has shut on the world and the two of us are completely alone. I feel my heart beating. I see the creases around her eyes and the downy hair on her cheek. I wait. An emptiness stretches on all sides forever.

'I see,' she says.

LIZZIE

It's another of those fulcrums on which the world turns into something other than it was a moment before. Do I jump and surf the tsunami to wherever it takes me or remain safe and dry on land? I know only one way to find out. We both know the deadly seriousness of this love - and its secret. That in its mortal danger lies the honeyed treasure. We must now lie together naked, without even a gossamer of a dream between us, and let whatever this is unfold.

DAN

She stands and moves in beauty like the stars at night into the bedroom. I follow her. We lie together and gaze into each other's eyes. A cloud of unknowing beckons me into a thousand stories. She smiles with that familiar warning and invitation in her green eyes. 'Hello, Dan,' she says. I fall again into the darkness of the deep. 'Hello, Lizzie.'

Drowning in this sea of feeling is like flying.

Chapter 20   Lost & Found

LIZZIE

Most who have a limb amputated suffer excruciating pain; the limb may be gone but the pain is horribly real. Surgeons say this pain usually begins immediately after the surgery when sensations of burning, stabbing, shooting pains and terrible itching are felt in the missing limb. Doctors say it's a response to mixed signals from the brain, but I think it's not only the brain. The whole body suffers the loss of what was once an integral part of it. The lungs, the stomach, the nerves, the glands, the muscles, the bones, the heart... the whole un-whole body grieves. Yet the most bitter of all losses, even more than an arm or leg, is the loss of a child. That never goes away.

Joey's birthday has arrived again. Every year on this day I go for a walk and imagine Joey by my side. We have conversations about his friends, school, his hopes and fears, his dreams. I never ask him about his family, his parents, his home; I've no right to ask him about such things. His adoptive parents gave him a home when I didn't. They were kept awake by his baby cries, teething and night feeds, not me. They nursed him through his childhood illnesses, not me. They held his hand when he took his first steps, taught him to ride a bike, swam with him in the sea, took him on picnics, bought him ice cream, dried his tears and kissed his knees better when he fell over. I have no idea if he has brothers, sisters or grandparents. I don't even know his name now other than the one I gave him that he had for two weeks. I exiled myself from his life and must therefore live with the consequences. As my mother often said, perhaps to herself as much as me, 'You've made your bed, you've got to lie in it.'

Once I visited a psychic in her booth on Brighton Pier. I told her nothing about myself yet she told me my son was far away from me but there was no need to worry, he had powerful spirits looking after him. I like to think I'm one of those spirits. If what happens to us can be genetic heritage, family history, luck, star signs, random events, destiny from a previous life, fluctuations in the quantum field, the machinations of dark energy beyond the event horizon of a black hole… why not an overarching transcendentally interconnected energy field that keeps Joey and me connected forever?

On previous Joey walks I've hidden my tears behind sunglasses. This year I walk along paths through the wetland, ponds and waterways of Burrs Country Park and I don't cry. The empty Joey-ness inside me is now so much part of me it *is* me. Plus, sharing it with Dan has eased the pain in my phantom limb into something gentler than a stabbing agony of guilt, shame and remorse.

DAN

After six months of back and forth between my rented flat and Lizzie's, it's clear we'll soon be living together again. Though I can't just go back to living with Lizzie in her place. She doesn't want that either. I find us a house.

It's on a leafy quiet road with a basement for my drums and some recording gear, a spacious kitchen, light and airy rooms, and a garden. She likes it. Within a couple of months we're in. There are boxes everywhere and we're living in chaos, but this is the first home that belongs to both of us. We also have the room for parties. Whether the new neighbours enjoy our parties as much as we do, I'm not so sure.

LIZZIE

I come home to find Dan has cooked a meal, bought a bottle of Chablis, laid the table and lit candles for dinner. I'm touched that he's made this effort. I'm not sure why we're eating dinner so early until Dan explains, there's a party at the Arts Centre to celebrate a grant they've just received and Obsidian are playing. 'I know it's Joey's birthday but it's a last minute thing,' he says. 'Do you want to come?' 'Thanks but no,' I say, 'though you'd better get going or you'll be late.' 'Thanks Lizzie,' he says, 'I knew you'd understand.'

Yes, I understand that Dan cannot understand. How could he? Non-parents do not understand the depth of the loss and parents do not want to imagine such a loss. I straddle one of the great divides that runs through our culture like a river separating one country from another. I am both a mother and not a mother, and inhabit the no-woman's land between these territories. Once I went to a self-help group for women who'd given away their babies. It didn't solve anything but just being with each other was a relief. We all knew the shame that cut into us like knives, that we'd committed the worst sin of all, given our child away to be cared for and loved by strangers.

I have a friend who wrote a book about motherhood. She wrote that to be effective as a mother you had to put yourself first. If you didn't then you lived through your children, made them responsible for your happiness and your buried resentment at not living your own life erupted as righteous condemnation of any woman who dared to live differently. When she gave readings mothers spat at her with fury and attacked her saying she was a terrible person, a disgrace, the worst kind of mother, a selfish one. Which rather proved her point. But why such heavy condemnation?

I stare out into the night hoping for clarity. There's the rustle of night creatures and the faint swish of traffic but no answers. It's another of those times when you sit alone and grapple with the vague shapes of things in the dark hoping you'll salvage a degree of wisdom but are as likely to sink into despair, reach for the valium or give up on introspection entirely and watch a soap on TV. Gazing into darkness however is like staring into a crystal ball, sometimes things reveal themselves. After all, the Hubble telescope transformed astronomy when, instead of focusing on stars it focused on what appeared to be empty space. Gradually the faint light from nebulae and galaxies millions of light years away, even events just moments after the big bang, were detected. The act of gazing into darkness revealed the story of the universe. Perhaps if I gaze long enough into the darkness of my story of motherhood, the very looking can create some light. Certainly I can expect no enlightenment from patriarchal attitudes embedded within culture and society. Perhaps it's about power; it usually is. And mothers have a terrifying power.

We come to life within her and for a while she's our whole world, with absolute power over us - and we all know what absolute power tends to do. Freud said the guilty secret that binds society together is the hidden wish in all men to murder the father; perhaps a deeper secret is the wish to annihilate the mother. Maybe our sentimental expressions of love in flowers and cards on Mother's Day are attempts to hide the collective secret that however much we may love her, we would also like to be free of her. After all, until we expel her from our psyche, she is a constant reminder that we do not belong only to ourselves but also to each other. Our mother's very existence intrinsically threatens our separate individual identity. Perhaps this is why our individualised society cannot deal with the power of the mother and so condemns her to a life of self denial and sacrifice else be vilified. And look at how many dead mothers there are in Hollywood movies. It's no accident the most individualised cultures have banished the Goddess to a far off wilderness and projected the Mother's omnipotence skyward onto a male God in his heaven.

I open a bottle of wine and roll a joint; tonight is not a night for cold sobriety and abstemious self-denial. Especially as the only redemption possible for a mother who gave her child away is in a love that has seen into our human darkness and survived it. And this love is not a pearl of great price created in the gritty irritation of life, it is a diamond, forged two hundred kilometres under the surface of the Earth at a temperature of 800C in a pressure 50,000 times atmospheric pressure - the hardest of all loves. This is the only love that can redeem a mother like me, a failed mother, an abandoning mother, a 'bad' mother. To save myself I must gaze without flinching into the heart of my darkness and stare into our collective denial of the awful power of the mother. This is the only hope for a hybrid non-mother mother like me, one who gave her child away to strangers.

I pour another glass of wine. What I need is not out there; I've looked. I have to find it myself. Religion, self-help books, yoga, valium, the seven secrets to unlocking your true potential and becoming amazing, none of these are going to help me. Not even meditation can shed light on this one. I smoke the joint and drink the wine but even these old friends of humanity, tobacco, marijuana and the fruit of the vine, can't help here.

Perhaps it's not just me. Maybe all mothers are 'bad' mothers. Maybe they have to be. After all, it's the complexity of a mother's love that makes us human. The uncomplicated loves of grandparents, dogs and therapists might be balm for psychic wounds but this love is not the love that forces us into our humanity. That power belongs to a love with a mother who was once our whole world, the one we loved with the absolute totality of innocence and then had to leave to become a separate and unique self. And it is the mother who throws us out of this paradise. She has to. It would be impossible to leave a perfect mother, the one all mothers are supposed to aspire to - why would anyone turn their back on paradise?

Becoming our own person is a far more complex operation than a cut through an umbilical cord and requires a much tougher love than the unconditional acceptance we're supposed to give our children. This love is real and struggles with being and non-being, existence and annihilation, self and other, war and peace. It's the love in the mammalian bonding between a parent and child that must ultimately give way to freedom. It's the love you find in long marriages where we suffer each other's darkness to the end. It's the love that knows our human darkness and capacity to inflict pain yet still finds forgiveness and redemption. These are the loves that render us human, loves where despite our failings, terrible mistakes and whatever dreadful harm we've dished out, still there is love.

The sky turns dark. It's a clear night. I look up and see not only the stars but also the vast emptiness that lies between them. Surely not only childless mothers suffer, all mothers do. It's the price of our humanity to love your child more than yourself and then give them the freedom to be themselves even if that means they leave you.

Yet though our children must become free of us, we are never free of them. Even when we give our children away they are always with us. Today Joey is eighteen, a man. If Joey wants to he can now find me. It's up to him.

DAN

It's a great party. Lizzie should be here not moping at home. Loads of people ask where she is. I don't think she has any idea she's such a figure for people, they're always asking me about her. Nevertheless, the band has its following too, and there's a load of them here. They're shouting out requests and we're playing them. Obsidian is flying. Tonight is ours. We kill it. Lizzie would have enjoyed herself.

I'm a little worse for wear but stagger home from the party in not too much disarray. Lizzie is asleep on the sofa in her jeans and sweater. Two empty bottles of wine and an ashtray overflowing with cigarettes and joints are evidence that she's had quite a night too. This is the third time in a week Lizzie has drunk herself into a stupor or been so stoned she's gone over the edge into oblivion. That's not all. She lights a cigarette, smokes half of it, leaves it smouldering in the ashtray and lights another. She picks up a book, flips through it and puts it down; there are six lying open about the living room. She's restless as if waiting for something to happen but doesn't know what, when, where or how it's going to happen. OK, most of life is like that, but there are other ways to deal with it. You can distract yourself, keep calm and carry on, write poetry, read Schopenhauer, stare into the void and wait for it to stare back at you, share with a friend, a therapist or a stranger on a train, play a timpani roll for an hour in a 'shit happens' T-shirt... What you *don't* do is lock yourself into an endless run back and forth between a rock and a hard place while mind fucking your way to nowhere. Which is what Lizzie seems to be doing.

In the morning I ask if she's alright. She says, 'I'm fine.' I think, OK, she'll tell me when she's ready. But it's been weeks now. I approach her carefully; I know how easily she slips into dark places.

'What's up, Lizzie? Do you want to talk about it?'

'Nothing's up. I'm fine.'

'No you're not. Sit with me on the sofa and tell me what's going on.'

I pat the cushion next to me. She remains standing.

'I keep telling you, there's nothing going on. Except what's going on because I'm pissed off you keep going on about something going on even though I keep telling you there's nothing going on.'

'Lizzie, I am not trying to get at you. I'm concerned. You're drinking too much every day for a start.'

She glares at me. 'Who are you to judge what's too much for me? Especially given you smoke weed most days and whatever else is going round when you're with the band.'

'Firstly I don't do it every night. Secondly it's not just the drinking. Look at you.'

'What do you mean? Are you telling me how to live my life, like you always say I'm telling you? To repeat your words back at you, I'm just being me and living my life so get off my back.'

I sigh. 'This is what I mean, Lizzie. I'm trying to reach out to you but you keep batting everything back as if I'm out to hurt you.'

'Well clearly you are useless at reaching out if this is the way you do it, accusing me of all sorts as if you're some kind of saint.'

I stand up and hold up my hands in front of me. If she doesn't want to talk there's nothing I can do. 'I was only trying to help but OK, Lizzie, I'll back off.'

I take my jacket and walk towards the front door.

'Dan, I'm...' I turn. 'I'm sorry. I'm just... just not... you know...' She stares out the window.

'No I don't know Lizzie, that's why I'm trying to find out. But if you keep insisting it's all fine I'm not going to throw you to the floor and restrain you with handcuffs until you confess.' I turn and open the door. 'Let me know when you're ready to talk.'

'Dan...' She walks over to me and puts her hand on my arm.

I pause with my hand on the door handle and look down at her hand on me. 'Yes?' I say and look at her. She can probably see I'm losing patience because I'm frowning.

'Nothing,' she says and turns away.

'See you later,' I say, and leave.

LIZZIE

Dan's left. I pull out the letter. It's a creased official brown envelope that is not an electricity bill, a bank statement or a tax demand. I read it for the tenth time.

DAN

I've no idea where I'm headed. For once I don't want to play the drums. I wander into the park through trees fringed with the first colours of autumn. There's a bite in the north wind and I wish I'd brought a scarf. I sit on a bench and put my hands in my pockets to keep them warm. A collie runs over to me, drops a ball at my feet and looks up at me panting. I reach for the ball to throw it but he's playing a different game. He grabs it before I can and runs away, his tail wagging in triumph. Is Lizzie playing some kind of game? Is she doing all this because of something I've done?

I look back through my crimes and misdemeanours over the last months and find nothing to explain her behaviour. I forgot to close the window one time when I went out. I was late home from a couple of gigs but she knows that's how it goes. Matt, Oumar and Chris came over one time and we left the place in a mess with pizza boxes and empty cans of Heineken lying about. She went off on one but I apologised and hoovered the whole flat, even the areas that looked completely clean to me. None of this explains why Lizzie's staggering about in some no-man's land like the militarised zone between North and South Korea. A thought occurs to me, I'll go see Jan and Michelle. They might have a useful angle on this.

I walk through the park to Newsome Street where they live with their three-year-old son Carl. He's a cute kid. The other day I took him out for a play and we kicked a ball around. It was more fun than I'd expected and he's apparently been pestering Jan and Michelle for us to do it again.

I ring the doorbell. Jan answers in an apron with blue paint on her cheek and hands.

'Hi Dan, come in. As you can see, I'm encouraging Carl's creative self expression but he thinks it's more fun to paint me.' I follow her through to their kitchen. Carl is jabbing a paintbrush onto a sheet of paper. Jan points to the splashes of primary colours on the floor, the chairs and Carl. 'I should have stuck to crayons,' she says.

Carl leaps off the chair and runs to me. 'Play football!' he shouts and punches me in the leg.

'I've come to see your mummies,' I say. 'Perhaps later.'

'No now,' he says. And pulls me towards the door.

'How about we all go for a walk in the park? I can talk with your mummies while you have an ice cream and then we can play football.'

'Yes! I want ice cream! I want ice cream!' He punches me in the leg again.

I look questioningly at Jan.

'I guess it's the only way we'll manage a conversation,' Jan says. 'I'll get Michelle.'

We are walking through the park. Carl is kicking through leaves and jumping in puddles. 'What do you want to talk with us about?' Michelle links her arm through mine. 'Is everything OK with you and Lizzie?'

Once in the middle of a fight, Lizzie had insisted we go to see them. Michelle was doing a course in counselling and Lizzie thought she might be able to help us. I hadn't wanted to go but hoping to get Lizzie off my back I agreed. We ended up on the sofa in their living room facing them both. I was tense. I sat with clenched fists and a frown expecting to get it in the neck. I mean two feminist lesbians and Lizzie's oldest friends were hardly going to take the side of a privileged man against a woman oppressed by the patriarchy. They didn't. But then they didn't take Lizzie's side either. I was so relieved I wasn't in for an ego-bashing confrontation that when they asked me what was really going on behind my tension and self-protection, I wept. Out came the story of my alienation from my family and how with Lizzie I tended to defend myself against something similar happening by pushing her away. We then entered deeper territory and Lizzie ended up telling them about Joey. It turned out they'd been hurt by Lizzie's inexplicable coolness when Carl was born. After tearful sharings all round, from Jan and Michelle as well as Lizzie and me, we ended up laughing. Since then I've felt they are friends of mine too. Not my first port of call in a trouble, that would be Matt, Oumar or the drums, but in this situation with Lizzie it felt good to be asking their advice.

We arrive at the cafe and weave through pushchairs, bags of baby paraphernalia and young children in full on emotional states from ecstatic breastfeeding to howling despair, and park at a table by the window. They sit down while I weave back through the pushchair jungle and queue for cappuccinos and an ice cream. I bring the tray to the table, place the cups of coffee in front of them and the tub of ice cream and orange juice in front of

Carl and sit down. 'Enjoy,' I say to Carl and wink. He dives into the ice cream with a small wooden spoon.

'What do you say?' Michelle says to Carl.

'Fank you,' he says with a mouth full of ice cream. We take advantage of his raspberry ripple happiness.

'It's Lizzie,' I say. 'Something's up but she won't talk about it. I'm worried about her. Has she said anything to either of you?'

Jan shakes her head. 'Not to me she hasn't. Has she to you?' She turns to Michelle. Michelle purses her lips.

'Has something happened recently between you that you've forgotten but she's still hurting?'

'I can't think of anything.' I shrugged. 'But then I'm not always the most sensitive of people when it comes to Lizzie's complex inner world.'

They nod. They know what I'm talking about.

Jan suddenly stops slurping her froth and bangs her cup back in its saucer. 'The date! What year is it?'

'Oh my goodness,' says Michelle.

They both look at me. The penny drops.

'Oh my God,' I say. 'It's Joey. He's eighteen.'

I push back my chair and stand up. I promise Carl I'll play football another day. He's happy for the moment with his ice cream and nods. ''morrow,' he says. I kiss each of them in turn and rush back to Lizzie as fast as I can.

Lizzie's sitting on the sofa staring into space. I sit next to her without taking off my jacket.

'It's Joey, isn't it,' I say.

'Yes,' she says.

I hold her hand and with my other hand stroke her hair.

'I'm sorry I didn't realise.'

'I'm sorry I wasn't able to tell you.' She squeezes my hand. 'Stay here. I want to show you something.' She goes into the kitchen and returns with her bag. She reaches into it and pulls out a creased official looking envelope with her name typed on it. 'Here read this.' She passes me the letter in the envelope. 'It's a relief in a way,' she says and sits back down next to me.

I read the letter aloud.

'Dear Miss Loughran, We are writing to inform you that there has been a request from Mr. J Newton d.o.b. 16.04.69 for information regarding the identity of his birth mother. Please contact Mrs Brown, Sen. Social Worker at this office Extn: 25 who is dealing with this case. Yours sincerely, Hull Social Services.'

LIZZIE

Dan sits beside me when I call Mrs Brown. She tells me Mr Newton had contacted them a few months back but it is a legal requirement for him to have had counselling before going forward so he can understand the full implications of his desire to meet his birth mother and to ensure this is the right decision. This is now part of the process for people who were adopted under the old regulations and had been assured there would never be contact between the child and his or her natural mother again. I give my address and occupation. I give my date of birth and that of Joey and where he was born. And I confirm I am willing to go forward with meeting Mr Newton. I have a million questions rushing through me but Mrs Brown's official matter of fact manner stops me asking any of them. Two weeks later Dan and I drive to Hull.

We sit in the waiting room of the Council Offices. The chairs are hard plastic stackable ones. The green and cream walls have posters reminding you to always wear a seat belt and the dangers of fireworks. There's a torn one with information about the new Poll Tax and another about the increased penalties just come in for Class A drugs - life imprisonment. Here it is, the day I've been dreading and longing for eighteen years.

A tall woman with brown curly hair wearing a dress with a pattern of daisies and what look like fish approaches. They're clouds not fish. 'Hello, Miss Loughran, I'm Mrs Steadman. If you'd like to follow me.' Dan and I stand up. 'Just Miss Loughran,' she says. Dan sits back down. 'I'll wait here,' he says. She shows me to a room with a table, four chairs and high windows through which I can see only sky. It looks like a police interrogation cell. 'Mrs Brown will be in to see you soon.' She turns to leave, pauses and, with the first sign she recognises the human drama in this situation, asks if I'd like a cup of tea. 'Yes please,' I say. I'm left alone to read more posters. She returns with a tray and carefully places a pot of tea, three mugs and a plate with three digestive biscuits on the table. I'm left alone again. The clock on the pale green wall ticks. A car drives into the car park outside, its engine idling. Somewhere a phone rings and a door bangs. I sit suspended in the in-between place where what has been is gone and what will be is yet to arrive.

A woman enters. She introduces herself. It's Mrs Brown. 'I'm just checking in with you before I fetch Mr Newton. Do you have any questions?'

My mouth is dry and my heart is racing faster than Dan beats drums at the frenzied height of his drum solo. 'I'm fine,' I say. She leaves. She returns with a tall man with dark hair that reaches his shoulders. He's dressed in a green sweater and denim jeans, is wearing a bag crosswise over his chest and he's smiling. I stand up. There are tears in my eyes that I would wish away if I could.

'Hello Joe,' I say.

'Hello Miss Loughran,' he says. 'I think you are my mother.'

'I am,' I say.

I walk over to him to shake his hand but he pulls me into a hug. I am hugging a man who many years ago was a tiny baby called Joey. I am hugging my son.

'Please call me Lizzie,' I say.

'OK,' he says. 'Is this tea for us?' He sits down. 'I'll be mother' he says, and grins. My heart nearly drops out of my ribcage in relief. He pours tea into the three mugs. The third is for Mrs Brown who is with us, I presume to check nothing untoward happens. I'm smiling too now.

'Obviously I have loads of questions but I'm not sure here is the right setting for that.' He looks about the room with its fluorescent lighting and interrogation room vibe. 'Perhaps we should meet somewhere more relaxing.' He looks at Mrs Brown. 'I suppose that's alright now we've actually met,' he says.

'I agree absolutely,' I say before Mrs Brown can interfere. I pick my bag up off the floor. 'How about we go for a coffee? I'm sure you must know somewhere in Hull that's the right setting for a woman to meet her eighteen year old son for the first time.'

Suddenly I feel less afraid now I've named what's happening. I'm even a little excited that I'm about to get to know a man, my son, who is smart, funny, handsome and looks more like me than I'd dared to imagine.

'I know just the place,' he says. He holds out his arm for me to link in with him. 'Let's go.'

I pause at the door. 'Thank you Mrs Brown.' She nods.

We walk through to the waiting area where Dan is sitting with one leg up crossed over the other, his ankle on his knee, tapping out rhythms on his calf. He sees us and leaps to his feet.

'Joe, this is Dan, my partner. Dan, this is Joe, my son.'

When an atom splits a tremendous energy is released. When atoms come together and fuse, as happens in the heart of the sun, many times more energy is released than when they are split apart. A new family has come into being. We walk out together into Hull city centre and into a million unknowns. What was split apart has come back together.

Chapter 21   1st Counselling Session

Dan

Why am I here? Because Lizzie insisted. She said it was make or break and we'd split unless I agreed to come. I'm hoping this counselling will sort things out. I don't know if it will.

Lizzie

I'm hoping this will help Dan see what he's done and that somehow we'll find a way through. It's not only what he did, and that was bad enough, it was that he lied about it and kept things secret from me. He seems to think he's done nothing wrong.

Dan

I kept it from you because I knew what you'd do. You'd not understand and go crazy. Which is exactly what you did.

Lizzie

Of course I'm upset and angry. Anyone would be. You had a scene with Jodie, whatever her name is at WOMAD and when you came home, you carried on seeing her behind my back.

Dan

It's Josie, her name is Josie. And I didn't carry on seeing her. We spoke a few times, that's all.

Lizzie

That's all! If I hadn't overheard you saying in that creepy voice you get when you're trying it on with someone, that you'd get her tickets for your next gig, I still wouldn't know and you'd be having a sordid secret affair like your brother James gets up to. The only difference between you is that he does it on a yacht or in a fancy hotel and you do it in a field or at a mate's house.

Dan

It is not sordid. And I am not like James. Since this happened you've done nothing but attack me. When I try to explain you go off on one to such an extent I've stopped trying, which is why I'm spending less and less time at home.

Lizzie

Explain! What the hell is there to explain? You fucked Josie and didn't leave it at the festival. You brought it home, shoved it in my face and lied to me. That's why we're here, to sort this out.

Dan

I didn't lie to you. I never mentioned it, that's all. And I've not seen Josie since Womad. All I did was agree to get her a ticket and backstage pass for our Leeds gig. But you're so angry it's like I hatched some Machiavellian plot to betray you.

Lizzie

Then why are you here if you don't think you've done anything wrong?

Dan

I'm here because I care about us, and you going on and on at me is definitely not going to help. Counselling might be the way forward. Though I must admit, I'm not holding out much hope.

Lizzie

I go on at you because you refuse to deal with it. You pretend you did nothing wrong. Whenever the going gets tough, you run away into your drumming and the band and call up your groupie to offer her tickets for your next gig. Why do that unless you were planning on getting together with her again?

Dan

She's not a groupie. She's a journalist. She's doing a feature on us and wants to interview us as a band.

Lizzie

Interview you like fuck! This is getting worse. Pretending this is about publicity when it's nothing of the sort. I heard the way you were talking to her.

Dan

This is exactly what I mean. You don't get it. You and I, we're not married. You don't own me. You've no right to dictate to me how I behave. I'm a free agent with my own life to live. You go live yours and I'll go live mine. I'm sick of you going on at me like this.

Lizzie

That is what you always do, threaten to leave instead of staying to sort it through.

Dan

I'm here aren't I? But if we're talking about sorting it through, what about you? What's your side in it all? What about how much time you spend with Joe? You've even cancelled arrangements with me at the last minute in order to be with him.

Lizzie

Who's Joe? Oh, I need to explain. He's my son. A son I had at 15, who was adopted and found me last year. We're getting to know each other. It's been painful at times but wonderful. His adoptive parents understand but I'm sure it's not been easy for them either to have me suddenly on the scene. They're very different from Joe. He's into wildlife photography, music and travel, while they'd prefer him to have a steady job and work his way up the ladder. For Joe to find me is brilliant for him too. He's said he spent his whole childhood surrounded by people who looked different to him and it's wonderful to find someone who looks like him. But more than that, we're alike in other ways. We have similar loopy writing. We both like to walk on the wilder side of life rather than have a desk job or routine. We even like the same kind of food. It's amazing. Do I feel this has taken me away from Dan? Not at all! OK, I've spent more time away and when Joe's visits he stays with us but it's not like Joe takes me away from Dan. In fact Joe and Dan get on well. Dan took him to one of their gigs a while back and Joe loved it.

Dan

Naturally Lizzie's over the moon Joe has come back into her life. I totally understand that. And yes I do get on with Joe, he's a lovely lad, I like him, but he's not my responsibility. Sometimes I feel Lizzie wants me to be a stepfather and I don't want that role. And yes, sometimes it does get to me how much time she spends with Joe. But he's her son after all. And it was awful what happened when she had him. Do I think this might have played a part in me staying connected with Josie? I don't think so. Though I have been feeling a bit of an outsider recently. I don't really mind that much. I've plenty of mates to hang out with and of course there's Obsidian. It's just that since Lizzie overheard me speaking with Josie, she's been impossible to live with and I've spent even more time away.

Lizzie

How do I feel when Dan says this? I'm not sure. I hadn't really thought of how much Joe coming back into our lives would change things between Dan and me. But of course it has. I don't see why that should mean he goes off with another woman though. Naturally I want to spend as much time as I can with Joe; we've a lot of time we've missed and will never get back. I don't want to miss time with him now. Dan would be welcome to come with us anytime but he usually says 'no' when we ask him.

Dan

It's just not my thing, Lizzie, to sit around like you and Joe do, talking about ideas and politics. You know that's never been me. Besides I don't think you realise how much when you're together it's just the two of you and I'm on the edge of things. I mean I don't really have any connection with him except that he's your son.

Lizzie

But why haven't you said anything before now?

Dan

Well he's not a friend or cousin or anything is he? He's your long lost son. Your connection is important for you both. I know that. No way would I get in the way. It seems right that you have as much time together as you need. It's just that… I guess I hadn't realised until now how much I've been feeling left out of things.

Lizzie

Poor you! Get out the violins. But you're not going to get any sympathy from me. Having to accommodate the existence of my son is no excuse for you to fuck anyone you fancy. Am I angry? Yes I am. Anyone would be. Is this about more than Dan? Well let me ask you a question, would you be angry if your partner slept with another person behind your back and kept it secret that he was still in touch with her? Of course you would. And so am I.

Dan

What about that cameraman you went for a drink with, the one you got it on with in Helmsley? Yes I was pissed off but not like you are now. And I haven't even met Josie yet since WOMAD. All I've done is talk to her on the phone. You actually met that Keith guy and went for a drink with him. Talk about one rule for you and another for me.

Lizzie

What do you mean you haven't met her 'yet'? That proves you're planning to. Stop pretending you're the injured party here when it's me who's being lied to. Just be honest for fuck's sake.

Dan

OK, I'll be honest with you. I like Josie. I had fun with her. She's funny, clever and sexy. There now you have it. You can be as angry as you like, but I'm not responsible for your happiness. I'm not here to plug up the holes in your psyche. I'm here to live my life my way. And I'm fed up with your judgments of me when I don't do things the way you want me to. Am I saying this because I'm no longer in love with Lizzie? Not at all! I love her. But I've had enough of the shit she flings at me day and night.

Lizzie

How do I feel when he says these things? Angry. He uses our relationship like a tit to suck on, and when he's got what he wants, he runs off doing what the fuck he likes. He's not a man, he's a self-obsessed child who won't take responsibility for anything. You asked how I feel, I feel abandoned, betrayed, tricked, undermined, manipulated, hurt, used and abused by an immature narcissist.

Dan

I give up. This is too much for me. I have not done those things to her. She has serious psychological problems she should be telling you about, not flinging shit at me.

Lizzie

And you haven't a fucking clue how to be in a relationship because the slightest need in the other looks like a terrible demand that sends you running faster than a bat out of hell. You talk about me attacking you but you undermine me all the time. You want the comforts and ease of your life with me but none of the responsibilities of a relationship. In every area of your life, you want to have your cake and eat it. I'm an idiot to keep trying to have a relationship with a man who doesn't really want one. Am I saying I want the relationship to end? No. But I don't want to be with a man who without fail puts himself first whatever the price to me. I did that before and don't need to go through that again. So yes, I will leave unless he changes.

Dan

How do I feel when Lizzie talks like this? I feel angry with her for trapping me in a web of demand and responsibility that I never signed up for and never wanted. Do I feel there's any meaning in what she says? Well maybe there is. But I'm not going there while she's in full-on crusading jihad to convert me to my inadequacies and failures. She'll just stick the knife in. Her childhood was so brutal and fucked up she thinks no one loves her. It doesn't matter how many times I've tried to show her I love her, she just doesn't believe it. It's almost as if she tries to find proof I *don't* love her so she can stay with what's familiar. Which is that everyone is against her and is going to hurt her. Lizzie, tell her what your father did to you. Tell her how he tried to shoot you. Tell her how he beat you. How your parents rejected you, abandoned you, condemned you. She's not going to be able to help us unless you do. Because you're right, we need help. But I'm not the only one here who needs help, you do too.

Lizzie

You want to know about my father? Well, I've wandered around this story for so long and it's so much of a mess it's hard to know where to begin.

My father's mother died giving birth to him. He was sent to live with relatives who didn't want him. On his first day at school they found scars and bruises all over him. He was taken to the hospital where they found signs of malnutrition and evidence of old broken bones that had mended themselves with no medical attention. He was taken immediately into care and never went back home again. He was later fostered with another family but was regularly beaten by the foster father who didn't really want him. My father ran away repeatedly but was always brought back to more beatings. His spirit was so broken he died inside and became unable to love anyone. He was a lost soul and like had happened to him, he beat me and punished me in weird and wonderful ways. Eventually I ran away from home when I was sixteen and lived on the streets. And despite being at time hungry, cold and with all sorts of shit going down aoround me, being homeless was a hell of a lot better than being at home.

My father was so angry that his daughter was living in a way that reflected badly on him, he got hold of a gun and went looking for me to kill me. Fortunately he didn't find me. He was planning to look for me again the next day but my mother got up in the night, slipped the gun into her handbag, walked down to the river and threw it into the Humber. Though she blamed me for his breakdown. I had broken his heart with the depraved and immoral way I was living. It was my fault. And I believed it. Talk about denial - I believed they were great parents and it was me that was wrong, bad and worthless. I do now know this is not the truth but sometimes it all comes back and I fall through the cracks into that old void of shame and worthlessness all over again. I've concluded I have to live with this bleakness that comes over me every now and then and make the best of it. But you seem to be suggesting this darkness is not really mine but my father's. How can that be? I'm nothing like him. What do you mean?

Dan

I get it, Lizzie. She's saying your father knew such a level of pain and despair when he was a child that it was beyond his capacity to deal with. Yet it existed. And when energies exist, they don't just fade away and disappear, they seek ways to live just like all life does. And parents will, without knowing what they're doing, give their buried pain to their children. As I well know, above ground the family silver is passed down the generations, underground it's the family trauma.

Lizzie

So are you saying this terrible flaw running through the whole of my life is not really mine and not my fault? It's something I've taken on and am dealing with because someone has to? And if I don't, I'll pass it onto someone else? I have to think about this.

Chapter 22   2nd Counselling Session

Lizzie

We've had an interesting week - 'interesting' as in the Chinese curse 'may you live in interesting times'. I've been thinking a lot about what you said, that my demons are my father's trauma and he passed it onto me. I thought my bouts of feeling crushed by shame and guilt were because I was a deeply flawed person, irredeemably fucked up. After what you said, I'm beginning to sense maybe these meltdowns are not entirely my fault. How I deal with them is up to me but the experiences themselves could be natural, maybe inevitable given my family history. I've also seen how I've passed some of this suffering down the line onto Joe. Joe loves his parents and is delighted to have found me, but I'm aware, even if he isn't, that at two weeks old he suffered the sudden and devastating loss of his whole world. The familiar smells, sounds, sights, voices, all he'd known were suddenly gone and in an instant, everything became something else. I know this happened before any language or memory, but such a shock must cast a shadow over the rest of his life. Perhaps that's why I'm so intent on spending as much time as I can with him, and haven't really paid attention to how this might affect Dan. I can also see how when I feel Dan rejects me, it triggers what happened with my family and I go into an emotional free-fall that is too much for anyone to cope with. I'm still angry with him but I can see what I bring to this situation more than I did before.

Dan

Yes, she's still angry with me and that's been made very clear. She's cold, cut off, distant, doesn't respond when I speak to her and generally does all she can to make my life miserable. I mean what's the point of this counselling if it doesn't lead to any change between us? I'm pleased for Lizzie that she's finding things that help her, but nothing here is helping me.

Lizzie

Here we are again, Dan thinking only of himself.

Dan

Of course I think of myself. Are you trying to say I don't matter?

Lizzie

No. I'm simply pointing out that you focus on one thing - you. The rest of us are merely bit players assigned walk-on parts in the drama of King Dan Brewin.

Dan

If I'm the self centred arsehole you describe me as, why do you want to be with me? You insisted we came here after all.

Lizzie

I wonder that too sometimes. It might be I'm addicted to you because your charismatic energy gives me a hit of life that's an antidote to my despair. Which I'm beginning to understand is exactly what my father must have felt during all those early years of abuse. I mean broken bones that were left to heal themselves. Malnutrition. Loneliness. Apparently he'd be left for days on his own with just bowls of food left out for him like a dog. My father never spoke about any of it, in fact never went anywhere near any emotion or feeling ever. Now I know why. Because that kind of abuse swamps you completely. You think it must be your fault and so you drown in a terror spiral of such unspeakable shame and despair, all you can think to do is kill yourself. My father simply couldn't go there and so passed his unconscious despair, rage, and terror onto his children, mostly onto me. The only reason I know what happened is a friend of my aunt worked in Social Services and told her what she'd read in the old case notes, and she told my mother. And my mother, after a particularly vicious beating as a way to excuse him, told me.

Dan

Here we go again. You say I'm a narcissist who thinks only of himself and that's exactly what you're doing, focusing only on yourself. Perhaps it's you who's the narcissist, not me. How do I feel when Lizzie speaks about her father? Well it's clearly important for her but I can't see how all this ancient history is going to help us.

Lizzie

Thank you for your enlightened response, Dan. Very empathic and sensitive of you.

Dan

You see - that's what she does. Digs at me all the time.

Lizzie

I'll tell you what I do, I take care of you, listen to you and respond with love and sensitivity to your needs. As soon as I begin to tune into myself about things that matter for me, you attack me. Yes, I feel aspects of my relationship with Dan mirror my childhood. I ran away because there was no room for me in that house with my father and mother making me the scapegoat for all their unresolved issues. Well something similar is going on here. If Dan doesn't get what he wants from me he kicks off big time with no appreciation that I'm a person with my own life and needs. OK it took me a long time to realise this for myself, in fact it took Dan leaving me to get it, but now I have. And if he doesn't start to care for me on this level soon, he's going to lose me.

Dan

She's crazy! Of course I care for her. For a start I'm here aren't I? This is more of her childhood trauma acting out and her not believing anyone could love her. So she just pushes me away rather than seeing that of course I love her. OK, I am not going to become her lap dog doing everything the way she wants me to, but that doesn't mean we can't be together. Am I afraid of losing her? No. I'm more afraid of her entangling me in her wily schemes to make me what she wants me to be. Is this linked to my childhood? Probably. But I don't see how this in any way relates to the fact she keeps banging on about how I'm not doing it right, not taking care of her, not listening to her, not man enough, not whatever. You should be asking her why she goes on and on at me, not asking me how I feel about it. Though I'll tell you exactly how I feel about it, I don't like it, don't want it and won't stand for it much longer. If she wants me she'll have to quit attacking me. What do I think she's trying to say to me? I don't fucking know. If she'd just say it without this constant stream of criticism I might be able to understand.

Lizzie

OK, I'll say it as directly as I can. You seem to think my role in your life is to keep you happy and meet your needs. If that doesn't happen you either pull away or attack me. Like when I was offered work with Ken Loach. You were jealous and resentful and instead of celebrating with me, you walked off into the night in a foul temper. Like when I was invited to the premier and the after-party. You were invited too but couldn't bear to play second fiddle to me, which you wouldn't be by the way, so you backed out. I went alone and actually had a lovely time with people there, including Keith. And yes we met later that week for a drink because he wanted to know if I'd be up for a job in New York next year. I told you about the drink but not about the job offer because I knew you'd go off on one and so I planned to wait until the offer came through, if it did, and then tell you. You know how these things work. What's the point telling you if it's not going to happen? Another example, Joe called up and was coming to Manchester the next day for a photography exhibition. He wanted me to go with him so of course I said yes. This was the first time ever that he'd asked me to do something with him. I'm hardly going to say 'no I won't come with you because my boyfriend's playing a gig even though I've seen him play many times before.' But you went silent and cold and didn't come home until the next day. I never asked what you were doing as I didn't want to know. But I know you. I know how when you're threatened you'll do something, anything, to make me insecure, afraid and hurt in order to get power over me again. Have I said enough or do you want more?

Dan

Wow you really hold a grudge don't you?

Lizzie

There you have it. You haven't listened to a word I've said, you've just reacted, defended yourself and gone for an attack.

Dan

What do you mean, how am I affected by what Lizzie's saying? I feel she's getting at me in revenge for Celia and Josie. I feel she's trying to get one over me in order to control me. And I feel she's manipulating this session with you to try and get you onto her side. What do you mean, how do I feel about all those scenarios? Isn't it obvious? I don't like it and think Lizzie's playing a dangerous game. I'm not going to ever be what she wants me to be. Neither am I going to be one of your patients, clients, whatever you call them, who does what you want in order to please you. What? You wonder if I might be more afraid than angry? What makes you say that?

Lizzie

She's saying it because you appear so afraid of being trapped, manipulated, tricked, bullied, humiliated, judged or rejected that you'll do anything to stop whatever it is you're afraid of actually happening. It's as if you've made a vow never to let it happen to you so you defend yourself to the death.

Dan

You can keep your psycho-assassin insights and DIY psychoanalysis to yourself. I'm not paying for this counselling for you to take over the session and sound off at me like you do at home. I'm asking the counsellor, not you, why she suggests I'm afraid rather than angry.

Lizzie

I was only trying to say you look afraid to me too.

Dan

So you both think I'm afraid of how much Lizzie could hurt me. I hope this is not the sisterhood ganging up on me. But to answer you, yes, I think Lizzie could hurt me and she does. As a result I'm afraid, who wouldn't be? Is what I'm afraid of a repeat of my childhood hurt? Well yes, isn't that how it works according to you psychotherapists? Do I think I can discriminate clearly between the reality of Lizzie and my fear? How would I know?

Lizzie

He can't trust me because his trust was betrayed as a child. Because he can't trust me he continually protects himself from me. My frustration about it then proves I'm just out to use him and can't be trusted. It's a horrible double bind. There's more. Dan doesn't trust anyone so all he can rely on is himself. Fine when he's travelling unencumbered on the road, but in a relationship he doesn't see the reality of the other, just his fearful projections and so he's still on his own. A debilitating impossible Catch 22 that traps us both.

Dan

I don't know what to say. I hear the truth in what you're saying but I don't trust you. If I trust you, that would be it. I'd be lost in your world, taken over by your ideas, your control and completely overwhelmed by you. It would be the end of me.

Lizzie

My god, Dan, that's awful, to either be alone, isolated with just yourself or in relationship but without yourself. That's dreadful, no wonder you defend yourself to the bitter end. And I can see that anything another person says or does to help, in this case me, will look like more manipulation and interference and only make matters worse. That really is being stuck between a rock and a hard place.

Dan

I know I protect myself fiercely and fight. I know I say and do things that even while I'm saying and doing them I know will cause trouble. I know I've hurt you, Lizzie. And I'm sorry about that. But this is me. And I have to be me. Even if it means I hurt you.

Lizzie

Yes, you have to be you. One thing I've learned from you, Dan, is we have to be free to be ourselves because without that freedom, love is meaningless.

Dan

I didn't expect you to say that. I thought you'd go at me again.

Lizzie

Well being me I might still go at you but I'm not like your family, Dan. I don't want to entrap you in a golden cage where you can't be yourself. Anyway I could never compete on that front with your family. They offered you money, security, status, wealth, the whole world, if only you'd sacrifice yourself on the altar of the family and do it their way, and still you walked away.

Dan

I have a lump in my throat. No one has ever spoken to me like that before. I'd given up hoping someone could ever genuinely care for me rather than forcing me to be what they want me to be.

Lizzie

If you think about it, it's pretty amazing how we've managed to stay together as long as we have, given our childhood experiences of love and relationship were so awful. Maybe we should congratulate each other rather than going at each other. Though maybe neither of us can help making mistakes and then blaming the other because to take it all on ourselves in one go would crush us to death, so we dish it out to each other and take it back bit by bit in these fights and struggles when we're ready. In which case maybe it won't be endless conflict between us right to the bitter end, maybe one day we'll get through the whole damn lot and end up serene and wise, laughing at our old mistakes and displaying our war wounds like victory medals.

Dan

That's your fear, endless struggle and war. Mine is that I'll end up alienated from everyone, a frustrated non-entity surrounded by failure. Sometimes I think I'm headed that way even with you.

Lizzie

OK, our parents couldn't manage to get through this shit but maybe we can. They didn't have the opportunities we've had to deal with it consciously and creatively. Was there even such a thing as counselling when they were young? Certainly no one in working class Hull ever lay on a couch and had psychoanalysis that I've heard of. All they had was confession with a celibate priest who hadn't a clue about real human love. Maybe, Dan, we can deal with it by making enough love to redeem not only ourselves and each other, but our families going back generations, and then no one need ever suffer like we have again. How about it Dan? How about an adventure into love where we make the kind of love that can redeem even the crazy, fucked up broken people like you and me?

Dan

You can often see what I can't. I sense things that I can't put into words. But I do really love you, Lizzie. It's just sometimes a blind fury burns through me that wants to destroy everything. I can't help it. This is me. If I stop being me then I'm fucked as that's all I have - me. Either I'm me and fuck it up or I'm not me and fuck it up that way.

Lizzie

Meanwhile I fuck it up by *not* being me when what I need is to be more ruthlessly myself. Who designed this thing!

Dan

I'm not sure I want to be like you, Lizzie, and I'm damn sure you don't want to be like me. Though for sure I'm up for allowing this love of ours to become the wild rushing river it's meant to be. What other choice do we have anyway than to let our love be what we've always known it to be - a wind that blows through everything standing in its way, a flood that drowns even ancient mariners and carries them home to the depths, a fire that rips through a eucalyptus forest until all that's left is a devastation in which new growth blankets the hillsides in the wild colours of orchids.

Lizzie

Yes - let's go for it, Dan. Let's make enough love to hold us even when we're shaking with hate and fury, so lost in despair we want to die, so petrified we're frozen to stone. Let's then dance in graveyards where our feet will make the bones of our ancestors shake.

Dan

Yes! Let's make enough love to wake the dead and dance with them on rooftops until our songs call whole towns from centuries of sleep. And let's dance in the streets and fields even though the people watching will think we're insane because they can't hear the music. And, Lizzie, how about we go the whole way?

Lizzie

What are you doing on your knees, Dan? I hope you're not genuflecting to some mythical false god.

Dan

Not a false god, Lizzie, the only god ever worth praying to - love. Lizzie, will you marry me?

Chapter 23   Wedlocked

LIZZIE

Dan's busy with Obsidian. Now they're a 'serious' band apparently they must drink more booze, smoke more weed or whatever's going round, write darker more angst-filled songs and return home later than ever. Jenny, Oumar's new woman, has taken to calling me to moan about it all. I tell her, get used to it; in my experience most musicians are engrossed in their music to the point of infatuated obsession but at least that keeps them occupied and away from other temptations that come their way, especially those that approach them with sexy moves and smiles when they're flying on a post-gig high. I also tell her, don't worry, Oumar loves you, he told me. I hope it helps her. Being a rock star's woman is not an easy ride. There's always three in the bed, the two of you and their guitar. Or in her case a keyboard and in mine, a drum kit. Sometimes you find the whole band with you between the sheets. As for being a wannabe rock star's woman, that's worse. For a start you don't live in a mansion and can't distract yourself buying fancy clothes and jewellery. But that's not what's bothering me.

I'm struggling with how everything about Dan is irritating me. I should have doves flying about my head and choirs of angels singing as I gaze dreamily skywards bathing in a pink glow of happiness. Isn't that how you're supposed to feel when the love of your life has proposed and you've accepted? Yet I'm walking around tight-lipped, with a scowl and gritted teeth. I'm irritated by the clothes he wears, the mess he makes, and the way he chews his food. I can't stand that he's always late, forgets to put the toilet seat down, never cleans the sink or the taps, and drops his clothes by the bed and leaves them there. I could go on so it's just as well he's away so much with Obsidian.

DAN

I must admit, getting married seemed a natural next step to me and no big deal. I guess I haven't really taken on board what it means. Lizzie seems to be taking it far more seriously. She frowns a hell of a lot more for a start. She also regularly hassles me about what kind of wedding we're going to have, a simple do it yourself job with a few friends in a registry office or a grand party with family and invitations to all and sundry. I'm easy with it. I just tell her I'm fine with whatever. For some reason that irritates her. In fact rather a lot seems to irritate her these days. I'll have to sit down with her and find out what's going on. Though I don't know when. We've so much on getting ready for our next gig at Reading Festival, this time on the programme. OK in the Festival Republic Tent again but late afternoon and we'll be playing our own tunes. There's a lot of focus needed to get that together and so I'm away a lot. Maybe that's what's getting to her.

I'll get backstage passes for her and Joe. That'll sort it. I hope so. Her negative vibes are starting to get to me.

LIZZIE

It's Tuesday evening. I ride through the park on my bike to the Arts Centre where I'm running a workshop. The dusk deepens. I pedal through the trees through the smell of damp autumn leaves, the last songs of blackbirds and the rustling of hedgehogs and beetles. Dan's teaching a drumming class tonight at the Arts Centre too, though I'm trying not to think too much about him, partly because I feel guilty. He'd need to be an unimaginative deaf and blind egomaniac in a suit of armour not to notice the critical energy crackling off me in his direction. He tiptoes around me trying not to aggravate me, which just irritates me more. Fortunately, for both of us, he's spending most of his time working with the band for their album and the gig at Reading.

I arrive at the centre, park my bike and sign in. I turn up the heating and set out chairs for the workshop. Twenty of us are soon deep in dramas exploring our complex and muddled relationships with each other. We finish without resolving the predicaments of our human condition, but at least having managed to laugh at some of it. I leave my assistants to tidy up, say goodbye and walk over to my bike to unlock it from the railing. It's not locked to the railing. It's chained to another bike. Dan's bike. Dan has arrived for his drum workshop, locked his bike to mine and gone off with the key.

DAN

I'm deep in coordination exercises to develop four-limb independence when the door crashes open and a whirlwind enters. It's Lizzie. I tell the class of eight to continue with the exercises and I turn to see what's happened. The class is not interested in beating out rhythms with different right and left hands and feet; they're more taken with what's going down between Lizzie and me.

'What's happened? Are you alright?'

'No, I am not alright. I'm furious,' she hisses.

'What are you talking about? What do you mean?'

'I mean I'm can't get home because you've locked your bike to mine and taken away the key.'

'But, Lizzie, I...'

'Don't give me excuses. I don't know why you did it but perhaps you want to keep me trapped and unable to go anywhere. Well if that's your game you can forget it. I am not going to be shackled like this to anyone. Give me the fucking key!'

I find the key in my bag and hold it out to her. She grabs it and storms off.

LIZZIE

I unlock my bike, lock Dan's to the railings and leave the key on the reception desk. I ride home through the park at a speed that sends foraging mice, voles and hedgehogs running for cover. I sit on the sofa with a glass of Rioja. Why the hell am I so furious over a locked bike? I call Carole.

'I need you, can you come over? Or can I come over to you?'

'Has something happened?'

'Yes. And no. But I need to sort myself out.'

'I'll come over. Put the kettle on. Better still, open a bottle.'

Carole arrives and takes one look at my wild eyes, pours herself a glass of wine and sits next to me. I tell her I'm enraged that Dan had locked our bikes together and taken the key.

'Surely all this can't be about just a locked bike. It must be about something else.'

I'm telling her - yes, you're right, it's not about the bike, it's that Dan, as always, thought only of himself and chained us together without any consideration of how it would affect me.

'But Lizzie, you've been a couple forever, plus you've had a break-up and got back together, if you don't know by now what Dan's like then no one does. It doesn't make sense that you're only realising now he's a selfish sod.

Of course he is. They all are. But he's also gorgeous, funny and sexy, and adores you. So, Lizzie, what's this all about really?'

I'm stopped in my tracks. Of course this is not about the bike or Dan or a missing key. It's about the whole business of getting married - tying the knot, taking the plunge, walking down the aisle, hitching our wagons together and getting spliced. I'm terrified I'm going to be trapped in a suburban Alcatraz.

DAN

Lizzie's friend Carole is leaving as I arrive home. We meet on the path to the front door.

'I think you'll find she's calmed down now,' she says.

'That's good,' I say. 'Thanks.' Though I'm not sure what I'm thanking her for.

I open the door, warily. A heavy object might come flying at me. Lizzie's on the sofa. I join her. 'I'm sorry,' she says. I nod. She looks down to the floor. 'I thought I was easy with getting married and being together forever, but the truth is I'm afraid of being trapped, unable to run free and imprisoned for the rest of my life.' She looks up at me. 'Dan, I'm as afraid of commitment as you are.' She shakes her head. 'Who'd have thought it?'

'So this is why you've been a porcupine throwing off poisoned spines at me for the last few weeks. I thought it was because you were angry about how much time I've been spending with the band.'

'What can I say, Dan? I really am sorry.'

I'm not ready to forgive her just yet. 'You know, Lizzie, I only locked my bike to yours because you'd forgotten to lock it. Any passing stranger could have run off with it. You thought I was selfishly tying you to me when I was actually taking care of you.'

She hangs her head. 'OK, I guess I deserve a bit of punishment. Go on, take revenge. You've got a window of opportunity to freely punish me with no reprisals, and it starts…' She looks at her watch. 'Now!' She peers sideways up at me through her hair. Her green eyes flash with mischief. 'And now it's ended.' She bites my arm. 'You missed your chance!'

At times like this I wish I could channel Machiavelli or connect with my inner Genghis Khan or something, as it is I laugh, pull her to me and forgive her everything.

LIZZIE

How does this person, who was freaking me out like someone loudly chewing popcorn and talking during a movie or a fingernail screeching on a backboard, suddenly become a refuge from the storm? I've no idea. Yet Dan is once again my beloved comrade in arms, my partner in all sorts of crimes, my soul mate and the love of my life, with not an irritation in sight. Well there's still the mess after he's washed up and the pile of clothes on the floor but so what.

In another twist of the n-dimensional labyrinth of our humanity, I wanted love but my hidden longing was for freedom, and Dan wanted freedom but his hidden longing was for love. We each found what we most needed hidden behind what we least wanted.

DAN

We decide to go for a simple registry office wedding with just a few folk and the next day to have a ceremony we design ourselves. Followed by what most will consider the main event, the after-party party.

Lizzie books the registry office for the legal part; I book the Arts Centre for the fun part. I call my parents to tell them what's happening. 'Well, dear, if that's what you want,' said my mother. 'You know where to send the invitation.' 'This is the invitation,' I said. 'I see,' she said. An Ice Queen in her palace at the North Pole could learn a thing or two about frost from my mother.

LIZZIE

Saturday is to be the registry office, Sunday the main event. Joe is staying with us for a few days having come over from Liverpool where he's doing a degree in film studies. I ask him if his parents would like to be invited? He thinks not. 'You and Dan, well you're very different. They'd feel out of place.' I want to be sensitive to this situation. It was awkward enough when Joe said he wanted to train as a film cameraman and I asked Ken for advice as to the best way to go about this. He invited Joe to be a runner for a week on the set of his next film. This involved little more than being a courier, cleaner and general dogsbody but it was enough for Joe to get the bit between his teeth. His adoptive parents were not happy. They wanted him to study something useful like engineering or law. I told him, naturally they want you to be safe and secure in life, not struggling with the insecurities and challenges that creative artists tend to experience. So when he explains he doesn't think his parents would want to come to our wedding, I nod and don't question him further. Though I asked him to be the official photographer. 'You know this means you'll have to bribe me to make sure I shoot you in a flattering light,' he said. I hit him on his arm. 'You've blown it now, mum! You won't be able to hide from the camera and I'm going to zoom in on that scar on your forehead for sure.'

He'd called me 'Lizzie' to begin with. And that felt right. Last year he asked if he could call me Mum. 'Little Carl has two mums so why not me?' Eighteen months later, I still feel a shiver of pleasure when he calls me 'Mum'.

DAN

Lizzie seems to think she needs a different outfit for each stage of this wedding, the official form signing in the registry office, the do-it-yourself ceremony and the party. She goes with Jan, Michelle and Carole to Selfridges and Harvey Nichols and returns with shiny bright carrier bags and lots of tissue paper. It'll be a T-shirt for me. Though I promise Lizzie it'll be clean and without printed slogans denouncing the poll tax or a list of The Rolling Stones' Steel Wheel tour dates. Maybe to keep her happy I'll iron a crease down my Levis.

Joe and I make fun of the planning fest going on around us, like when Lizzie and Carole returned from the hairdressers with purple highlights, fake tans and designs of flowers on their fingernails, and we pretended to be jealous drag-queens. But as he's the official photographer and I'm the groom we can't get too carried away taking the piss. I lend him my Minolta camera. The rolls of film are easy to load and unload and the autofocus means you can point it and shoot easily even with a few drinks inside you. Within days he asks me for more film. He's taken loads of pictures of the ironing board, dangly earrings and the growing number of empty wine bottles in the kitchen. 'I'm creating a visual story using the contextual signifiers of time and negative space as well as patterns, textures and varying depth of field to construct a narrative of love,' he told me. I stared at him. He's been spending too much time in university lectures and not enough getting down on the dance floor.

It's then I notice his smile. 'Got you there didn't I!' He laughed and took a pic of me trying to pretend I knew all along he was having me on.

Matt and Oumar are my two best men. Oumar tells me Jenny is disturbingly interested in the whole drama of this wedding. I warn him, getting married is like getting into a boxing ring where there's no way out, you have to stay and fight. Lizzie overheard me and was not pleased at my description of marriage. I had to admire each and every one of her various designer outfits before she forgave me.

Chapter 24   Nothing Between Us and the Stars

LIZZIE

My parents are meeting their first grandchild for the first time at the wedding of their eldest daughter. It could be an episode of the new East Enders. Joe and I discussed how to handle it. Joe thought he should be introduced to them as the photographer and speak with them through the day about family, children, love, that kind of thing, and just before they went home, he'd say, 'oh, by the way, I'm your grandchild', and catch them on camera as their mouths fell open. I said, no way, that would be cruel. He said, but what about what they did to you, that was cruel. I said, yes but the class system, prejudice against the Irish, religious brainwashing, poor people being abused by the rich and other alienating and oppressive systems in society had been cruel to them. Instead of peeling the potatoes we got lost in a philosophical quagmire about the politics of experience and how humanity's alienation from its natural instincts, necessary for ordered communities, was in opposition to connecting with our natural instincts, necessary for happiness. We were on the verge of realising that this alienation *is* our nature when Dan yelled he'd finished cleaning the car and was dinner ready?

DAN

Over dinner Joe and Lizzie were playing off each other on one of their psycho-political wanderings. I let it wash over me until they asked me how I thought he should be introduced to her parents at the wedding. I thought I should introduce him. That would save Lizzie from whatever fall-out might follow and I didn't really mind how they reacted to me.

'I don't think so,' Lizzie says. 'You'd be rude and confrontative. I don't want to unnecessarily upset them, they're too old and frail now. I'll do it.'

'You're being way too understanding, Lizzie. You need to fight for yourself. Don't you agree Joe?'

'Absolutely! Mum, you should confront them. Not for me, I don't care. Do it for you.'

'What's the point? They believe they did nothing wrong and that's not going to change now. You have to pick your fights, so I'll give this one a miss. Besides, they're not evil, they're victims of circumstance.'

'I don't agree, Mum. You say you have to pick your fights, OK, but I reckon the fight against injustice is a fight worth having. And even if you don't say anything I might.'

'He's got a point, Lizzie. He's suffered from them too. You may have to let him have his fight with them even if you don't.'

Lizzie bites one of her fancy fingernails. 'OK you two, but how about you keep the fighting talk for another time, not our wedding party?'

Joe and I look at each other.

'I'll try,' I say. 'But I'm not guaranteeing anything. The last time we met them I had no idea what they'd done to you. This time is different.'

'I'll try too,' Joe says. 'But what's that Chinese saying you told me? 'If you would forgive your enemy, first you must wound them.' You see I do listen to you, Mum, you'd better be careful what you say to me in future!' He points the camera at Lizzie as she grabs a cushion to throw at him.

'An even older saying,' she says, ' in fact one of the first ever recorded, is, 'Listen to your mother as if it is the word of a god." The cushion flies across the table.

LIZZIE

I *do* fight for myself, fiercely, but against worthy opponents, not pathetic figures like my parents who don't need to be beaten down more than they've already been by inequality and poverty in a society that abuses the poor and under-privileged. Instead I've had those fights with Dan. Just as he's had his fights with me. In the great escape from our families' histories, we've fought each other. But it was a good fight. Dan didn't remain insulated from life by the cushioned superiority of privilege and I didn't stay locked into a religious ideology that dictates poverty is a virtue while accumulating more wealth than any other institution on the planet. No. I dived down into the depths and was drowned. Dan stepped into the fire and was burned. Then he pushed me into the fire and I pulled him into the ocean. If that isn't good fighting I don't know what is.

'I think it's best I introduce Joe in a very straightforward matter of fact manner. 'Mum, Dad, this is Joe, your grandson.' Their denial is so profound they will shake his hand politely, without feeling, and that will be that.' They didn't believe me but that's what happened. My father nodded and shook Joe's hand. 'Pleased to meet you sir,' he said and went off to the toilet. My mother frowned and said, 'I see.' She turned to me with an accusing stare but did add that maybe we'd all meet again, which was more of an opening than I'd expected. 'Weird,' was Joe's verdict. Dan just shook his head in disbelief.

DAN

The registry office segment was over quickly with just our parents, Carole and Matt, the witnesses, and Joe, the photographer present. After saying 'I am' and 'I do' a few times, popping on the rings and signing various forms, the nine of us go for tea in a nearby hotel. And so it was our parents met for the first time over sandwiches and cake in the lounge of the Piccadilly. I'd given into Lizzie's insistence and wore a tie and suit I'd bought from an Oxfam shop. Looking smarter than I'd been in over twenty years, I introduced them. 'Arthur and Patricia, this is Charles, my father, and Margaret, my mother. Father and mother, this is Arthur and Patricia.' We chewed on the egg and cress, the cucumber and the Battenburg with meringue, washed it down with tea and champagne and talked about whether it might rain. The 'real' wedding was to be the following day.

The ceremony was great. With everyone around us we solemnly promised to support each other, to be always honest with each other and to love each other through thick and thin. Though knowing I was likely to forget what to say, Lizzie had written it out and it was a far more poetic exchange than that. Someone played a flute, someone else read a poem, rose petals were thrown, and champagne was drunk in quantities. Later the heavy guns came out and Obsidian played. There was laughter, arguments, tears, drunken conversations that everyone hoped would be forgotten, hugs, kisses, crazy dancing and a fight. It was all a wedding should be.

LIZZIE

We both have work commitments that can't be changed so we delay our honeymoon. Dan has booked us into a hotel for the night. We drive into downtown Manchester and park. A night of love and romance lies ahead of us. Dan can't remember the name of the hotel, but it's a warm night and we stroll arm in arm, up close and in love. He'll soon remember.

The night is cooling. Dan is not remembering. I'm getting restless. I want to lie with my love in bed with champagne and candles, not patrol the streets of Manchester in the cold night air. We're no longer arm in arm. Dan has messed up our special night with his lousy memory but my memory works fine. I recall other occasions when he's messed up. I remind him of them in case he's forgotten them too.

Dan is silent, his arm tense, his neck tight. More walking around, more looking, more trying to remember the hotel's name. No hotel. We're walking more quickly now while I help him remember other situations when he's failed to come up to the mark. He mutters under his breath but I don't listen. I'm too busy explaining that I will never forget how he ruined up our wedding night because, as always, he doesn't give a fuck about anything other than himself. We arrive back at the car and climb in. I stare out the windscreen, a stone statue of righteous fury. 'I'm so angry,' I spit at him, 'I'll never forgive you!'

DAN

We walk the pavements of Manchester looking for this bloody hotel, which anyway was Lizzie's idea not mine. I'd have been happy with a pizza and a beer back home. I booked a bridal suite in a hotel only because she wanted it so I don't need Lizzie going at me like a murder of crows pecking into my brain with a long list of my failures and a detailed analysis of everything that's wrong with me. I feel bad enough already and know it's my fault; I don't need to be told again and again and again.

We're back in the car. She's staring through the windscreen like an ancient monument. At least she's shut up. The air is heavy and still, like the dead calm before a storm when the wind stops and there's a quiet that penetrates deep into your brain. But it's not the silence of peace; it's a portent of destruction. I turn to her stony profile and pronounce every word with scalpel-like precision. 'I hate you with every fibre of my being.'

LIZZIE

We sit in silence, a silence loaded with every single fucking thing there has ever been between us. Everything that's been said and done and can't now be unsaid and undone, it's all here. A concrete wall of hard reality slams into us, the hardest of all hards, human hard. We hate each other.

I stare out into the night. It begins to rain. This must be one of the worst wedding nights ever.

A giggle begins in my stomach. I try to suppress it but our complete absurdity hits me. All those vows to cherish and honour each other, to love and support each other forever, to always be there for each other, and a few hours later we're hating each other with the hardness of contract killers. We're utterly preposterous. I can't keep it in and the laughter bursts out of me. Dan begins to laugh too. We choke on our laughter and collapse. Tears run down our cheeks. We're in hysterics. We're helpless and gasping for breath between deep sobs of laughter and can't stop howling even though it hurts. Each time I'm about to get my breath back, I catch Dan's eye and we're bent over lost in uncontrollable gales of laughter all over again. Eventually I'm able to speak. 'That was the final ceremony.' I say. 'Now we're truly married.'

DAN

The car is steamed up from our laughter. I wind down the window for some fresh air and see the name of the hotel we're parked outside. I recognise it. We've been parked outside our hotel the whole time.

We climb out of the car and stand facing the hotel. I pull Lizzie to me and hold her close. My arms, my mouth, my legs, my stomach, my eyes, my lungs, my feet, my brain, my heart and my throat speak to her in the wordless language of the body - come with me, Lizzie, and let's fulfil our old promises to fly through vast skies into the heart of the sun, swim in wild oceans and drown into the depths, and make love until the sky falls in, the sea turns gold and the sun shines all night.

LIZZIE

Dan and I hold each other, two tiny particles in a universe so vast it drowns your dreams and drives you into a crazy wisdom that burns away all but the freedom to love. 'Yes, Dan, let's surf a tsunami in the sea of love until we're flying with nothing between us and the stars. Let's dive into the depths of the ocean where no light reaches and drown. And let's stay in that darkness until we make enough love to burst into an enlightenment that blinds even gods and ancient sages.' I lean into him and hold him close. 'Because if love can't save us, what else can?'

DAN

I stroke my cheek against hers. In a language as ancient as life I whisper into her hair, her eyes, her mouth, her breasts, her heart, her stomach and her bones, and tell her what our bodies already know. The love that redeems us, that forgives us our sins and heals us, this love doesn't come from a far away God in his heaven, it evolves down here, on Earth, forged in the struggle of warm-blooded mammals who must love one another or die. So it's up to us to make the love we so desperately need and, with our feeling bodies of soft animal tissue, our warm mammalian hearts and the tender organs of a creature-hood that bleeds and hurts and fights and dies, to make enough love to break our hearts wide open. Because if we don't, no one and nothing else will.

Our hearts beat like the ghost notes of a drum you feel but can't hear, a pulse so faint yet it sits under everything.

Let someone sober worry about what disasters may happen,
Lovers must be wild, disgraceful and crazy.
Because remember, in the way you make love is the way God will be with you.'

Jalal al-Din Rumi (1207 - 1273)

Printed in Great Britain
by Amazon

80512706R00139